B   SUMMER

Edited by Steve Berman for Bold Strokes Books

Speaking Out: LGBTQ Youth Stand Up

Boys of Summer

Visit us at www.boldstrokesbooks.com

BOYS OF SUMMER

edited by

Steve Berman

A Division of Bold Strokes Books

2012

BOYS OF SUMMER

ISBN 13: 978-1-60282-663-2

This Trade Paperback Original Is Published By
Bold Strokes Books, Inc.
P.O. Box 249
Valley Falls, NY 12185

First Edition: May 2012

CREDITS
EDITORS: STEVE BERMAN AND STACIA SEAMAN
PRODUCTION DESIGN: STACIA SEAMAN
COVER DESIGN BY SHERI (graphicartist2020@hotmail.com)

CONTENTS

INTRODUCTION

June. July. August. Don't we ask a lot of these three months, of summertime? We want bright sun shining down on us and nights warm enough for T-shirts and shorts. We want the welcome return of a wide range of smells from coconut to chlorine. We want the surf to be cool against our bare skin as we dare it on the beach, the rivulets of ice cream cool against our hands as we share such a treat with our friends.

In three months we try to wring as much pleasure, as much frivolity, as we possibly can. Vacations. Weekdays were nothing more than extended weekends. Maybe camp, maybe just lying idle in the grass. Abandoning work, unless you happen to *have* to work during summer, and then we still daydream about what we could be doing instead.

And romance. Winter may own Valentine's Day, but everyone knows the real season for finding love or mending broken hearts is summertime. Teenage boys strut around shirtless. Tan lines are maps to the heart…or places lower on a guy's topography. All that solar energy a gay kid has absorbed is just waiting to be released through a kiss.

So here are ten stories that capture the playfulness of the

season. What you hold is a permanent June in print, a never-ending July of first loves, a constant August of dog days and even daring adventures alongside the warm water.

And the best thing is, no matter what the weather outside, no matter how low the temperature might fall, you can always pick up this book and feel the sun shine on your face as you read these stories again.

Steve Berman

PORTRAIT OF THE ARTIST AS A YOUNG SWAMP THING
ANN ZEDDIES

At nearly sixteen, still spending vacation weekends with his parents, in a cottage on a not-too-distinguished part of Jensen Lake, was not Shane Kerry's idea of how things should be.

He had his own ideas of what an appropriate vacation should look like. It could be a beach resort on a turquoise-blue tropical ocean, one where his parents could lie in their beach chairs snoozing all day while Shane strolled the warm sands meeting interesting, well-tanned boys of his own age. Or, if it had to be a cottage, it should be a cottage on the grounds of a classic, Adirondack-style lodge with well-groomed trails, a tennis court, and a roaring hearth fire beside which Shane might be seen, looking pensive in the depths of a massive wing chair, long after his parents had gone to bed. There he might be recognized as a night owl and philosopher by a good-looking boy in artfully aged khakis and a faded T-shirt just tight enough.

Shane had a lot of good ideas about vacations. None of them started with collecting his half-eaten packages of Oreos and pretzels from the backseat of his parents' Toyota, then helping his dad lug the rest of their gear into the small cottage Shane's mom had inherited from her mother.

A normal vacation might even have taken place on Jensen Lake, if Shane's parents could have owned or even rented one of the larger places down on the point. They were spacious and new, with patios overlooking the lake, where lights were strung and parties happened, and docks where new boats and watercraft were tied up. The people who stayed in those places were always going off for a cruise on Lake Michigan, or a side trip to a gallery in Saugatuck, or having friends over for cocktails on the patio.

Instead, Shane's mom was firing up the grill to cook the brats they'd brought in the cooler, while his dad went down the road to buy firewood for the traditional after-dinner campfire on the pebbly little strip they called their beach. Shane dragged his duffel bag up to his room under the eaves. He opened the windows to air out the slightly musty smell. A rickety wooden outdoor stair served as a fire escape. He'd spent many an evening perched out there, watching life on the lake unfold. Rather than go down and make conversation with his parents, he took his phone and his sketching kit, and climbed out the window to the familiar vantage point.

He tried texting some friends back home. Mark didn't reply. Jana texted back @ *movies. L8r!* Shane felt a brief pang of jealousy that people were going to the movies without him, while he was stuck here. But he had to admit to himself that there wasn't all that much of a social scene for him at home, either. He'd dated a couple of boys, but it hadn't gone anywhere. He'd dated both Mark and Jana, for that matter. The date with Jana had been an awkward evening at a junior high school dance, after a comfortable friendship that had lasted through middle school and beyond. Toward the end of the evening, she'd asked him if he minded a personal question. He'd known what was coming, and confessed. It had been a huge relief to tell somebody. He'd still not been out to his parents then, officially. Then he and Jana had ditched the dance in favor of a celebratory midnight breakfast at the diner.

He'd tried a little harder with Mark. There had even been kissing in the back of the indie theater and in a secluded area of a local park. It was good practice, Shane felt. At least he knew *how* to kiss a boy. But he'd known Mark for years, too, and in the end they'd both admitted it was too much like homework. Diligent but not very rewarding. Safe, but sparkless.

Shane pushed the disappointingly silent phone away and flipped through his sketchbook. He'd practiced his drawing skills by copying some photos, trying to add a few touches of his own to bring the drawings to life. Here, a dark Adonis brooded with his face dramatically half-lit. On the next page, cleverly posed bodies lounged on a beach that was an idealized version of the one Shane knew. This, too, seemed too much like homework. Shane had faithfully reproduced perfect faces, but they lacked a spark.

Dissatisfied, he riffled the pages. Only one sketch held his attention. It was a quick, semi-abstract watercolor sketch, all blues and brilliant gold. He'd been watching a boy riding a Jet Ski, but in the painting, the boy had been transformed into a kind of carefree Icarus, careening toward the sun. Shane had captured his own feelings about what he'd been seeing, for a change.

Distant shouts and laughter distracted him. He flipped over onto his stomach and surveyed the lake. From here, he could see the dock at the Simmses' place. The Simmses were apparently in residence. Jason Simms and some of his friends were horsing around in the water. Having a good time. Too cool to invite Shane, even if they'd known he was here. The Simmses came up every year, just like Shane's family. One of Shane's classmates hung out with Jason, and Shane had tried to get into their group, but he seemed to be invisible to them. He'd given up trying. But he still fantasized, at times, that he'd somehow become much cooler, that he'd acquired the clothes, the hair, the new iPhone. He imagined strolling into one of their parties and being welcomed. He imagined going over there now. But he didn't have that much courage.

He sighed and pulled his sketchbook toward him again. He painted a fractured image of the scene in front of him, as if it were seen from the underside of the water—a confetti of clothing colors and glints of light, viewed from a dark lurking place. Even the sun seemed to shine brighter over there. Money gave them a special sheen. It was a yin-yang of the lake, and the shadow side was where Shane hung out.

"Shane!" He looked down to see his mother waving her barbecue tongs at him and calling his name. "Come on down, honey, supper's ready."

They sat at the picnic table and ate off paper plates. Shane's dad had already started the traditional after-supper campfire. At the end of the meal, he poked the paper plates and scraps into the flames.

"Ready for marshmallows?" he said cheerfully.

"Sure, Dad," Shane said.

"Come on now, let's have a little enthusiasm," Shane's dad said. "Don't start growing up on me. This is my only excuse to make s'mores. Help me out here."

Shane laughed, dutifully. He remembered when this was so much fun—fishing with his dad, toasting marshmallows, star watching and all the rest of it. He didn't want his parents to feel bad. But it wasn't enough for him anymore. At times like this he wished he wasn't an only child. If he had a brother, at least there would be someone to distract his parents' attention from him. There would be someone to talk to.

"I got a call from Cindy Huntington this afternoon," his mom said. "They've rented the Garrett place for the summer."

"Oh?" said Shane's dad. "What happened to the Garretts?"

"I think Cindy said they went to Palm Springs this year."

Shane let his parents' chatter flow around him. As an only child, he was used to hearing a constant stream of irrelevant conversation.

"You know Cindy and Don's son Chase is still at home," his mom continued. Shane's dad seemed about as interested as Shane was. He grunted affirmatively while spit-roasting his marshmallow to an even brown all over. That was one of the few things he and Shane had in common. They both liked carefully toasted marshmallows. Shane's mom liked to set hers on fire and eat them charbroiled.

"You remember Chase, don't you, Shane?" his mom said. Shane nodded around a mouthful of graham crackers and chocolate. What he meant was that he remembered such a person existed. He'd seen Chase around, but didn't know much about him, and cared less.

"I think he's about your age," his mom mused.

Uh-oh, Shane thought. At intervals, his parents would try to prod him into socializing with some offspring of a friend or relative. Shane tried to beam a repressive negative vibration in their direction. I can pick my own friends, he thought. Perhaps this called for some overt distraction.

"No, he's a year older," Shane said. "He's going to be a junior next year."

Shane's mother did not seem discouraged.

"Well, Cindy told me they have to make a quick trip back to Chicago, and apparently Chase has some kind of job or something that he doesn't want to leave. But she doesn't feel comfortable leaving Chase on his own."

"Why not?" Shane's dad said. "He's sixteen. Back in the day, he'd have been married and on some wagon train to Santa Fe."

"Yeah, seriously," Shane said, while keeping a mental reservation about the whole married at sixteen thing. "What is he, some kind of short-bus refugee? You wouldn't hire a babysitter for *me*, would you?"

Shane's mom seemed somewhat nettled. "She told me that a lot of kids in the area have been hosting keg parties and things. There was a big deal a couple of weeks ago with a graduation party in town, where they trashed the house."

Things were coming back to Shane now. He remembered a little bit about Chase. He'd been a big gangly kid with a bad haircut and a goofy smile.

"Chase is a big dork," he said. "He'd never host a kegger. I don't think he has ten friends."

Parents! he thought. They invent stuff to worry about.

"Well, I'm sorry you feel that way about him," his mom said. Now she was clearly irritated. "Because Cindy asked if we could keep an eye on him for the next few days, and I said of course we will. Cindy and Don are very nice people, and it's the neighborly thing to do."

Oh, crap, Shane thought. You mean they're very rich people and you want to stay in good with them because—he wasn't sure exactly how it affected his father's business. But he knew his parents were supposedly friends with quite a few people he didn't think they really liked. People who invited them to big cocktail parties, but not to dinner or the movies.

"What do you mean, keep an eye on him?" Shane said. He had a feeling of doom already.

"Well, I said he could stay with us. I'm sure he won't be any trouble. Cindy said he works nights, and the poor boy has to eat somewhere."

"With *us*?" Shane said. "What do you mean, 'us'?"

"He can have the spare bed in your room."

"Oh, wait a minute!" Shane said. He rose from his place by the fire and stabbed his toasting fork into the ground. "Mom! You could have at least asked me!"

"Oh, for heaven's sake, honey. I suppose I should have, but it's just for a couple of days. We can't make him sleep on the couch."

"Why can't he sleep on his own damn couch?" Shane said. "He's got a driver's license. He's practically an adult. He can drive himself to a motel if his parents don't trust him to stay in his own house. Why is that my problem?"

But he'd gone too far with that, and his father decided to get involved.

"There's no need to raise your voice to your mother," he said. "It won't kill you to share your room for a day or two. I'm sure the Huntington boy is a nice enough kid."

"That's just it," Shane said, striving to sound reasonable. "You're treating me like a kid. Like you can just put someone in my room without asking."

"Well, I'm asking now," his mother said. "I'm sorry, honey. I didn't think it was that important to you."

"Jeez. How would you feel if I just offered one of my friends crash space in you and Dad's room? I like my privacy, too."

"I'll remember that next time. I appreciate knowing how you feel about it."

Shane knew his mom had read a lot of books on how to raise children, and he felt as if she were just reciting her lines. But he knew she was really sorry. He couldn't resist it when she used her Mom-voice on him. His dad hadn't read any child-raising manuals. His dad just ignored the whole controversy and went on toasting marshmallows.

"How about you owe me one?" Shane said.

"I think I can live with that." His mom smiled.

Shane felt at least he had come out of this with his dignity. Though he wished he could get a signed IOU. His mom had a tendency to forget what she owed him when the moment for payback came.

"Want to go out in the boat and do a little night fishing?" his dad said.

Shane was not sure if this was meant to be a bribe. He didn't think his father had been paying much attention.

"Okay, sure," he said finally. He never knew if his father was trying to get them to bond over fishing, or whether it was just one of those things his dad absentmindedly did and dragged Shane along because he was there. They seldom talked much. But Shane enjoyed floating around doing nothing in particular. Being out on the water gave him a feeling of freedom, especially at night when all the daytime boundaries disappeared into mysterious depths.

His dad put out safety lights and used the trolling motor to move them around the upper edge of the lake toward the boundary of the state park on the other side. Looking back, Shane could see the little glow of the lamp on the screened porch, where his mother was sitting with her book. There were lights on at the Simms place, and at the Garrett place next door. Evidently the Huntingtons hadn't left yet. There were people out on the patio. They obviously had company.

There were a couple of little islands just offshore, with roots and fallen logs providing underwater shelter where fish could lurk. Shane's dad lowered the lights and the chum bag into the water and put out the poles, and they settled in to wait for a bite. Shane rummaged in the storage box under the seat for some bug repellent.

"I'm sorry you're going to be stuck with a roommate," his dad said. "You know your mom. She's a soft touch for anyone who needs a favor."

"Yeah, I wouldn't mind if *she* was the one doing the favor," Shane said. He wasn't really that mad about it anymore, but he couldn't back down.

"Oh, come on," his dad said. "Your mom will be doing the

cooking and whatnot. All you have to do is sleep in the same room with him. Get over yourself."

Irritably, his dad shook the chum bag in the water. Under cover of the darkness, Shane glowered at his back. Now he felt worse than ever. It was like having come out to his parents added a layer of ambiguity to everything. Was his dad mad at him because he was sulking over nothing? Or was he disturbed because he was thinking of Shane sleeping next to another boy, and how it wasn't the same as if Shane had been straight?

It wasn't the same. Shane couldn't explain to his father how he was worried about what some other boy might say about him. He didn't know Chase. Chase could go to the other kids, afterward, and say stuff about him. Tell them about how he had to sleep with the fag. Shane didn't think that would happen. He didn't want to think that. But it was possible.

"Dad—" he said. But before he could try to explain, his father put his hand on his shoulder and gave it a squeeze.

"Sorry, son, I'm not trying to give you a hard time," he said. "Maybe we can make it up to you later this summer. Think of something fun you can do on your own. Okay?"

"Okay, sure," Shane said.

The fishing poles twitched and dipped. Shane's dad smacked him on the back.

"Oh boy!" he said. "Looks like we've got something! Come on—help me out here!"

They'd hit a school of crappie, and went home with six sleek fish. Cleaning them before bed was the not-fun part of night fishing. Shane's dad was adept at the process. It kind of made Shane gag, but he could do it. He cleaned two to his dad's four.

"You're catching on," his dad said encouragingly.

Yeah, Shane thought. At least I didn't cut myself on the knife this time. He did feel pretty good about it, though, once the guts and scales were dumped and he'd washed his hands and rubbed lemon on them. He liked the plump sheen of the fish and the multicolored glint of their scales. He also enjoyed knowing that delicate white filets for tomorrow's dinner were packed away in the refrigerator in a Ziploc bag. It was the process in between that he didn't like.

❖

He lay in bed thinking about how you'd paint the change from live fish to dinner. You couldn't just portray a plate of fried fish. That would be lame. He glanced over at the other twin bed with its matching cowboy bedspread. He sighed and wished he'd talked his parents into bringing Mark along. Then there wouldn't have been room for a guest. He'd thought about it. Honestly, the reason he hadn't was that he'd had a secret hope he might meet someone this time. On the beach or somewhere. And if Mark had been there, it would have been awkward. Well, now he was going to meet someone. Just not the way he'd hoped.

He wondered if maybe you could paint a plate of fried fish. Like Warhol. Plates of fried fish in different colors to match the scales of the live fish. Or a fish that was made of lots of fractal filets, kind of a mosaic... First he'd have to learn to paint fish, though. He wanted acrylics for a messy, tactile surface. He needed to bring more art supplies up to the cabin. And if his mom owed him one, maybe he could get her to redecorate his room. Matching cowboy bedspreads couldn't even be passed off as ironic. They were just tacky and childish. He rolled over and turned out the light.

❖

In the morning, he got hold of his friends at home and discussed the injustice with them in detail, promising to keep them up to date as events unfolded. He felt better after hearing their assurances that his parents were insane, and listening to Jana laugh about the cowboy bedspreads.

In fact, he felt good enough to take the kayak out and cruise slowly past the Simms house to see if anyone was around. He was in luck. A group of guys was getting ready to go tubing behind the Simmses' new powerboat. One of them was Scott, the boy who had been in his English class last year. Scott actually waved to him, so he slowed his stroke and drifted alongside.

"Hey, how're you doing."

"Howzit," Scott said, giving him a pretentious Hawaiian hand gesture. Shane happened to know that Scott had been on vacation to some time-share resort in Hawaii once or maybe twice. That didn't make him an islander.

"It's good," Shane said.

"Hey, are you going to the bonfire tomorrow night?" Scott said. Shane saw by the look exchanged between the other two that they hadn't planned on inviting Shane. He tried to think fast how to answer in a way that wouldn't reveal he hadn't known there was a bonfire planned.

"Maybe," he said. "Did they decide where it was going to be?"

"Well, it turned out the Petersons were going to be home after all, so we couldn't do it there," Scott said. "And Chase said no. Can you believe it? His parents are actually going out of town for the weekend, and told us he wasn't interested in partying."

Shane shook his head in a way that said "Some people."

"Yeah, so we're just going to do it at the park. It's the middle of the week. With any luck Smokey the Bear won't get there till it's too late."

The guy driving the boat revved the engine impatiently.

"Later!" Shane said, and got out of the way before the wake hit him.

He came into the house before supper and saw that someone was talking to his mom. Glimpsed from the kitchen door, the stranger intrigued him. He was tall, with thick dark hair that straggled over his collar in little curls and ended up in a ducktail at the back. His outline from the rear was attractive—thin and rangy with long arms and legs. His sleeves were rolled up, revealing tanned hands and forearms. Shane stepped through into the kitchen.

"Hi, Mom."

"Oh, hi, honey. Good timing. Chase just stopped by."

OMG, Shane thought. Please don't tell me I was just cruising Chase Huntington.

Chase turned and smiled, sticking out his hand.

"Chase. How're you doing," Shane said—thinking, WTF, he's going to shake my hand? Who does that?

"It smells good in here, Mrs. Kerry," Chase said. Shane thought, What a suck-up. It did smell good, though. It smelled like his mother's peanut butter chocolate chip cookies.

"Thank you, Chase. I just made some cookies. Why don't you boys take a plateful out in back and let them cool enough to eat."

Chase offered to carry the plate, plus napkins. Shane rolled his eyes behind his mother's back. Could she get any more corny? Anyone would think Chase was some poor, starving orphan instead of the son of an investment banker.

At least she hadn't poured them glasses of milk. Shane pulled a bottle of A&W root beer out of the cooler on the porch, and Chase accepted a Diet Coke.

"So your mom was telling me about her bird watching," Chase said. "She said you knew a lot about birds, too."

"Not really." Shane shrugged. "She's been working on her Life List since I was a kid. I used to go out with her sometimes."

"I think it's cool to know about birds. Birds are not my specialty."

"What is your specialty?" Shane said. Thinking: Could this get any more Aspergers-y? We'll be talking about how to breed hamsters next.

"Amphibians," Chase said, like that was a perfectly normal topic of conversation.

"Really," Shane said. His eyebrow shot up before he could stop it. Chase looked fazed for a minute. Then he shrugged and fit half a cookie into his mouth.

"These are good," he said, chewing. "See, amphibians are the early warning system of the ecology. They're dying now, or turning up deformed, and we don't know why. Global warming, pollutants? We haven't figured that out yet, but we need to, because ultimately it will affect humans, too."

In spite of himself, Shane was intrigued by the audacity of a geek who would just go on saying what he wanted to say.

"How did you get so interested in amphibians?"

"My uncle is a biologist," Chase said. "He's like the black sheep of the family. So we had that in common. And I really wanted a pet turtle when I was a kid, and he started telling me why that was a bad idea. I guess he could see that made me really sad, so he promised to take me out to see some turtles in the wild, and I got into it. I started hanging out in swamps on my own. I like wetlands because they're liminal."

"They're what, now?" Shane said. Actually, he had some idea what the word meant. It had come up in a movie he'd seen about cave art.

"On the edges of things. Changing from one state to another. Wet to dry, dry to wet. Air to water, water to land. Amphibians move between environments. Also, they're very sensitive to conditions. Like frogs. Frogs have absorptive skins."

He paused and looked at Shane. He sighed. "Okay, I know it's not a popular topic. You asked." He slumped back in his chair and took another cookie. "These are good. Did I mention? Yeah, I guess I did. So what do you do when you're up at the lake? I haven't seen you hanging out on the Simmses' dock."

"We just got here," Shane said. "I haven't had time to hang out much."

He hoped Chase would get the subtle implication that Shane was not having time to hang out because now Chase was here. Chase gave him a look from under the locks of hair falling over his brows. The look said he knew Shane had just dodged the question. Okay, maybe Chase wasn't as clueless as he appeared. Shane noticed his eyes were very dark. You'd almost think they were deep. If, Shane corrected himself, you didn't already know it was just Chase.

Chase reached out one long arm to the edge of the table, where Shane had left his bag of art supplies in a jumble when he decided to take the kayak out. He picked up the notebook.

"Is this your mom's?"

That was exactly the wrong thing to say. Shane could feel his face reddening, though he willed it to stop. Art was girly, art was not something a normal boy would care about. He had to fight back that notion every day. Not that anyone said it to him. But he was afraid they would. He heard it in his own head.

"No. Mine," he said shortly. He reached for the notebook, but Chase held it just beyond his grasp.

"Oh. Cool. Mind if I look?"

Shane did mind. But what could he say? "It's private"? That would only let Chase know he was touchy about it. A sure way to get more unwanted attention.

"Yeah, whatever," he said begrudgingly. Thinking: I don't care. Don't give a shit what he thinks. What does he know?

Anyway, if Chase gave him any crap about his sketches, he'd have the excuse he needed to stop even pretending to be polite to him.

He waited to see if Chase would linger too long over his drawings of handsome men, if Chase would make any comments. Chase browsed through the pages attentively, but didn't appear to pause on one more than another.

He looked up and smiled, his gaze browsing over Shane's face as if it were another drawing. His smile was not bad, Shane thought, surprised. Interestingly crooked, a little crinkle around the eyes, and a glint of humor or things unsaid that brought life to his expression. It might even have been attractive, to someone who didn't know he was just Chase.

"You're good," he said. "I didn't know you could do that. I like the kind of abstract ones the best. They have a flavor to them. They're different."

"Thanks," Shane said. That was a conversation stopper in the opposite way from what he'd expected. He hadn't expected Chase to appreciate his painting.

"So, are you planning to be an artist? Are you going to go to art school?"

"I don't know yet."

"Well, you should. You're that good."

"Yeah, well, my parents aren't that impressed. You know how it goes. They want you to do something practical. My dad thinks I should get a business degree and then go into advertising or marketing or something."

"Yeah, I do know how it goes." Chase smiled wryly. "My folks couldn't figure out why I wouldn't want to go to Chicago with them. They're attending a Republican fund-raiser. For some guy who doesn't believe in global warming. Law school—that's what they want for me. They know I'll never get into Harvard like my brother. But anybody without a law degree is a loser as far as they're concerned."

At that point, Shane's mother called them in for dinner. She'd fried the fish in beer batter and made potato salad and corn bread. Chase ate like there was no tomorrow, and kept the compliments flying as fast as his fork. Shane had started liking him more, but he started hating him again while he watched Chase make conversation and ingratiate himself with the adults. Everything was great and wonderful, and Chase jumped up to help every time Shane's mother had to take anything out to the kitchen.

"So, Chase, what's this job that's so important you wanted to stay here?" Shane's dad asked. This was a sore spot with Shane. His dad was always hinting it was about time Shane got a job. Shane loved his summers. He knew he'd have to work sooner or later, but he was trying to put it off at least until he was sixteen and could drive.

"Well, sir, it's not really a job, I guess, because I don't get paid. It's volunteer work."

"What kind of volunteer work?" Shane's mom said.

"My uncle works at the Biological Station in Kalamazoo," Chase said. "He's coordinating volunteers for the frog census in western Michigan. I'm helping him with that."

Shane's mom laughed. Probably disappointed he isn't working for Mother Teresa, Shane thought.

"Frog census? What on earth is that?"

"We're trying to find out how many frogs there are in the area, and what kinds," Chase said. "You can't actually go out and catch them, because they're too elusive. So someone has to go out to their habitats and listen for their songs. You sign up for a certain route that goes to different sites, and then you record your observations over a given time period. It's kind of technical, but it basically means I have to go out in a boat and listen for a couple of hours every night. If I'd gone back to Chicago with my parents, it would have left a big hole in my observations."

"Let me get this straight," Shane's dad said. "You have to go sit in the swamp at night, and this you do for free?"

"Yes, it's good experience if you want to be a biologist," Chase said.

"Sounds crazy to me," Shane's dad said. "This is what they spend our tax dollars on—counting frogs."

"No sir, this part is all volunteer," Chase said. "It doesn't cost you anything."

That shit-eating smile stayed plastered on his face even though they were obviously laughing at him, Shane thought.

"I think it's cool," Shane said. "Most people don't understand the importance of amphibians in the ecology."

He said it just to irk his parents, because he was fed up with their know-it-all attitude. Chase shot him a look of astonished gratitude, a genuine smile lighting up his face.

"Anyway, it's not that much different from night fishing," Shane said.

"Night fishing gets you dinner," Shane's dad said, ostentatiously spearing the last fish filet. Too late, Shane remembered that he'd meant to keep his parents in a good mood.

"I will have a job later this summer, though," Chase said. "My uncle has a lab tech position lined up for me, starting in a couple of weeks. I'll get paid for that."

Shane's dad gave him a "There, you see" kind of look. Once again, Shane resented Chase.

It wasn't the best moment to ask, but he figured it was now or never.

"Hey, Mom and Dad, remember how you were saying that maybe I could do something fun later," he said. Thinking: To make up for having Chase here!

"Well, I saw Scott this afternoon—you know, Scott Blanchard from my English class? And he invited me to a party tomorrow night."

"What kind of a party?" his mom said.

"Just a beach party. A campfire. Jason Simms and those guys are going to be there."

He could see his mom shaking her head already. "Oh, honey, I just don't think that sounds like a good idea. Will there be adult supervision?"

"I guess so," Shane lied. "I didn't really ask. Come on, Mom, you know those kids."

Too late, he wished he hadn't mentioned Jason. He didn't want his mom to get the bright idea of calling Mrs. Simms to ask about the party.

His mom looked at his dad. His dad didn't look welcoming to the idea, either.

"No, son, I don't think so," he said. "You never know what's going to happen at something like that. Drinking, party crashers. Kids do dumb things in a group. And besides, you have a guest."

"I'm sure Chase could go, too," Shane said. Taking Chase along was the last thing he wanted, but he'd do it if he had to.

"Thanks, but I can't," Chase said. "I'll be finishing up my survey."

That really burned Shane. Chase could at least have put up a good front. Supported him. Obviously the guy had no friends and didn't know how to be one.

"I can help with the dishes," Chase said. "Then I should get going."

Shane wanted to choke him—and also his own mom and

dad—but he wasn't ready to give up and burn his bridges yet. If Chase could suck up, he could, too.

"Could you use an assistant?" he said. "It sounds kind of interesting."

"Do you wear a life jacket?" Shane's mother said.

"Yes, Mrs. Kerry, I have a whole list of safety protocols I have to follow. Don't worry—my mom already grilled my uncle about this."

"When are you going to get back?"

Chase looked at Shane for help. Shane wasn't going to give him any.

"Uh…well, I guess I never timed it. I'm pretty sure I'll be through by midnight. Would that be okay?"

"Fine," Shane's mom said. "If you boys will be back by midnight, that should be all right. Shane—I want you to take your phone with you. Text me every hour so I know you're okay."

❖

The Huntingtons had a nice fiberglass powerboat. But for this job, Chase took the old rustbucket rowboat. He threw Shane a life vest.

"We're not really going to wear these, are we?" Shane said.

"Damn straight we're going to wear them," Chase said. "Go on—put it on or get back on the dock. Listen, that water is cold. And it's muddy and full of weeds at the bottom. I've fallen in before. It's not fun."

The boat had a motor, but Chase used the oars instead.

"The quieter you are, the more you can hear the frogs," he said. "Also, they'll clam up if there's a lot of noise."

Shane had to admit that Chase looked all right at the oars. There was easy power and no splashing in his stroke. The boat glided through the water almost silently, leaving hardly a ripple in its wake. A waning moon rose above the pines on the shoreline, and mist hovered over the water, smelling of reeds and mud.

"Want me to row awhile?" Shane said. He wanted Chase to see that he could handle a boat equally well.

"Thanks, but no. I know where I'm going. You can have a turn on the way back, if you want."

The hull whispered through reeds and lily pads. They reached a shallow place where cattails and arrowleaf reached over their heads. Chase put out the anchor and handed Shane a headlamp with a red filter over the lens. Shane remembered those from star-watching expeditions with his father.

"Sorry I only have the one light," Chase said. "You can use it. Take my notebook and check off the frogs as I call them. You'll get the hang of it pretty soon."

Shane didn't hear anything at first. Then he became aware of an intermittent chirping and trilling.

"Those are the Gray Tree Frogs," Chase said in a low voice. "Now hear that 'plunk, plunk'? Kind of like a flat guitar string? That's a Green Frog."

Shane listened harder. "That one?"

"No, that really loud one, like a honk, those are the Bullfrogs. But put a check mark for the Bullfrog. There! That was the Green Frog."

Shane got interested in spite of himself. It turned into a Frog Jeopardy game, with the two of them competing to push an imaginary buzzer first and name that frog. But even with liberal applications of Deep Woods Off, the mosquitoes located them and passed the word.

Shane stood it as long as he could, but when he had to spit out bugs, he reached his limit.

"Jesus H., how do you do this every night? I'll be covered in welts."

Chase shrugged. "Used to it, I guess. Maybe they don't like me as much as they like you." He glanced at his luminous watch. "Just another fifteen minutes and we'll be done for the night. I think we're doing pretty good. I was hoping to maybe hear a Pickerel Frog. They sound kind of like marbles clicking together. But they're rare. There are actually only thirteen species of frogs in Michigan, and really only the big three I told you about are mating right now."

"Mating! You didn't tell me that's what we were listening for! You mean the frogs are getting it on and we're listening? That's gross."

"No, no, we're just listening to the frog singles bar. Those calls are what they call 'advertising.' The frog is trying to lure potential mates. They're like, 'Here I am! Where are you?' Or maybe, 'Hey, I'm a Green Frog. How 'bout it?'"

Shane realized he'd been hearing a low buzzing noise for the past few minutes. It was getting louder. Then his heart jumped and he yelled involuntarily, as a bright light seemed to be coming right at them and the sound became unmistakably the noise of a motor right next to them. The other craft swerved around them at the last minute, leaving a wash that agitated the reeds and rocked the rowboat wildly. He heard laughter fading away into the dark, and a motor revving in the distance.

"What the *fuck*," he gasped, clutching the gunwales.

"Assholes," Chase said.

"Jesus Christ, what was that?" Shane said.

"Jet Skis," Chase said. "That's the second time they've done that. If I had a wild guess, I'd say it was Jason Simms and a couple of his guys. He's got the new Jet Ski. It's totally illegal to ride them at night, but I can't report him because I never know if it's really him. Who else would be that big a douche, though. Assholes."

He reached for the notebook. "We may as well quit now. We'd have to wait too long for the frogs to come back. They've been scared straight, for now."

Shane laughed shakily. "Scared straight? Are there gay frogs? The Gay Tree Frog? Is that what you said?"

As he packed up and reached for the oars, Chase's legs tangled clumsily with Shane's. Their fingers brushed as Chase grabbed the notebook. He jerked hastily away.

"Homosexuality is not uncommon in the animal kingdom," he said repressively. "But I don't believe it's been observed in frogs. They don't have mammalian sexual organs, you know. Both sexes have a cloaca, which—"

"Jesus, stop now!" Shane said. "I almost got run down by a rogue Jet Ski. I don't need a lecture on frog reproduction. Gross."

Homosexuality in the animal kingdom, he thought. Who talks like that! His cheeks burned, from the shock and from suddenly wondering if Chase was trying to tell him something. Like, that he knew Shane was gay. Who would have told him? Probably most of the kids at school knew, but Shane had never bothered to announce it to anyone up here. Maybe Scott talked, and it got around. Scott never did know when to keep his mouth shut.

Shane didn't try to take the oars. This was Chase's goddamn project. Let him do the work. The Jet Ski encounter had made him forget why he came out here in the first place, but now he remembered. He hadn't had any time to soften Chase up, but if he didn't mention it now, he might not get another chance.

"Listen, Chase, I wanted to ask you about that party," he said. "I really want to go. I wish you'd come with me."

"But your parents said no," Chase said.

"Yeah—but what they don't know won't hurt them. Come on, we could just head up the river into the state park, park the boat and walk over to the beach. Spend just an hour or so, just enough to have some fun. We'd be home before they know it."

"I don't want to go," Chase said. "Your parents have been really cool to me. I'm not gonna lie to them. Anyway, I have my observations to complete. I promised my uncle."

He sounded as dorkishly deadpan as ever, but Shane could tell he was agitated because he was splashing with the oars.

"Well, okay then, you could just drop me off. Drop me off, do your observations, I'll call you and then you can pick me up and we'll go home. No harm, no foul. Right? Everybody's happy."

Chase was silent for a long time. Shane kept quiet, hoping he'd talk himself into it.

"I don't get you," Chase said.

"What do you mean? I want to go to a bitchin' beach party. What's weird about that? I'm normal!"

"No, I don't get why you want to hang out with those guys, anyway. If you don't have the clothes and the shoes and the Jet Ski and the trip to Hawaii, they're not gonna notice you. They think they're all that. You aren't like them."

It stung, it was too close to the truth. It made Shane cruel.

"So who do you think I should be like, then—a Swamp Thing like you?"

He couldn't see Chase's face in the darkness, but he felt the boat jump in the water as Chase yanked harder on the oars. Chase's voice was still steady.

"Just stop caring so much what they think."

"Oh, right. Like you? You totally care! You suck up to my parents like whoa! Maybe you want to be me, is that it?" He wanted to turn his back and stomp away, but he couldn't, because he was stuck in a boat.

Chase quit rowing. They drifted in the middle of the lake, like two astronauts lost in a rift, stuck in the same space capsule.

"Yeah, sure, that's it. I just want to be you, because you're *so* cool."

He was mad now. He was out of breath, and his voice shook. "Yeah, maybe we *should* switch. You can have my perfect parents and their perfect stuff, and go to the perfect college and be a clone like my perfect brother. And I could have the parents who would do stuff with me and actually notice my existence. But no, that wouldn't work. They'd never trade Normal Shane for a geek like me. So forget it—you can have my life if you want it so bad, and I'll just—I'll just be screwed. Ah, fuck it."

The boat spun slowly. Shane couldn't believe he was having a fight with a guy he hadn't even known last week. Chase kept saying things that actually meant something. It was like he could see into Shane, and knew where to punch him so it would hurt. Why couldn't he just talk about nothing, like a normal person? This wasn't normal.

Chase picked up the oars and spun the boat back toward shore. The night was silent, except for the sound of his breath huffing.

"Oh damn, I forgot to text my mother," Shane said. Chase didn't say anything.

The boat grated on the pebbly shore in front of Shane's cottage. Chase got out without looking back and went into the house. Shane heard him say, "Oh, hi, Mrs. Kerry." Apparently his mom was still up. When he went into the living room, she was curled in the shabby arm chair. Chase was already gone.

"Mom, hey, I'm sorry I forgot to text you," he said. "We were just listening to the frogs and stuff and—"

His mother closed her fat paperback novel. "I actually got so wrapped up in this book I forgot to check the time," she said. "Oh well, it's not midnight yet and you're home safe and sound."

"Okay, cool then, I guess I'll go on upstairs. I'm pretty tired."

His mom started to smile and nod, but then peered up into his face and caught him by the arm as he tried to slip past.

"Are you sure everything is all right, honey? You look upset."

"I'm fine," Shane said. But he could see he wasn't convincing her. She glanced up at the narrow stairs where Chase had gone, and lowered her voice.

"Is there something—well, you know, going on between you and—" She nodded toward the stairs.

Shane just stared at her. This is one of those moments they describe in books, he thought. Where the blood drains from your face.

"Mom! For God's sake! No. There is *nothing* going on. Nothing like that! Nothing at all." He also lowered his voice, to a venomous whisper. "Except that I can't stand the guy. Mom, for God's sake, he isn't even gay. Just—please, would you mind your own business? This is so embarrassing I can't believe it."

He tried again to leave, but she wouldn't let him go.

"You know you could tell me if there was something like that," she said. "I hope you would. I know I'm not the best at talking about things like this, and I guess neither is your father, but we know you're growing up now, and—"

Shane rolled his eyes. This was definitely one of the stranger evenings in his life.

"Seriously, Mom. Not happening. Your houseguest is driving me crazy, but no. Not in a good way! So can I just go to bed now?"

She reached up and gave his hair a little pat. "All right, honey. See you in the morning."

All Shane wanted was for Chase to be asleep. But he

walked in on Chase pulling his shirt off. He had his back to Shane. Shane's eyes widened slightly. Nice muscles. All that rowing had been good for something. And tan. Shane couldn't help wondering how far the tan went.

"Bathroom's yours," Chase said without turning around. When Shane came out, Chase was rolled in his blanket, under the cowboy coverlet. Shane turned out the light and tried to pretend he was asleep.

"Look," Chase said, voice slightly muffled by his pillow. "I didn't mean—I mean, I'll drop you off at the beach tomorrow if that's what you want."

"But you—okay. Thanks." Don't ask questions. Don't make him change his mind, Shane told himself. Maybe this was Chase's way of apologizing.

Chase rolled over in a great thrashing of blankets.

"I never said I wouldn't. I just—I was trying to make a point about those guys." He sighed. He had the blanket pulled almost all the way over his head. Shane could hardly see the shape of him in the dark. It was easier to talk to people you couldn't see.

"What do you have against them, anyway?"

"I thought you knew, but maybe you don't." Chase sighed again. "Before my mom called your mom, she called Jason's mom. They made up some lame-ass excuse why I couldn't stay. Not that I wanted to. I used to hang with Jason when we were up here. But the thing is, once they found out I was gay...I mean, the guy's a douche anyway. It's not like we were really friends. Those guys are totally shallow. I don't even want to talk to them. It's just...awkward. When you talked about gay frogs, I thought you were talking about me. It's the kind of shit that—"

"Wait, what?" Shane interrupted. He hadn't thought this could get any weirder than it already was. "You're gay? I thought you were talking about me. I thought one of those guys must have told you."

"Told me what?" Chase said.

"That I'm *gay*, dumbass." Shane was trying to keep his voice down. Having his parents overhear this little chat would be like the perfect storm of aggravation.

Chase rose up on one elbow.

"You, Mr. Normal? You're putting me on, right?"

"No, I'm not putting you on. Jesus."

Chase flopped back onto his back and slapped one hand over his eyes. "Well. That's…awkward. So you weren't mocking me with the gay frogs comment."

"No. For fuck's sake, I was just joking. Just saying any dumb shit that rolled out my mouth. Because that Jet Ski about scared the crap out of me."

Chase snorted. "Yeah, I just about pissed myself. That was crazy."

Shane was quiet for a minute, trying to absorb the latest shock. "You know," he said finally, "maybe the reason they don't like you isn't that you're gay. Maybe you're just too weird. Maybe they're scared of you."

There was silence on the other side of the room, and Shane wondered if he'd overestimated Chase's social skills. Maybe he truly couldn't take a joke. Then he heard smothered laughter. "That could be it," Chase said. "I like it." Then he growled *"Swamp Thing"* in a deep bass voice.

"Yeah, okay," Shane said. "Going to sleep now."

He didn't go to sleep, though. Not for a long time. He was pretty sure Chase was asleep because he could hear Chase snoring gently. But Shane lay there with his eyes wide open, thinking WTF. Thinking: What else does the whole world know that I don't? And: Why didn't someone tell me?

❖

Shane thought the next day would be super awkward, but it wasn't. Chase insisted on cooking breakfast—pancakes and eggs. Shane's mom gushed over his ability to keep sunny-side-up yolks unbroken.

"Good job, Chase!" Shane said in a perky, teacher-like voice, and Chase actually got it and rolled his eyes at Shane behind his mom's back.

They spent the day doing things that didn't require a lot of talking. They took the kayaks out and Shane enjoyed showing Chase that he knew a few tricks Chase didn't. They landed on the state park side, where the dunes were, and Shane got Chase to pose for some sketches. Chase kept talking, even when he was facedown in the sand so Shane could capture the lines of his back. Shane admitted to himself that he didn't really mind all that much. It meant that Chase had to listen when Shane wanted to geek out about the difference between art and illustration, and how he wanted to have his own show before he graduated.

"I know this is awkward," Chase mumbled into the sand. "It's not like we have to be BFFs because we're the only gay kids on this side of the lake. Anyway, my parents will get home tomorrow and I'll be out of your hair."

"Shut up, I'm trying to draw you," Shane said.

Shane captured the fluid lines of Chase's arms stretched out over his head, as if he were diving. He smudged in shadows to suggest the curve of muscles under tanned skin. It felt as if he were touching Chase with his eyes. He wondered what it would feel like to touch him for real. His skin would be hot from the sun beating down and the gritty caress of heated sand.

"Stay right there," Shane said. To distract himself, he quickly switched to his watercolors. He captured Chase's flesh in the warm tones of sand, wavering as if seen through shallow water. He layered blue and green into Chase's tousled hair, let his hands spear out ahead of him like fins. Instead of the jeans that gapped away from Chase's hip, casting a blue shadow, he splotched Chase's lower body with green and brown tendrils like water weed. The rest of the page was the colors of water. What had been a boy was a sleek stripe of movement, one with the lights and shadows.

Chase sat up and brushed sand off his chest. "I'm getting broiled," he complained.

The paint was still wet. Shane hadn't had a chance to close the sketchbook and hide it away. Chase reached for it.

"Let me see."

He looked, then looked sideways at Shane. His eyes were deep, for sure. Even if he was just Chase.

"Can I have this?" he said.

"No, I made it for myself. Part of my *oeuvre*."

"Then you can make another one for you. I want this one. I like it. Portrait of me as a Swamp Thing."

"I'll make another one for you."

"Nope. This one. That's my price for taking you to your dumbass party."

Their fingers met on the page, smudging both with the same colors.

"All right, all right—you can have it. When it dries."

Shane felt hot, breathless. The sparkle of sun on water was too dazzling. He needed shade and a cool drink. He followed Chase to the beached kayaks and paddled home.

❖

Before supper, Shane's mom got him alone on the pretext of having him carry the laundry basket upstairs.

"I had to do some grocery shopping today," she said. "So I

went into town." She had a plastic bag from the pharmacy in her hand. "And, well, I know you said everything was fine last night. But I just thought—you know, in case—"

She held the bag out for him to take. Shane wanted no part of it. Suddenly he knew what was in there. His mother had little red spots of embarrassment in her cheeks.

"Mom!" Shane said. "This is so totally unnecessary. I'm prepared. Not that I need to be, because nothing is going on."

"Well," his mom said, reverting to her normal Mom-voice, "if you're talking about that condom you've been carrying in your pants pocket for months now, I think you should know that you put it through the wash at least once. That thing has been around the block and needs to be retired. Now take this and stop being so stubborn."

Reluctantly, Shane accepted the bag. "Mom, this is so embarrassing."

"Oh, honey. It's normal to think about these things. People didn't talk about it when I was your age, but I wish they had. I just want to know that you'll take care of yourself."

"Okay, Mom, I promise I'll do that should the day ever come. But this is not that day!"

She made the little hand gesture that meant "I'm all done with your nonsense" and started putting clean clothes away.

"Thanks," Shane said to her back.

❖

That night, Shane equipped himself with a flashlight and made sure his phone was charged. He considered putting on some aftershave, but realized the scent of Off would destroy the effect.

Chase rowed him across the lake with great energy,

determined to dump him on the far shore and get back to his frog survey.

"You probably think I'm really shallow, but I just want to do this, you know?" Shane said. "Don't you ever want to just do something? Like, to know what it would be like?"

"Sure," Chase said, rowing steadily. "But I already know what Jason's parties are like. Call me, okay? I'll be out here in the swamp."

Shane jumped onshore without getting his pants wet and jogged down the road that crossed the park to the Lake Michigan beach beyond the woods. He could smell woodsmoke before he got there. As he crested the foredunes, he could see the blaze of a driftwood fire. He heard voices and spotted a crowd of dark shapes moving between him and the fire.

He walked boldly into the middle of the crowd, anonymous as anyone. He didn't see any familiar faces. A lot of the people there seemed bigger, older than he was, like townies. And there were girls, of course. Girls everywhere. People were dancing, flirting, making out in the shadows. He got into a conversation with a couple of girls as he filled himself a paper cup of beer and drank it, and started to loosen up a bit.

"Hey, man—you made it here." It was Scott.

"No problem," Shane said, feeling very cool.

"How'd you get here?"

"I got a ride. You?"

"Jason and a couple of the guys rode the Jet Skis. I hitched a ride behind Jason. Night riding is awesome."

"Did you come down the river all the way to the big lake?"

"No—parked them on the Jensen Lake side."

Shane made a note to himself to be careful when leaving and not run into any of them on the way back. He didn't want them to meet up with Chase.

Scott was hanging out with the usual crew plus a few strangers. They'd brought a couple of six-packs in addition to the keg. "Here, you gotta see this," Scott said, pulling him into the shadows behind the dunes.

"Fireworks! Cool, huh? We're going to light them off later. After everyone's shitfaced. Freak them out."

Jason stepped out of the firelight into the shadows, to grab another can of beer. He looked as if he'd had a few already. He was with several of the bigger kids Shane had noticed.

"Hey," Jason said. "So you finally ditched Frog Boy, huh?"

Shane didn't know what to say. He just took another gulp of beer and shrugged.

"Listen, you know what?" Scott said. "We're gonna take the Jet Skis and see if we can find him later tonight. We can buzz him again. We sideswiped him last night and you should have heard him squawk. Like a frog. Want to come along?"

He glanced at Jason for approval. Jason didn't seem that happy to see Shane. But if Shane just laughed and said it was cool, he figured he could join up with them. At least for the duration of the party. He'd drained the last of his beer, and he had to say something.

"Why?" he said. "What's the point?"

Scott's smile faded. He still didn't quite get that Shane wasn't thrilled to be part of this.

"Dude, because he's such a loser!" he said. One of the other kids laughed. "Yeah, he's so gay. Gay for frogs."

Shane crumpled the paper cup in his hand. He surprised himself by speaking. "Your plan sucks ass. It's lame." He tossed the cup at Jason's feet and turned away.

There was astonished silence, and then a lot of noise and laughter.

"Don't go away mad! Aww, what's wrong?"

"Maybe he's gay, too—gay for the little froggies."

"Yeah, he is—gay for Chase!"

There was general laughter, like that was clearly impossible.

Shane didn't think anyone heard him say, "Maybe I am," as he walked away. He heard them behind him, picking up their six-packs and heading back to the fire.

Shane didn't know what he was going to do. He just knew he was mad. He paced back and forth behind the dunes. Finally he picked up his cell and called Chase.

"That was quick," Chase said.

"Meet me by the landing in ten minutes," Shane said. "But watch out. The Jet Ski boys are back in town."

"Okay," Chase said, like he understood more than Shane did. "I'll be there."

Shane pulled off his sweater. The fireworks were unguarded. He stuffed a bunch of them into his sweater and made a bundle of it. He thought there was enough left that they wouldn't notice. He didn't know what he was going to do with them yet, but the thought of things exploding made him feel better.

By the time Chase arrived with the boat, Shane knew what he wanted to do. But it scared him a little.

"Taxi's here," Chase said. "Where do you want to go?"

Shane waded into the water, not caring if he got his pants wet. He handed Chase the bundled sweater, and his cell. "Don't let that get wet," he said. "It's fireworks, and my phone. And hand me that life jacket. I might have to go all the way in."

Chase rested on his oars and gave Shane that crooked smile. "Dude, what happened to you out there?" he said. "This is like superhero Shane. This is not normal for you."

Shane climbed into the boat, splashing. "You know what happened with the Jet Ski last night? I found out who did it. They're planning to come by again tonight. I just—I guess it made me mad. I'm not gonna take this anymore."

"How are you going to stop it?" Chase reached over and put the paw of the Swamp Thing on Shane's shoulder. Shane realized he was shaking.

"Dude, take a breath," Chase said. "I've been there. But what can you do? They're not worth getting into trouble."

"The first thing I thought of was dropping a dime on them," Shane admitted. "But I don't want it to get back to me. I have to spend time up here and they could make it hell."

"Exactly," Chase said.

"But then I thought, suppose their Jet Skis had been improperly secured—which they probably are anyway. Suppose they just happened to drift away from shore and it was no one's fault. It just happened. Know what I mean?"

Chase was starting to smile again.

"Then they wouldn't be able to bother us tonight. And possibly they'd get busted for driving the Jet Skis at night, which is not cool."

"And what about that?" Chase said, nodding toward the bundle.

"They were going to set those off later. They still have a bunch of them. So…maybe if these happened to go off prematurely…it could be that someone else would call the rangers. And if not, oh well. We'll be out of here anyway."

"That's brilliant," Chase said.

He rowed along the bank, while Shane used his flashlight to scan for the Jet Skis. He found one pulled up on the bank, and two more moored to a log.

"I'm going in," he said.

"Wait, I'll help." Chase pulled into a stand of reeds and anchored the rowboat. Then he slid over the side and into the water.

"This is everything you're not supposed to do," he said. "Leaving the boat? At night? Such a bad idea."

"Shut up," Shane said, heaving at the watercraft to push it offshore and into the water. "They only used sandbag anchors—so I guess they just dragged. Too bad."

One by one, they pushed the Jet Skis into deeper water.

"Someplace they won't see them right away," Chase panted. "Past the reeds there, it's all mudflats. Put them aground. They'll be safe but hard to—"

"Eww!" Shane found the mud by floundering into it up to the knees.

"Lie back—your float vest will hold you up and you can float out of it," Chase said. He'd slipped, and his arms were muck to the elbows.

"It stinks," Shane said. "I stink. Nature is disgusting."

"No, it's not," Chase said. "It's just nature. Swamp Thing, remember? Swamp Things rule. It'll wash off on the way back to the boat."

There were a few minutes of panic when they couldn't find the boat. But it was there.

"I'm taller, I'll boost you," Chase said. Shane scrambled up his back, got a knee on his shoulder, and Chase's wiry arms pushed him up into the boat. He put his weight on the other side so Chase could flop his long legs over the gunwale without swamping them.

Shane tried to wipe his face and just smeared more mud over himself. "And now, part two. Oh crap. Matches. I didn't bring any."

Chase smirked. "Reach under the seat. In the metal box—my emergency kit. Never go out without it. There's a lighter in there."

"In case you need to smoke a bong?" Shane said.

"I don't use drugs," Chase started to explain seriously. Then he stopped. "Oh. You're kidding, right. Ha ha."

Shane fumbled for the fireworks in the dark. He had half a dozen strings of firecrackers and several rockets.

"If I could give you some advice, 007," Chase said. "You don't really want lighted explosives in the boat with you by accident."

He sculled back toward the log. "Put them on here, light them, and then I'll row like hell."

Shane got everything set up in a line, then leaned out of the boat and lit every fuse as fast as he could. Chase pulled away fast enough that Shane nearly fell into the water again. He'd passed the grounded Jet Skis when the firecrackers started to go off. The explosions were deafening even though he'd been expecting it. Chase passed the point and reached the shelter of the little islands as the rockets' red glare faded from the sky. When the last of the firecrackers died away, Shane could hear screen doors slamming and saw a few lights coming on in nearby cottages. Indignant residents came out to see what was going on. He could imagine that the park ranger office would be getting some phone calls soon.

"That was awesome," Chase said.

"And now—back to the frog census?" Shane said.

Chase shipped the oars and let the boat drift under the dark branches of the tamaracks on the island. "Um—no—I'm done. I finished early on purpose." He sounded kind of funny, the way Shane did when he was nervous and his voice became unreliable.

He leaned forward and put his hand on Shane's shoulder again. "Could you ever—I mean—have you ever wanted to— kiss a Swamp Thing?" he said.

Shane didn't say anything. But when Chase leaned toward him, he didn't move back. He put his hand on Chase's other shoulder, to brace himself. And kissed a Swamp Thing.

It wasn't anything like homework. At first there was the smell of Off, and mud, and a touch of Banana Boat coconut-scented sunscreen. Then there was just the taste of Chase, and warm wet lips. Who knew? Shane thought. Something else the whole world knew and not him—that kissing Mark hadn't been practice for anything. This wasn't technical. It was wet fireworks and burning water, and the sun coming up at night in the middle of a swamp. It was also kind of like wrestling on a ladder, as they tried to wrap the maximum amount of arms and legs awkwardly around each other while not capsizing the boat. And the mosquitoes found them and congratulated them enthusiastically.

They broke apart, breathing hard.

"*This*—is not happening in a boat," Chase said.

"No," Shane agreed, though he felt that it almost had. "But—"

"Yeah, I know," Chase interrupted. Shane knew they were both seeing the same thing—single beds with matching cowboy spreads, and Shane's mom and dad down the hall. "I've got an idea this time. Think about cold water, and frog mating."

When they reached the Kerrys' cottage, Shane stopped on the screen porch, opened the door, and stuck his head inside. "Hello? Mom? We're back."

Both of his parents were up, his mother in the kitchen putting things away.

"Oh, Shane! You're early. Come in—why are you standing in the doorway?"

"We're kind of muddy," Shane said. He spread out his arms so she could get a good look at him.

"Oh my goodness! What on earth happened to you?"

"We went aground," Chase said. "We had to get out and push."

"I'll get a towel," Shane's mom said.

"We had another idea," Chase said. He managed to look politely apologetic, under the mud smears. "There's a guest bath at my house. We could go clean up over there and not track mud through your house."

The Kerrys only had one shower, upstairs.

"It's no trouble," Shane's mom said.

"Well, there's another thing," Chase said. "I'm kind of worried about leaving the house empty."

"What do you mean?" Shane's mother looked at Shane. "Is something going on out there? We heard a commotion a little while ago."

"Yes, ma'am," Chase said. "We heard it, too. It sounded like fireworks, maybe at that beach party. A lot of kids know there's nobody home at my house. So I wondered if it would be okay if I slept over there tonight. Just to make sure nobody tries to come over and trash the house."

Shane's mom looked from one to the other, as if she suspected they were up to something but wasn't sure what.

"I wouldn't be alone," Chase said. "That is, if Shane could come with me."

"Mom, we'd be *right* next door," Shane said. "I'll call you if we see anything that doesn't look right."

"Oh, let them go," Shane's dad called from the other room. "I doubt they can get into much trouble." He appeared in the kitchen doorway. "Just stay out of your dad's liquor cabinet," he said to Chase.

"Yes, sir," Chase said sheepishly.

"Yeah, I was young once," Shane's dad said. "Go get cleaned up before you catch pneumonia."

❖

Shane stood in the foyer of the Garrett place, looking around, while Chase went to get more towels from the laundry room. Everything in there was new and top of the line, from the coffee maker to the big-screen TV. All perfect stuff, the kind of thing Shane had always envied.

It didn't seem to matter any more. He'd fallen for a Swamp Thing, for a geek with a spark in his eyes and wiry, calloused hands, for a guy who smelled like gunpowder, Off, and mud instead of Axe or Lucky. And he felt like everything about this vacation was finally the way it was supposed to be.

Chase came back, leaving a trail of muddy droplets across the white tile floor. "Do you want the first shower?" he said.

Shane brushed a bit of water weed off Chase's bare chest, and let his hand trail slowly down to that tantalizing gap between damp jeans and a glimpse of untanned flesh. He felt Chase flinch from his chilly fingers. He closed the space between them and felt Chase's warm breath on his neck. Shane rubbed his hands over the rhythm of bone and muscle he'd only glimpsed earlier, drawing the shape of Chase in his mind's eye. "We can shower later," Shane said. "Swamp Things forever." They pressed together, rib to rib and belly to belly, and body heat rose up through chilled skin as creatures in dark water rise to meet the light.

GET BRENDA FOXWORTHY
SHAWN SYMS

I got off the blue Niagara Transit bus and crossed the road, entering the yard behind Simcoe Street Public School. Walking alone at night put me on edge. The schoolyard was empty, and I felt totally nervous.

God fucking damn it, Rickie told me she'd be here a half hour ago. Leaning against the fence, I pinched my arm as punishment for swearing, though I hadn't even said it out loud. Tapped out a nervous rhythm on the pile of dusty pebbles under my discount-store sneaker. Sweat slopped onto my brow, courtesy of the late-summer humidity that weighed down the air even in early evening. I wiped my forehead with the back of my hand. Tonight, we were going to do something outrageous, like nothing I'd ever dared before.

The three of us agreed to meet behind the elementary school in order to draw as little attention as possible. Where could be quieter than the backyard of a grade school in August, especially this late at night? We all worked at the Village, but Preet had the night free to take his mom and dad to a temple in St Catharines for some Hindu holiday. Rickie's shift ended at nine o'clock and she said she'd hurry over. Preet was picking us up before ten, as soon as he was back in Niagara Falls. I thought about where we were going: Brenda Foxworthy's house. There wasn't sufficient skin on both my arms to pinch myself enough times for all the swearing that nasty girl's name inspired in me. For once I wanted to do more than just swear, though.

And I was off work because Ed hadn't scheduled me any shifts at all that weekend. What a prick. I pinched my arm again, wished my boss wasn't so good-looking. Ed managed us parking-lot attendants at Maple Leaf Village every summer. Nineteen and a typical macho jock, he was in the law-and-security program at Niagara College. You got the feeling he liked being in charge. He liked to wear tight shirts that showed off his arms and chest, both of which possessed wiry spirals of manly hair. When he wasn't ruling the roost at work, I would see him trolling around Clifton Hill in his white Trans-Am. Checking out the chicks, I guessed. He was ridiculously proud of that stupid car, bragged to all the guys at work about it.

I was pissed about the time off. I needed that summer job. Not all of us had rich dads to pay for school clothes, let alone shiny white cars. When he saw me looking at the schedule in the office yesterday, Ed came up to me with a fake-looking smile and patted me on the shoulder. "Sorry about that, buddy. Too many guys on the team this year, I can't fit everybody in every single weekend."

His firm hand on my shoulder had caused some stirring in my underwear, but I willed my groin back under control. What a phony. Ed was not my "buddy" at all. One time when he and I were alone in the office and I complained about having to work late, he actually put me into a headlock with my face in his armpit till I said *uncle*. I remembered the smell—and the shame. The scent I secretly liked, the feeling of defeat I sure didn't. I never told anyone. Ed had pet names for all the parking guys; to my face, he called me Supermodel because I'm thin. I knew he called me "Dean the Queen" behind my back. Then again, who didn't? Preet and Rickie, that's who.

If there's one thing the three of us never spoke about, it was anything related to sex. Maybe that made us atypical eleventh graders, but for each of us the topic was a sore spot. Rickie was a loner who only had male friends. Her and Preet hung out and played basketball together. "Rick's just one of the guys," Preet had explained once. "I basically treat her 100 percent like a bro— the only thing we don't do alike is use the same washroom." I'd never seen her use a bathroom at all, in fact.

I had been friends with Preet since grade eight, when his family moved to Canada. Mrs McDowell, my homeroom teacher, asked me to befriend him when he first arrived and spoke only Punjabi. Over time, he became well liked—Preet was smart, friendly, great at sports, and very handsome. He was able to run in the popular circles at school, with friends on both the football team and student council. He was nice to all the teen leaders, but he kept most of those people at arm's length. He maintained a close friendship with me even as the others christened me "queer of the year."

I'd known Rickie even longer. One day when I was in grade five, she started following me home and threatening to beat the shit out of me for calling her adopted brother a chink. She'd gotten bad information. Her brother was a tough little kid—there was no way I'd have provoked him, even though he was two years younger than me. And of course I'd have never said that word; I pinched myself again just thinking it. It wasn't the first time someone chased me home or beat me up, and it certainly hadn't been the last. But I had both Preet and Rickie to watch my back, which was a relief. Would I ever stand up for myself? Yes, I thought. Tonight.

A screech of tires a block away tore me from my thoughts. A sleek black car gunned up Armory Street like a drag racer, though there was not another vehicle in sight to compete with. Instinctively I drew closer to the fence. As the car passed, I heard a guy on the passenger side laugh as he tossed a crumpled Coke can out the window at me. The car skidded to a halt at Victoria Avenue, then quickly pulled around the corner and out of sight, a chorus of yelping neighborhood dogs barking in its wake. Soon all was quiet again.

Blocks away, tourist trap Clifton Hill was loaded with noisy idiots: loud American visitors buying cotton candy for kids up well past their normal bedtimes. Drunks from around the world stumbling down the street in search of a greasy burger. Honeymooners destined for heart-shaped hot tubs. A few late-night sightseers at the foot of the hill arguing about which Niagara waterfall was the best. What a bunch of losers. I yawned just thinking about it.

"Hey, Dean." Her low, gravelly voice came out of nowhere. I jumped, and actually shrieked a little. Rickie had walked through the schoolyard instead of up the street, surprising me from behind.

"Thank God you're here. You scared me!" I put my hand on my chest and shook nervously.

Towering over me by three inches, she put a reassuring hand on my shoulder. With her short, dark near-crewcut and bulky build, Rickie looked like a football player. In my imagination, the high school football team set the bar in terms of masculinity—and I always fell short. Never wearing makeup and with a strong, self-assured demeanor, Rickie had it down without even trying. But while just thinking about those guys filled me with nervous anxiety, Rickie's presence had a calming effect.

I turned to her and smiled. "How was work?"

"The usual."

"Anyone barf?"

"Nope, believe it or not."

"Anyone jump?" Rickie operated the giant Ferris wheel at the Maple Leaf Village amusement park. It was two hundred feet tall. Someone tried to jump once this summer. Rickie hadn't been working that day, though. I don't know why she was acting so sensitive. The guy didn't actually die.

"Hey, that's not funny, kid…" She grabbed me half playfully by the scruff of the neck. She was always calling me "kid" even though we were both sixteen. Her father used the same expression all the time. A single dad, he was a mechanic at Niagara Falls Auto.

I paused before my next question. "Did you see Brenda?"

Rickie's eyes locked with mine. "She's still there." Her voice cut like glass. In three short, sharp shards, you could hear exactly how Rickie felt about Brenda.

I had no idea why Brenda Foxworthy even had a job. Her father was an alderman and her mother was a real-estate agent. Still, she worked at the Village like the rest of us Niagara teens. She sold fudge to tourists in a booth where she dressed in a uniform with a short white skirt. What a princess. What a bitch. I didn't bother to pinch myself for swearing anymore. Brenda was still at work. Good. Everything was going according to plan. Now if only Preet would get here—time being our great enemy at the moment.

Rickie carried the rope in a brown paper bag. Preet was bringing the metal hook. In my knapsack, I had the long, sharp knife.

The three of us lived within blocks of one another, all worked on the same gaudy tourist strip, and we usually ended up in a lot of high school classes together. But right now, the main thing binding us was our intense hatred for Brenda. Rickie and I both turned when we heard the low rumble of an automobile engine. It was Preet, approaching slowly in his brother Vijay's black Mercury.

The car pulled up and we got inside.

"Hey, how's it going?" Preet called out over the car stereo as Rickie took the front seat and I got into the back. He shook hands with both of us. Preet usually did that; it was one of his macho behaviors that, to me, felt both alien and adorable at the same time. As we passed all the drunken yahoos outside the Caverly Tavern, Preet rolled up the windows and turned on the air-conditioning. "Shit, it's a hot night."

We made nervous small talk as we drove to our destination—Brenda's expansive house in the city's tony north end, Stamford Centre. I kept quiet—because Preet's taste in music drove me crazy. I hated ZZ Top. Why did he always have to play the hard-rock station? In my bedroom by myself, I listen to new wave. Preet told us how they barely made it to the temple because both his brothers had come home drunk and started an argument with his father.

We all had our own reasons for what we were about to do. Why did I hate Brenda Foxworthy? Well, for years I'd disliked her as much as the other rich poseurs who made up the gifted program at our school. I was supposedly smarter than average, but I always felt like a fish out of water in that group—most of whom had been "gifted" since birth: gifted with violin lessons, showered with trips to Europe, granted anything they ever wanted.

I'd always been a wallflower in that program, until we got involved in the Board of Ed's problem-solving competition last year. We were put into teams to strategize solutions to social issues like acid rain. I unexpectedly came to life in our preparatory sessions. It involved both creative thinking and stuff that I cared about. For once, I felt motivated in my otherwise unhappy high school career.

At least, I did until Brenda announced the morning of the Niagara South competition that she was dumping both me and Andrew Horsgill to join another team with some of her snobby friends. Each team needed a minimum of three members and we couldn't get anyone else to hook up with us under such short notice. Brenda's team won, and went on to win a North America–wide competition in Illinois a few months later. So Brenda Foxworthy was the 1986 problem-solving champion—accepting a trophy at a banquet in Chicago while I sat alone in my room feeling like a loser.

Preet had the inside scoop on Brenda's house because he'd been there before. They had actually gone out for a month, culminating in a final date where they had sex on Brenda's bed while her parents were at a Lion's Club banquet. She dumped him the next day. That was three weeks ago. Preet looked like he was going to cry when he told me. Red-faced, he confessed she'd made a disparaging remark about his penis. "She's got a gigantic stuffed animal sitting next to her bed. How was I supposed to keep my dick hard with that fucked-up thing right next to me?" Out of respect for Preet, I managed not to laugh. But I did try to picture him and her naked together. I'd never even seen another guy's cock—I had a shy bladder and preferred bathroom stalls to awkward rows of public urinals.

Preet's erection malfunction wasn't the only reason for the abrupt breakup, though. She told him she needed a boyfriend with a more wholesome image because of her parents' standing in the community. Preet was one of the most clean-cut guys in our whole school. The only way he differed from Brenda's other boyfriends was the color of his skin. Soon after, Brenda started dating Angelo Mancuso, a nineteen-year-old with a dumb gaze and a five o'clock shadow. I found it bizarre she'd dumped Preet, then started seeing Angelo. Her family and friends were such WASPs I was surprised they would even consider an Italian guy to be white. But his parents owned a construction company.

Rickie had her own reasons for hating Brenda, but she wouldn't tell either of us. I only know because I saw what happened. It was at the end of football season, the day our team kicked Westlane High's asses. The cool kids had spiked their

7-Eleven Slurpees with gin at the game and everyone was acting punchy. I was kinda surprised to see Rickie at the game. Then again, same with me, but for weeks it was all anyone talked about. It was more or less mandatory; afternoon classes had been cancelled so everyone could go to the game. I'd tried to hide in the school library, but they shut it down for the rest of the day. In a less-populated corner of the football field I saw Brenda beckon for Rickie to follow her behind the bleachers. This was weird; I sneaked closer to see. Brenda kissed Rickie full on the lips, and took Rickie's hand and placed it on one of her breasts. After a few seconds she pulled away. Brenda stared at Rickie. From where I stood, I couldn't see Rickie's face. "There," Brenda said. "At least you know you're not a faggot, anyway." She walked away. I was confused. What a weird thing to say. Rick wasn't even a guy, right? It was some stupid prank.

I never mentioned it to Rickie because I wouldn't know what to say.

Part of me wished I understood why Brenda liked to hurt people. The other part of me only wanted to hurt her back.

I might never have dared if not for Preet, though. The whole thing was his idea. Rickie had enthusiastically agreed. I was afraid—but liked the idea of getting revenge for the first time ever. If Rickie and Preet were in, I was in. After all, it was me who supplied the knife. Grow some balls, I reminded myself. That's what my boss Ed had told me after I said *uncle* and he finally released my face from the aroma of his armpit. He'd looked disappointed in me, staring after me as I walked away.

Turning onto Stamford Green Drive, after about a half block we reached Brenda's house. Her red Camaro was nowhere to be seen—but a brown Lincoln Continental, presumably her parents', sat at the far end of the driveway. Some lights were on in the house, too.

Preet slowed down, pulled just past the Foxworthy residence, and parked in front of the next-door neighbors' house—far enough not to be noticed, but close enough for a quick getaway. Despite the air-conditioning, I was clammy.

"Remember everything we talked about?" Preet asked quietly.

We both nodded. Preet handed me the heavy metal hook, and I put it into my knapsack.

"Any questions?"

We shook our heads.

"We have to be extremely quiet starting now. Got it?"

We nodded. Preet opened the door and got out, and we followed suit. Closing our doors as quietly as possible, we tiptoed through the far edge of the yard toward Brenda's bedroom window, on the west side of the house—on the second floor.

Her light had been left on. As Preet had anticipated, Brenda's window was open. And as he had already told us, the sill was made of painted wood. I unzipped my knapsack and handed the rope to Preet, followed by the heavy metal clasp. Preet had explained it was an extra-durable piton used by his older brothers when they went rock climbing. It hurt my arm when I pulled it out of the sack. I guess I needed to grow some biceps, too.

He secured the thick length of rope to the piton, angling it with the sharp talon facing forward. Preet launched it toward Brenda's window, where it landed on the sill and sank into it with a muted thunk. Thank God for all his years of basketball—if it had been me, I'd have broken a downstairs window or missed the house altogether. I sucked at sports. I couldn't throw or kick to save my life. Or who knew if I had any athletic talent or decent aim. I usually seized up with fear any time people even looked at me.

Preet turned and smiled. Rickie gave a thumbs-up. Preet

walked over to where the rope hung down neatly along the side of the house and gave it three or four firm tugs. He started to climb up.

Once he reached the top and clambered inside, Preet gestured for Rickie to follow. I watched with amazement as the piton held in place, supporting her beefy frame as she scaled the side of the house. She pushed her way through the window frame; now it was my turn. If Preet hadn't ordered me into silence earlier, this was just the moment I'd have started blubbering and babbling. I was terrified, but I grabbed the rope and started to hoist myself up. Trying to be rational, I told myself if it could support both Preet and Rickie, the rope could support a beanpole like me without breaking. So this was what it felt like to break and enter. As I found my footing, I actually started to feel a bit excited—and strangely honorable. I was like a cat burglar stealing back my own dignity.

So far so good. Once I got up about eight feet, I could see into the Foxworthys' kitchen; the window was a few feet over. It featured an island in the center of the room with a grey marbled counter top. The room was spotless, as if it had never been used. It was also empty, thank goodness. I kept moving, looking neither up nor down. After an eternity, I reached Brenda's window. I used both hands to pull myself in and tried to still my adrenaline-fueled panting. Thankfully, the door to her bedroom was closed. I caught my breath and looked around.

Rickie stalked the room, her eyes narrowing as she took in the luxurious surroundings. Brenda's four-poster bed was adorned with a sleek white satin spread. She had five pillows, whose cases had pretty floral designs. Next to the bed was a matching white dresser with a large built-in mirror. The glass had ornate etchings around the edges.

Sitting on the dresser was a thick copy of the Concise Oxford Dictionary. Brenda had been the kid in kindergarten who got the

64-colour box of Crayolas when most of us had gotten the eight basic hues. I had to touch the dictionary just to determine if the spine had been cracked—to see if it had ever been opened. I walked over and picked it up—and saw something next to it that startled and surprised me. A little bound book with a chocolate-brown cover and a gold lock. With ornate letters, the cover read *My Personal Diary*. It went straight into my pants pocket. Here might be my answer to finding out why Brenda was such a sadist.

Preet stood in front of his prey, over in the corner of the bedroom closest to the window. He hissed at me: "Dean, give me the knife." Pulling at one shoulder strap and then the other, I removed the compact orange knapsack from my back and tossed it to him. In it was the largest knife from the Ginsu set my dad ordered my mom off the TV for Christmas last year. Preet pulled it out. The blade was large and full of serrated teeth.

He stood in front of an extra-large stuffed teddy bear, which wore a yellow felt hat as big as my head. Plopped down next to Brenda's bed, it was over three feet tall even seated. The bear's plush fur was dark brown, with a lighter tan fur lining the inside of its ears, the pads of its feet, and a circle that surrounded its nose. A smile had been sewn into the tan fabric using thick black thread. I wondered if a teddy bear like that would have the power to take away my own erection like it had to Preet. I'd never had to perform sexually for another person, let alone in the presence of a Godzilla-sized Pooh bear.

Brenda had told Preet she'd had the stuffed animal since she was a little girl. When her parents first gave it to her, it was taller than her. Bits of fur were missing here and there, like the patchy bald spot on the back of my dad's head we weren't supposed to mention. Its eyes were two plastic hazel buttons. They looked strangely sad.

"Fuck you, bitch," Preet whispered. He stabbed the stuffed

bear roughly below its throat, pulling the blade out and shoving it back in several times in a downward motion until he'd carved a jagged line that would have split the animal's rib cage in two—had it possessed one. Though gutted, it still offered that same sad smile. Rickie and I watched in silence as he kicked the bear between its legs several times, causing the little white Styrofoam balls that comprised its innards to fly across the room.

Then Rickie walked over to Brenda's dresser and took a tube of crimson lipstick from an open box full of jewelry and makeup. She applied it to the stuffed bear's lips, giving it a surreal sneer like some kind of circus clown. She looked at Preet standing next to her, and put out her hand. Preet gave her the knife. Rickie used it to cut the bear's head right off and dropped it on the ground in front of the ruined animal. I was startled by my friends' violence, but I felt like a live wire myself. If I had a match I might have set the decapitated bear on fire.

That's when I noticed the trophy. It sat on a small white table between the bedroom door and the closet door, next to a miniature clock encased in a glass dome. The trophy had a wooden base, upon which sat a pewter cup with handles on either side. The base had a small metal plate screwed to its front, engraved with *Tomorrow's Leaders Problem-Solving Contest, Chicago, Illinois, First Place.* I stared at it blankly, unable to draw my eyes away.

Preet looked at me, then at the trophy. He walked to the dresser, grabbed the winning cup, and placed it on the floor in front of him. Then he unzipped his pants, reached into his underwear, pulled out his penis, and began to urinate into the trophy in a steaming waterfall.

"Whoa, man!" Rickie called out in shock. No matter what Brenda had said, Preet's dick looked beautiful to me. I couldn't help but stare. Rickie was gazing right at Preet's pecker, too, as gushes of urine pumped out of it and poured into that hateful goddamned trophy cup. As Preet's stream slowed to a trickle, I wondered if I could get over my pee-shyness and fill it up the rest of the way myself.

Right then the bedroom door pushed open. Brenda's little sister Becki, her head barely reaching the doorknob, stepped into the room, pointed at Preet's penis, widened her eyes, and screamed. Preet stuffed it back in his pants and darted toward the window, Rickie lumbering directly behind him, Becki screaming all the while. I heard a rumble from behind her as someone started up the stairs.

I looked over at the now-full trophy cup and its specially inscribed square base. I took two steps toward it, then stopped. I felt a moment of inner calm. With the inside of my right foot, I kicked the trophy's base as hard as I could. With immaculate aim, it arced into the air toward the corner of the room and landed, upside down, on the bear right where its head used to be. As it came down, a torrent of piss soaked the giant teddy bear's white Styrofoam guts. Then, like an avalanche descending the side of the mountain, the trophy toppled downward, rolling in circles with the effect of gravity till it landed upright at the bear's feet. Right on top of its chopped-off head. One edge of the base stabbed the smiling stuffed animal directly below its black plastic nose.

A wave of euphoria I'd never experienced before passed through me. I felt like the star football player who'd just kicked a fifty-yard field goal and won the game. Becki continued to scream. I took one more look at the yellow-stained bear and the trophy at its feet, the rim of its cup still wet with drops of Preet's urine. I bolted for the open window. I heard Rickie's voice call upward from the ground below, "Dean, hurry up!"

That's when I heard Brenda's voice in the hallway, calling out Becki's name. Fuck. I'd just been ready to hop out the window and climb down the rope. I stuck my head out the window and hissed, "Guys, just leave. Do it."

My stomach was doing flip-flops just like yesterday when

my handsome boss Ed put his hand on my back. But I willed myself to stay calm. I can handle this, I thought. In the distance, I heard Preet and Rickie pull away in the car.

I turned to face her arrival, but Brenda didn't even notice me. Her straight platinum hair spun as entered the room, her eyes boring a hole into tiny Becki where she stood, dwarfed by the enormous defiled bear. I noticed that Brenda's perfect white uniform skirt was soiled with the green and brown smear of a mint-chocolate fudge stain. She addressed her baby sister coolly.

"Why would you wreck my tired old stuffed animal, you little twat? I'm sick of that thing anyway. I would have just given it to you, greedy bitch."

Becki, who looked about five, howled as if she hated her sister as much as the rest of us did, then she pointed to where I stood on the other side of the massive bedroom, my skinny frame next to that of the window. Brenda glanced at me and then stared her sister down once more. With a look of supreme menace, she snapped her fingers and screaming Becki went silent.

An adult male voice called up from downstairs. "Is Becki all right?"

"She's fine," Brenda called out in a loud, crisp voice. Then she shut her bedroom door. Still mute, Becki crouched down behind the remains of the large stuffed animal.

Brenda turned to me and our eyes met. She smirked at me, self-possessed as ever, as if her enemies broke into her home all the time. "Dean the Queen. I wouldn't have thought you'd have the balls."

"What are you doing here?" My nostrils finally tweaked at the smell of all that sodden piss. Why wasn't Becki plugging her nose?

"Shouldn't I be asking you that? I live here." Brenda affected an imperious tone, like she was a princess or the star of her own TV show. "Some American fag in a purple T-shirt barfed all over the front of the fudge stand. We shut down early. I got a ride home from the parking-lot manager. I assumed he was gonna grope my legs, but he didn't. Another fag. Just like you and your friend Preet." She paused, looking around the room dramatically. "Sometimes I feel like I am surrounded by fags." Brenda looked at the bear, and she looked at me. "Like right now," she taunted.

What a strange moment. Inside, I felt like I was swimming up a river, and every time Brenda said *fag*, it was as if my leg felt the tug of the undertow. I wasn't going to show it, though.

"Your words can't hurt me."

In the corner, Becki sniffled loudly, and Brenda snapped her fingers in her direction again. The kid paused mid-sniffle.

"You have no idea what I'm capable of." Brenda sneered. She looked over toward the window, the hook, the rope. "I could push you right back out of my room the same way you came like a fucking burglar." She paused. "A turd burglar." Brenda seemed pleased with herself. I knew she was hateful, but she'd never said such mean things to me before. At school, she had such a veneer of respectability and popularity. Was this the real Brenda after all?

On the floor between us lay my orange knapsack and my dad's Ginsu blade. I'd almost forgotten it earlier. Brenda followed my glance, her own eyes showing a glint of mania. I was sure she wasn't crazy enough to try to carve me up in revenge for her hacked teddy. At least I hoped not. I didn't want to find out. She started to walk toward me. Brenda looked dangerous.

"Your words can't hurt me," I repeated as I pulled her diary out of my back pocket, its lock glinting in the overhead lamplight. "But I think they could hurt you."

Brenda froze. "Give me that back."

"Maybe my friends want to read what you said about them in here. Maybe your own snobby clique might be interested in your true thoughts about them. Or maybe your parents would like to read it. Why don't you call them up here right now?"

"Give that to me. Please," she said.

"I don't have to do anything you say, Brenda. I'm not afraid of you." In the corner of the room, Becki looked up. And she smiled.

Brenda stared at me. "Now *back up*," I told her, raising my voice and brandishing the diary like it was a Bible and she were a vampire. Brenda retreated several steps. I wondered about the book I had in my hands and the power it clearly held over her. What was in there? Brenda sat down on the edge of her bed and played with the hem of her skirt. She wouldn't look at me. I snapped my fingers in her direction to get her attention.

"Where do you get off calling my friend a fag, Brenda? Preet deserves better than you. You messed with Rickie, too. Even if I was attracted to girls—and I'm not—I wouldn't touch you with a ten-foot pole. You're toxic."

I waved the book in her face. "You're the one who doesn't know what I'm capable of." I walked over to Becki crouching in the corner and handed her the diary. "Go downstairs now and give this to your father." Becki took the book, got to her feet and opened the door. She looked up at me. "Don't let your sister push you around anymore either." Becki exited the bedroom.

I slowly walked past Brenda, who had lain down on her bed as if I wasn't even there, flat on her back. Her bangs sat as straight as the edge of a tombstone. I picked up my knife, put it in the knapsack, tossed it out the window, and climbed out carefully. Before my descent, I looked over at Brenda one last time and surveyed her mess of a room. It smelled like shame. This is not where I belong, I told myself, grasping the rope and lowering myself downward.

When I reached the ground, I grabbed my knapsack, traversed the yard, and emerged onto the sidewalk. Time to go home. I'd call Rickie once I got there so my friends would know for sure that I was all right. Maybe they were even waiting for me a block or two from here. I reached the end of Brenda's street and turned onto Portage Road. After a minute, I heard a car pull up behind me on the dark and quiet street. I hoped to see Preet and Rickie, but when I turned around I was greeted by a white Trans-Am. The tinted window on the passenger side rolled down, and the driver leaned over. "Dean, you live around here?" Ed still wore his white uniform shirt from the Village parking lot. The top two buttons were undone. I leaned into the car window. In the hot night, I could already smell his sweat, and I liked it.

"No. I live downtown near Simcoe Street School."

"Get in, then."

As I opened the door, I saw Ed reach over and turn the radio off. I sat next to him, not bothering to buckle my seat belt. I locked the door next to me though. "What are you doing around here, boss?" I was nervous, but I wasn't going to let it show.

"I had to give one of the fudge girls a ride home. A friend of mine from over the river was partying on the Hill, and he ended up barfing all over the Village fudge stand. It was kind of funny." He laughed awkwardly. Ed seemed nervous for some reason. I wasn't used to that. "Since then," he said, "I've just been… driving around."

"Your friend. A guy in a purple shirt?" The fag had Brenda mentioned.

Ed raised one eyebrow. "Yeah, his name is David…do you know him?"

"Nope. I just heard about him." I looked closely at Ed's face for what felt like the first time. Other than when he made me say *uncle* alone in the office that time, we'd never been this close before. Such short, short hair. Perfect eyebrows. Seal brown eyes. "That girl you drove home, what did you think of her?" I searched his expression.

"Nothing. I didn't think anything of her at all. You want a ride home?" Ed put his right hand on my knee. Inside, I felt like everything I understood about the world was being turned upside down. But I wasn't going to let him know. I turned to face him.

"The schoolyard near my house is nice and quiet. Maybe we could drive there, then take a walk together. Let's go," I said and placed my hand on top of his.

CAVE CANEM
DIA PANNES

From our porch, I could see clear down to the corner. There hadn't been much traffic all afternoon—we don't exactly live on the way to anyplace, unless you count Collin's Feed and Tackle Shop, which I don't—and things showed no sign of picking up. I'd been waiting for Dad for almost two hours.

"I'm sure something came up."

"Something always comes up where your father is concerned." Mom snorted. "Are you going to waste your whole night waiting on him to show up?" She shook her head. "That's the trouble with bad boys, Wyatt. They break your heart."

"I guess not." I pulled my phone out of my pocket and started to text. "Maybe Jacksie wants to do something."

"Not the best idea you ever had, but better than this." Mom smiled. She always talks like she doesn't like Jacksie, but deep down, I think she has a soft spot for my flamboyant best friend. Four years ago, she won a radio contest, and the prize was two tickets to see *Hairspray* on Broadway. She insisted Jacksie and I should go—paid for the train trip into New York and everything, and called the whole thing a rite of passage. We'd just turned thirteen at the time. I hadn't really known what she was talking about then—Mom knew I was gay before I figured it out myself. Jacksie's known since forever. "Our fabulous adventure!" was how he'd referred to the trip.

My phone buzzed. *Sorry*, Jacksie's text read. *Stuck w/ gruesome 2some.* Jacksie had two younger brothers, Hunter and Steve. They were seven and nine, and completely annoying. Even their own parents couldn't stand them, which I suspected was why they went out all the time.

"That stinks," I muttered.

"No luck with Jacksie?" Mom asked.

I shook my head.

"Sometimes you have to make your own luck." Clyde, my mother's idiot boyfriend, spoke up. "They're getting things set up for the fair. I saw lots of kids hanging out there. You should check it out." He glanced at my mom, sideways, real quick. "Lots of pretty girls."

I glared at him, but he kept right on talking. "Here's some money. In case you want to get something to eat." He handed over a twenty. "Or whatever."

"That's a good plan." Mom sounded relieved now that the great mystery of what Wyatt was going to do with his Thursday night had been resolved. "Don't worry about your father. If he decides to show up—"

"Doubtful," Clyde said.

"I'll deal with him," Mom continued. "You go have a good time."

What the hell, I figured. I might as well go. Twenty bucks is twenty bucks, you know? And it was obvious they didn't want me hanging around the house. I didn't even want to begin thinking about why. "I'll go check it out."

I hopped off the porch.

"You want the car?" Clyde asked.

Mom and I both turned to stare at him. I'm not what you'd call the world's best driver. I've had my learner's permit for fourteen months now. In that time, I've gone maybe fifty miles. Mom hates driving with me, and I'm not exactly thrilled about having her screaming in terror every time I go faster than thirty miles an hour.

"He can't, by himself," Mom said. "I can drive him down there and he can walk back on his own later on…"

"It's all right," I said. "You don't have to do that." I walked everywhere that summer anyway—to my job, to the animal shelter where I volunteered, back and forth from Jacksie's house. Since school let out, I'd probably put close to a thousand miles on my sneakers.

What was another three or four miles to the fairgrounds? And if Clyde was right, and there were pretty girls hanging around, chances are that there'd be guys there too. Some of them might be worth looking at.

Stranger things have happened. Not usually to me, of course, but you never know.

❖

I understand that county fairs are big deals almost everywhere. I get it. It doesn't matter where you go. If there's a fair, crowds of people are going to show up. Some come for the rides, and other ones come for the funnel cakes and deep-fried Twinkies, and some folks just love the demolition derby.

It says something about Randsville that our crowds start showing up way before the fair opens. It doesn't matter that that Ferris wheel and Graviton are still loaded on flatbeds, or that the ticket booths aren't assembled, or that the bearded lady had, at best, a five o'clock shadow: something was happening, and that's such a rare event here that people turn out to bear witness. In this part of the state we're just that desperate for entertainment outside of the single movie theater in town.

They were bringing in the cattle trailers when I got there. Huge pickups towed perforated silver trailers, moving slowly so the show cows didn't get their udders in an uproar and curdle their milk. I saw a couple of kids I knew from school riding shotgun with their parents. They waved and I waved, and that was enough—they had things to do, and I was hoping I had people to see.

Actually, the most interesting thing I saw at the fair was this tall black guy in his twenties reach out and grab the collar of a guy around my age. They disappeared around one of the staff buildings. Out of bounds. We don't get muggings in this part of New York, but I had to follow.

So, I have seen two guys kiss before. Jacksie has downloaded a ton of gay movies onto his purple netbook. Nothing nasty—Jacksie has always said that the proof porn's boring is that no one ever says anything with more than one syllable. But we've watched *Trick* and *Were the World Mine* and daydreamed about Mr. Right.

But seeing these two kiss just a few yards away was something else…especially since I crushed hard on the kid the black guy was making out with. He had dark hair, short and spiky. Black tank top that showed off how summer tans love biceps. The silver chain from belt to pocket was simply a loop for the guy to grab on to.

I had to remember to breathe while gawking at them. And then, because I'm a stupid seventeen-year-old, I took a couple steps back and snapped a quick picture with my phone.

While cooling my blood with a cherry snow cone, I sent the photo to Jacksie. *Check him out!*

Jacksie's reply came almost instantly. *I love Bad Boys!*

Me too, I sent back. I guess taste in men was genetic. Only, I didn't really want to end up with the sort of losers my mother had.

❖

It was later, much later. I'd made my way back home and was almost asleep when I heard my mother's boyfriend running his mouth. "Well, doesn't he have a father?" Clyde asked. "He could go stay there."

"Get real. Dave didn't even manage to show up today, after he promised Wyatt he would." My mom's voice was steady and almost too calm. I don't know if Clyde ever heard her sound like that before, but every time I have, I wound up getting in some of the biggest trouble of my life shortly thereafter. In the dark, I smiled. Maybe she'd be kicking this loser to the curb soon. "I promised Wyatt he'd never be in a position where he had to depend on his father for anything, and I'm not about to change that."

"It just makes me uncomfortable," Clyde replied. "With me staying here now…and Wyatt being how he is."

"And how is Wyatt, exactly?"

"You know. The gay thing."

"You've got a problem with Wyatt being gay?"

"People have a problem with Wyatt being gay. And if I'm here, a grown man in the house with a gay teenage boy—well, they're going to talk. I don't want people to get the wrong idea."

"And if I had a teenage daughter, would we be having this conversation, Clyde?"

"That's normal. A woman's got a daughter, everyone knows that situation is gonna go nitro. Any man with a lick of sense keeps 100 percent hands off."

"But you're not going to be able to keep your hands off of Wyatt?"

I wanted to throw up. It was bad enough to think about Clyde and Mom being together. The thought of him touching me with those bloated, fat hands of his was absolutely revolting.

"What if he comes onto me? Teenage boys are full of hormones. They don't know how to control themselves."

Mom burst out laughing. "You have got to be kidding me."

Clyde sounded angry. "I'm not. You have to understand, Irene. This is a small town. People talk. They tell everything they know, and what they don't know, they're going to make up. You having that boy here is setting me up to be accused of all kinds of things."

"You think I don't know that people talk? I'm the one raising Wyatt. He's been gay since he was little. He wanted to marry Batman when he was three. I've spent my whole life listening to people talk, and so has Wyatt." I could hear Mom pacing now; four steps across the bedroom, five steps back. "It's not a new experience for us. I understand that it might be for you. But you're either going to have to man up and deal, or you're going to have to spend your nights in your own bed. I'm not putting my boy out on the streets for you."

"I'm not asking you to," Clyde protested.

"What do you think sending him to his father means, exactly?"

"Calm down—"

"*Don't* you tell me to calm down. This is Wyatt's home. And it's going to be Wyatt's home as long as he wants it to be."

"Of course. Of course it is. I'm sorry." I could hear Clyde get up—the bedsprings gave a sigh of relief when his lard butt moved—and kiss Mom. "I didn't mean to upset you. I'd never want to do that."

Jacksie never sleeps. I scrunched down in my bed and texted him. *OMG Clyde thinks I'm hot for his fat ass!*

LOL! U a chubby chaser now?

EWWWW. Laughing did make me feel better.

He wishes, Jacksie sent back.

He wants me out.

There was a long pause then, so long that I thought that

maybe Jacksie didn't get the text. I was about to write him again when he replied: *You can come here if you have to. Always.*

That made me tear up a little bit. Even though he was my best friend, I wasn't expecting him to say something like that. Of course, I wasn't expecting to ever need anyone to say that.

Thanks. Mom won't let him do it tho. It's ok.

Anytime, Wy.

It was hard to get to sleep after that. Not impossible, but hard.

❖

"Oh, Wyatt, wait until you see the sorry-looking mongrel we got in today!" Miss Vivian started screeching at me the minute I walked into Happy Valley Animal Rescue. "I told him we were in the business of saving lost causes—but between you and me, I'm not sure there's any hope for him!"

I rolled my eyes. My boss was almost fifty, but she liked to act like she was fifteen. "There's always hope, Miss V."

"You always say that, Wyatt."

"Only when it's true."

When Miss Vivian laughed, the reluctantly rescued alley cats we've got confined in cages stopped their scrapping and looked up in awe. There wasn't a tom in the place that wouldn't have cut his own nuts off to be able to yowl like that. I, on the other hand, was trying to figure out exactly how painful it would be to puncture my own eardrums.

"Let me check out this mongrel situation." Miss V. waved me to the back, intent, as always, on whatever she was reading on the computer screen. I was expecting some awful nip-happy Chihuahua-beagle mix...not the hot guy from the county fair.

Yet there he was, sorting out bags of donated pet food. Cat

food to the right, dog food to the left. There was always more dog food than cat food, even though cats outnumber dogs three to one most of the time. People just don't care about them as much, I guess.

"Hey," I said.

He looked up, brown eyes widening a little as he studied me. "Hey, I know you," he said. "Or I think I know you. You go to RCS."

I nodded. "I'm a senior this year."

He laughed. "I would be too, if I'd stayed in."

"When were you there?" RCS isn't a big high school, and I definitely would have remembered this guy.

He waved his hand vaguely. "Nearly two years ago, maybe? I only made it a couple of times before things went bad. But you were there. You're Wayne or Winston or some shit."

"Wyatt. Wyatt Haynes."

"Brody," he said. "Brody LeBeaux. Here to entertain and serve—for the next 196 hours and twelve minutes."

I raised an eyebrow. "What's that about?"

"Community service. Judge told me I had a choice. It was this or go to jail. I didn't really want to spend the summer in lockup."

"Can't blame you there. What'd you do?" I asked. "To get in trouble?"

"I was just in the wrong place at the wrong time. That's how us lost causes get started, you know." He rolled his eyes toward the front, where Miss Vivian sat.

"She's not so bad," I said. "Just loud."

"I don't think she likes me much," Brody said. "What about you? What did you do to wind up stuck here all summer?"

"It's kind of like an internship deal." I could feel my face flush. I wanted to be a vet someday, but who says stuff like that? "I'm pretty good with working with the troubled dogs. The ones that have been abused and shit. I'm hoping it helps me get a scholarship."

"So they're not paying you either."

I shook my head. "Nope."

"You wouldn't be better off working somewhere and saving up the money for school?" Brody narrowed his eyes. "Seems like that would be more of a sure thing for you."

"I go over and clean Stuckey's in the mornings," I said. "That pays all right, I guess." Mopping the bar, hauling empty kegs down to the basement, and getting all the empty bottles and cans bagged up for returns paid twenty-five dollars a day during the week, fifty on weekends—plus whatever cash I happened to find while I was cleaning. The ladies' bathroom was usually good for at least another twenty.

"Stuckey's? That's a cop bar." Brody's face looked like he had just been slapped.

I shrugged. "It's an empty bar when I'm there."

The dogs were getting bored with our conversation. They're smart, and they know when I show up that playtime is coming. By this point, they were going nuts, barking and jumping around. You couldn't even hear yourself think in there, much less have a conversation.

"What's wrong with the dogs?" Brody asked.

"They want to get out of those cages. Who's ready for some fun?" I asked. A dozen dogs howled in response. "All right!" This was the best part of the job. I pointed down toward the far end of the room, where the older dogs are kept. "Why don't you grab Sheba and Max and the twins, and I'll get these guys out."

Have you ever seen what happens when a dozen dogs who have been cooped up all day finally get a chance to run and play? It's total chaos. It's hard not to get caught right in the middle of it. I stood out there, sweating as I ran up and down the yard to throw tennis balls for the dogs to chase.

That's what I was doing when I heard Miss Vivian snapping at Brody. "I thought this community service thing meant you were supposed to be working! Not taking a nap with the dog."

I stopped and looked. There Brody was, sitting along the yard wall in a patch of shade. In his lap was one of the oldest dogs we had at the animal rescue, a big fat hound dog named Ponder.

"I asked him to do that, Miss V.," I said, right off. "You know Ponder won't go to just anyone. I think it's a good sign that he's so comfortable with Brody."

She snorted. "Dogs love everyone. They don't know any better."

There are dogs that do love everyone. These dogs are the lucky dogs—dogs that haven't been beaten, or starved, or loaded up with BBs by drunk rednecks "target practicing"—dogs who haven't seen humanity at its worst. These are the dogs that will wag their tails and roll over for everyone. You've seen these dogs. They expect the world to scratch their belly and give them a treat, and because they're lucky dogs, that's what happens. But not all dogs are lucky dogs.

The dogs who aren't lucky don't love everyone. They know better. Life has taught them that they have to be watchful and wary. They figure out fast who they can trust, and who they need to avoid. It's like they develop a sixth sense, an early warning system that lets them know if a person is a friend or a foe. If these dogs don't like you, they've got a reason. And if these dogs, these unlucky dogs, give you a chance, odds are you're a pretty decent person.

Ponder is one of the unluckiest dogs I've ever met. When he came into the shelter, he had burns and broken bones. Some idiot had poured battery acid onto his head, burning away fur and more than a little scalp. He was blind in one eye. I'd been working with him for months, and he still wouldn't take treats from my hand. But there he was, curled up in Brody's lap, fast asleep without a care in the world.

It was a good sign, if you asked me, that Brody couldn't be 100 percent bad boy.

The rest of the day flew by. I spent it showing Brody the ropes—including my foolproof trick of rubbing Vicks VapoRub under my nose right before tackling the nastiest cages—and working up the courage to ask him what his plans were after work. I still had that twenty bucks from Clyde. Maybe he'd want to check out the fair. You know, just hang out and stuff.

Mostly, I was hoping for stuff. I could fill out a note card with all the stuff I've done with another guy. No, more like a Post-It note.

The plan was to ask him after work, once we were out of earshot of Miss Vivian. There was only one problem with that plan. As soon as we were done, Brody was through the door and gone. There was a blue car waiting in the parking lot, motor already running. Behind the wheel of that blue car? The tall black guy from the fair.

❖

That pissed me off all weekend long. Not that it should, really. I'd seen Brody with the guy the night before. I knew he was in the picture. But I didn't like it. It was just wrong, fundamentally wrong, that the hottest guy I'd ever seen—who also happened to be gay!—wound up working in my animal shelter, only to have a boyfriend.

My mom thought the family reunion would distract me. I'd tried to get out of it—hanging out at Uncle Stan's farm watching all my kinfolk tear it up isn't exactly my thing anymore. I loved it when I was little. The barbecue, the bonfire, swimming with my cousins in the creek: it all used to be fun. But then my cousins started growing up into full-fledged rednecks, and I could think of five hundred other places I'd rather be.

No such luck. "I need you to come, Wyatt. Otherwise I'll be on my own."

"You're bringing Clyde." She wasn't making much sense.

"Exactly. I don't want to be on my own, with Clyde, at the reunion. It's too much of a change for everyone." She dropped her voice, afraid perhaps that her idiot boyfriend would stop paying attention to the pre-pre-race show and actually listen to her. "Some of my family still misses your father. More than you might think."

"It happens." Mom looked really sad when I said that, so I agreed to go to the stupid reunion. How bad could it be?

It turns out that the answer to that question is actually pretty bad. Things were going all right, at first. There was barbecue and fireworks and little kids running around with sparklers. Everyone else was having a good time. Clyde especially. The bonfire was still going strong by the time he ran out of beer. He'd searched the cooler for another can three times before giving up.

"Well, that sucks," he announced to the world. Then he staggered three awkward paces and sat down in a lawn chair right next to mine.

Had I been smart, I would have bolted right then and there. I don't know why I didn't. It's a ton of work, avoiding Clyde. Maybe I was just tired of it.

"Tell me something," he said, and I knew I was trapped.

"What's that?"

"You see that girl over there?" He gestured toward the edge of the fire, where my cousin Eileen was talking with her boyfriend. "Those legs? Those tits? They don't do anything for you?"

"Dude. You're sick. She's my cousin!"

"Forget she's your cousin for a minute. Just look at her like a woman. That's something any normal guy can do. Someone put her together right, that's all I'm saying. You can't even appreciate that?"

I shrugged. "Not my thing."

"Have you even tried? Been with a girl?"

I shook my head. "Nope."

"So how do you know you don't like it?" Clyde leaned closer, whispering with drunken volume. "It's the most amazing thing in the world—and you've never even given it a chance."

"How many men have you been with, Clyde?"

He sat back, affronted. "None!"

"So how do you know you don't like it?" I bit back the "It's the most amazing thing in the world" since I only suspected that was true.

Clyde looked at me for a long moment. I could almost see the drunken path of his thoughts as they traveled through his skull. Wrinkles formed on his forehead. I bet, if it wasn't so dark, that I'd be able to see smoke curling from his ears. "You know what, Wyatt? Gay kids run away all the time. No one is surprised by it when they come up gone." It took him three slurred attempts before he managed to finish his thought. "You'd better think about that before you say sick shit like that to me. Think real hard about it."

Then his eyes started to roll, and he passed out and fell over.

I thought about pissing on him then, I really did. But Mom apparently noticed that Mr. Wonderful was having a rough time.

"What happened?" Mom asked. She studied my expression intently, as if the answers she was seeking were engraved on my face.

I shrugged. "We were talking, and then he passed out."

"You didn't hit him? You look really angry."

"I wanted to, but no." I pointed at Clyde, facedown in the dirt. "He did that all on his own."

"What were you guys talking about?"

"He wanted to know why Eileen didn't turn me on."

Mom's eyes widened. "Does he realize she's your cousin?"

"Apparently that doesn't matter to straight people," I said.

Mom laughed. "Don't be an idiot." She looked down at Clyde. "We've already got one more of them than we need."

❖

You should tell your mom. Jacksie had been texting me nonstop since I'd told him about what Clyde had said. "He's threatening you."

He was drunk. Harmless. Too fat to do anything, I replied.

You never know.

I was beginning to be sorry I'd said anything at all to Jacksie. I know he meant well, but really? What was I supposed to do? I knew Clyde was a moron, but as long as Mom was into him, he was there to stay.

To distract Jacksie, I snapped a quick pic of Brody, who was having a great time treating the latest batch of kittens for ear mites. *Check out our new volunteer!*

Bad Boy!

I know. He's here all summer.

AWESOME! MAKE YOUR MOVE!

Can't. He's got a BF.

Chickenshit excuse.

I laughed right out loud. Brody looked up, one mewling gray kitten still in his hand. "What's so funny, dude? I've got like nine million scratches here."

I dropped my phone on the counter. "Sorry. Let me help you out."

We'd dosed maybe half of the kittens when Miss Vivian came into the back room with a weird smile on her face. "Hey,

Brody boy, what you been up to? The police just pulled up out front!"

Brody stood up. "What? I ain't done nothing!" He sounded angry, but he looked really, really pale all of a sudden.

"Then why are the state troopers out front?"

"Beats me. Why don't you go ask them?"

"Yeah, maybe they're here for me," I said. I was trying to break the tension. "Distract them while I make my getaway."

Miss Vivian snorted. "Wyatt, for you, I would do that." She gave Brody a nasty look. They definitely had not gotten any closer as the summer went on. "I can't say the same for everyone."

"You never heard me ask you," Brody said. "And you won't."

"Good thing. Because you'll know what my answer is before I even say a word." Miss Vivian turned on her heel and left.

"Bitch." Brody said it softly, one half second before Miss Vivian passed through the doorway. Her shoulders stiffened, but she didn't turn around.

The state troopers hadn't come for Brody. They never asked for him, and as far as I can tell, never even looked for him. They were way more interested in getting rid of the dog they'd picked up.

"We're not doing you any favors with this one," one of the cops said to Miss Vivian. "Meth dealers were using him to guard their lab. It doesn't seem like they were feeding him real regular. Boy's got a hell of an attitude."

It was true. The dog they were holding onto was the skinniest pit bull I'd ever seen. I could count his ribs from across the room. There was a terrible scrape on his left flank. He was definitely on guard, holding himself at attention, almost trembling with the tension. Every breath he took had a growl that went with it; a steady, rumbling threatening sound that filled the room like thunder.

"Let me see him," I said.

"I don't know about that." The cop looked at Miss Vivian. "I'm telling you he's not real friendly."

"It's all right," I told the cop. "He's just scared. Let me see him. I'm the aggressive dog specialist here." Miss Vivian was saying something, but I wasn't paying attention to her. Moving calmly, I stepped over and took the lead from the cop's hand. "It's going to be all right."

The dog looked up at me, and I looked down at him. I'm not sure what he saw in that moment, but it was enough to make the growling stop.

I squatted down so he could look me in the eye.

"Wyatt…" Miss Vivian's tone lowered. "You better be careful."

I ignored her. All of my attention was fixed on the dog in front of me. I wanted him to see me. If he could see that I wasn't scary, that he had a friend, then maybe we would be able to take him in and give him the help he needed. It all hinged on this moment.

"Are you hungry?" I asked him. "Do you want something to eat?"

The dog's tail began to wag. He stepped closer to me, some of the tension melting out of his body.

"Look at that!" The cop was amazed. "None of us could get that close to him."

"You have to make him feel safe," I said. "He has to be able to trust you."

"Food doesn't hurt either." Miss Vivian laughed. "Wyatt, why don't you take—" She turned to the troopers. "Do we know if he has a name?"

They shook their head.

"He looks like a Killer to me," Miss Vivian said. "Or maybe a Psycho."

"Cujo!" one of the cops suggested.

"No," I said. I reached out and patted the side of his head. "You're not a Killer, are you?"

He had brown eyes and a multicolored coat, with brown, black, and white all mixed together. It's a look dog breeders call a brindle. Two large black patches were on the top of his head, near his ears. "We'll call you Mickey," I said. "This is the day when your life starts getting better."

"Good job, buddy." One of the cops leaned forward to pet Mickey. But as soon as he stretched out his hand, Mickey's hackles rose, and the growling started again. The cop quickly pulled his hand out of range. "If you can pull it off, that is."

❖

Two days later, Miss Vivian pulled me to the side. "I wouldn't get too attached to this one, Wyatt. Not everyone can be rehabilitated."

"I've got to give it a shot," I said. "That's what the pros do."

"But you're not a pro, not yet, and this dog…"

"Mickey." It was really important to me that she called him by name. "His name is Mickey."

"Mickey is…these drug dealers…he may be too violent for you to work with. It might not be safe."

"You only know what the cops told you."

"Those troopers don't have any reason to lie to me." Miss Vivian crossed her arms. "Do you know what your problem is? You're too trusting. You believe too much. In dogs—and in your little friend back there." She nodded toward the back room and raised an eyebrow. "You've got a good head on your shoulders. Use it."

"What are you talking about?"

"Brody. He's not the nice guy you think he is."

"What makes you say that?"

"He's not here for shoplifting lollipops, that's what I'm saying. Keep an eye on your things. Protect yourself. Don't get too close. I went back there earlier, and do you know what? That little sneak was messing with your phone. He put it right back quick when he heard me coming, but I knew what he was doing."

I opened my mouth, and shut it again without saying anything. I didn't really know what to say.

"It's all right. You're just learning how people are in this world. It's an awful lesson, but we've all got to learn it someday." Miss Vivian shook her head, like she was really sad. Then her phone rang. She glanced at the number and smiled. "I've got to take this. Why don't you go back there and see what our mongrel is up to?"

Closing time couldn't come fast enough for me. My mind was spinning with what Miss Vivian had said. Did she really see Brody messing with my phone? It didn't seem possible. We'd only been working together for a few days, but he didn't seem like he'd try to screw with me.

If I couldn't trust my instincts, I could trust Ponder's. Ponder loved Brody. That old dog didn't love anyone, but when Brody came around, he'd start wagging that long tail back and forth. Almost every day included a snuggle session, where Ponder would climb up into Brody's lap for some affection. If this dog who didn't trust anyone trusted Brody, didn't that count for something?

I wasn't having nearly as much luck with Mickey. There would be pauses when he wasn't growling—mostly when I was offering him food—but he had tried to bite me more than a few times. Getting him to a point where he could live a normal life again might be more than I was actually capable of. But I wasn't about to tell Miss Vivian that.

Four o'clock finally came. I grabbed my phone and headed for the door. Brody was close behind me.

"See you later, Miss Vivian!" I gave her a wave as I left, even though I was really pissed at her.

"Bye, boys! Have a great night!"

"She's cheery today," I said.

"She's probably got a hot date." Brody looked all serious, at least until I burst out laughing. Then he smiled.

I was surprised when he starting walking down the shelter driveway with me. Normally, he'd wait on the steps until his boyfriend picked him up. "No ride today?"

Brody shook his head, shoving his hands down into his jeans pocket. "Nope. He's all done with me, I guess."

"What happened?"

Brody laughed, a short, bitter bark. "Everything was fine till he found out my birthday."

"Huh?" That made no sense. "When's your birthday?"

"Six months later than it needs to be. I turn eighteen the week before Christmas."

"Big deal. What's six months?"

"Three years for corrupting the morals of a minor. That's what his parole officer said. Now, she's a real bitch. Comes over all the time—late at night, first thing in the morning. Near as we can figure, she's hoping to catch us messing around and wham!" He smacked his hands together, hard. It sounded like a gunshot. All the crickets stopped for a moment, the fine, high whine of their wings shocked into silence by the sound. "Parole violation and he's back in jail."

"Dude." I'm sure there are appropriate things to say in this situation. I'm just not sure what they are. "That's messed up."

"Shit happens." Brody kicked the edge of the road, sending a chunk of the crumbling asphalt free. He kicked it again, this time with greater force. The asphalt picked up speed, bouncing over the dusty shoulder toward the irrigation ditch. I watched it go. The ditch was near dry—we'd needed rain for as long as I could remember—so there was no splash marking the asphalt's arrival. Only a final little puff of dust; a mushroom cloud of sand stretching toward the mindful sun.

❖

The next morning, Mickey's cage was empty. Empty and clean. There was no food in the feeder, and no water in the bowl.

"Hey, what happened to Mickey?"

Brody shrugged. "Beats me. He was gone before I got here this morning."

I wandered up to the front. "Hey, Miss V. What happened to Mickey?"

She turned and looked at me. "I didn't tell you? I've got wonderful news. I called pit bull rescue, and their people came and took him. They're going to rehabilitate him and find him a home." She was beaming. "His chances are much better with them. They're specially trained to deal with dogs with issues."

"No kidding?" Brody asked. He was standing behind me. "That's a lucky break for Mickey."

"It is." Miss Vivian narrowed her eyes. "Very good luck indeed." The phone rang, and she rushed to grab it. "Happy Valley Animal Rescue," she said, waving us both back toward the back room.

We'd barely passed over the threshold when Brody grabbed me by the shoulders. "Wyatt!" For one amazing, perfect moment, we were half an inch apart, nose to nose, eye to eye. It only lasted a second, but in that second, I couldn't think. I couldn't even breathe. I wanted to kiss him. I wanted him to kiss me. Then he shook me. "Could you try using that big old brain of yours for just a minute, please?"

"What?"

"Think about the situation! It doesn't make sense. Purebred rescue people who come in here, driving their Volvos and Jaguars—they've got money. Maybe not big money, but still."

"And?" I could almost, somehow, still feel Brody's fingers on my shoulder.

"What are people like that going to do with a dog like Mickey? He's way too beat up to be a show dog. You yourself said his nuts are gone—"

"I said he'd been neutered."

Brody kept on going like I'd never said a word. "Not fun times for Mickey. No breeding, no money."

"He could be a pet." I could hear the fail in my words even as I said them.

"He's nasty. He's mean—and he's mean-looking! Do you really think one of these rich bitch do-gooders is going to trust Mickey around her kids?"

"He just needs some time..." Lots of time, if I was going to be honest. Months. Maybe years. I'd seen a lot of messed-up dogs over the summer, but Mickey—he was the most hostile, aggressive dog to come in yet. He'd been with us for a week, and in that time, I couldn't even bring him into the yard with other dogs. He'd attack them on sight.

"Get real." Brody shook his head. "There was no pit bull rescue that came and got Mickey."

"So where did he go?"

"I don't know. Not yet. But I'm going to find out."

❖

That night, I couldn't sleep. I kept thinking about what Brody had said. He was so sure that Miss Vivian was lying to us, that there was no pit bull rescue, that something else had happened to Mickey. Miss Vivian was so sure that it was Brody that was the problem. I thought about what she said about my phone, and how I was too trusting.

And then my mind drifted to how it felt when Brody had his hands on me, and we were standing nose to nose, and every thought of Miss Vivian went right out the window. It had felt so good when he touched me, and now that his boyfriend was out of the picture?

Maybe Brody'd be interested in touching me some more. I'm not ashamed to admit that I was thinking about that...um, pretty intensely...when someone tapped on my bedroom window.

I just about jumped out of my skin.

Brody stood outside my window.

"Dude? What's up?" I tried to keep my voice steady. Who knows how long Brody had been standing there while I...well, who knows what he had seen?

"I did it, Wyatt. I found Mickey."

I began picking clothes up from the floor and pulling them on. "What do you mean, you found Mickey?"

"There's no time to explain. Not if we want to save him. Just come on."

"Mom," I called. "I'm going out!"

"You are? Now?" It was almost ten o'clock. I never went out this late.

Before I could answer her, I heard Clyde talking. "Let him go," he said. "It's good for a boy his age to get out and have some fun. It's normal."

Mom murmured something, and Clyde murmured something back. They both laughed, softly. I could feel my stomach knotting up. Before they could say anything else, I shouted, "See you later!" and bolted for the front door.

Brody had a motorcycle parked out front. "You ever ride one of these before?"

I shook my head. "I don't even have a helmet."

"You don't need one where we're going." Brody climbed on. "Just hang on tight, and lean the way I lean, all right?"

I got on behind Brody, wrapped my arms around his waist, and took a deep breath. "Let's go!"

It was dark, and it was hot, and it was like magic, being on that bike behind Brody as we cut through the town. We went uptown, going past the restaurants and strip malls so fast that their signs became a neon rainbow blur. The bike was screaming as we went through the industrial park. I wasn't even trying to pay attention to where we were, really. My stomach was flattened against Brody's back. My chin was inches from his shoulder. All I could smell was him. He smelled like leather and sun and a little bit of motor oil, a male scent that I wanted to breathe in and in and in forever.

I knew we were racing to find Mickey. Speed was of the essence. But I wanted this to last forever, the feeling of Brody tight in my arms, the heat of his body next to mine. I could feel myself getting hard, and for half a minute, when we went around a wide, long curve, it seemed like Brody could feel it too. He pushed his ass back against me, and we were pinned to each other, skin to skin, until the straightaway.

When he stopped the bike in front of a battered warehouse, it took everything I had to get off without making it totally obvious how much I wanted him. I also didn't want to look directly into his face in case he wore a smirk.

"Where are we?"

"Nowhere, exactly. They do a little bit of everything here."

Brody turned to look at me, his eyes traveling down to my crotch for one long moment before returning to meet my gaze. He smiled, just a little, the corners of his mouth turning upward. "Not much of it is legal, you know? Probably not any of it. You gotta be cool, all right?"

"Mickey's in here?"

Brody nodded.

"Then I'll be cool."

Being cool turned out to be harder than I thought. The warehouse was packed with people, most of whom wore leather or tattoos or lots of both. It was dark and smoky. I don't think it was Marlboros either.

We edged around the crowd, staying close to the wall. I could hear dogs growling, and there were people shouting. "What is this?" I whispered to Brody.

He hushed me. There were rows of crates set up along one wall. He climbed up on top of one, reaching back to pull me up after him. From there, we could see everything.

We could see everything, and it was terrible.

There was a squared-off ring on the floor, with pallets turned up on end to form walls around the space. Inside, two dogs were tearing each other up. One was a German shepherd, and the other one looked an awful lot like Mickey.

It was not the best day of that German shepherd's life. Mickey had ripped right into his side, opening up a scarlet moon that went from haunch to belly. I thought I'd seen stuff, working in the shelter, but nothing had prepared me for the slow, steaming slide of intestines toward the floor. The noise that dog was making was nothing that human ears were ever meant to hear.

The crowd was going nuts. People were screaming even as the shepherd went down on his side. Mickey was still going after him. There was blood everywhere. It took everything I had not to puke my guts out—and when I saw the handfuls of cash being passed around after Mickey was declared the winner, I stopped trying.

"How could she give Mickey to these people?" That was the first question I asked after I stopped being sick. I was so angry I couldn't even see straight. "What was she thinking?"

"She didn't *give* Mickey. And she didn't *give* a shit. She must have been paid good money for Mickey. There's no way that was Mickey's first fight. He's a trained fighting dog, and they're not cheap," Brody said. "I bet she made a thousand dollars on him."

"What are we going to do?" There were people everywhere, laughing as the ring was hosed down.

"I don't know," Brody said. His shoulders slumped. "I thought maybe we'd be able to snatch him and go…"

"Yeah, that's not going to happen." Mickey was enjoying his victory dinner, bolting down great gulps of food the way only a starved dog can. "I think we should get out of here."

Brody nodded, and we slipped along the back wall toward the doorway. We'd just made it outside and back to where he parked the motorcycle when it hit me.

"You know what, bro?"

"What's that?"

"Just because Mickey won this time doesn't mean he'll win the next time."

Brody shook his head. "Nope. Nobody wins forever."

"We've got to do something. We can't let him die like this."

He shrugged. "What are we supposed to do?"

I took a deep breath. "We could call the cops."

He snorted. "You can call the cops. They're not about to listen to me."

"So I'll call them." I pulled my phone out of my pocket. My fingers were trembling.

"You know that means the end of everything. The shelter. Your internship. It's all going to be gone if that bitch gets arrested."

I thought about that for a long minute. I'd been working at the shelter for almost a year. Working with the dogs was my best bet at landing a scholarship. Miss Vivian was going to write me a letter of recommendation. Mom sure didn't have the money to pay for vet school.

"Let me call Jacksie. He can call the cops and send them here. They never even need to know about us."

"The cops aren't going to listen to Jacksie. He's a little too... he burns a bit too bright...for them. They don't listen to people like that."

"How'd you know that?"

Brody blushed. It was the first time I'd seen him do it, and it was fascinating, watching his complexion slowly redden. "I, uh. Might have looked at your phone. I saw you take a picture of me, all right?"

It was my turn to blush, especially after I remembered the conversation Jacksie and I had had about that particular picture. "I'm sorry about that."

"Don't be sorry." He shook his head. "I don't want you to be sorry."

Brody was watching me closely then. I think that's what crystallized it all for me. If I couldn't stand up and be a man in his eyes, how was I going to be a man when I looked in the mirror?

"You know what?" I said. "That doesn't matter. If it's got to be me, it's got to be me. If I can't save one dog, this dog, what business do I have even trying to be a vet?"

"Besides," Brody said, "who knows how many other dogs she's done this to? This isn't the type of situation you find by accident, you know what I'm saying?"

I handed him the phone. "You want to call?"

He shook his head. "Life's too short. These people," he said, nodding his head toward the door, "they don't know you. They don't know your name. They got no business with you. You're not burning any bridges."

"Just trashing my future. That's all." I made the call. It went much faster than I expected. It only took a few seconds to tell what was going on and give the address.

"Come on," Brody said after I hung up. "We don't need to stay here to watch the fireworks. They're gonna arrest everyone they find."

We bugged out of there, crossing over the railroad tracks until we got a good vantage point. And we waited, and we waited, and we waited some more. Nothing happened. No cops came. No patrol cars. No sirens. Nothing.

The night grew thin, graying into dawn. From a safe distance we watched people leaving the warehouse. The sun came up over our backs.

"What a joke." I said.

Brody shrugged. "What do you expect? The cops are useless. If they want to burn your ass, they'll follow you around twenty-four seven. If not, you can burn the whole damn town down, and they can't be bothered."

"It's the last night of the fair," I said. "Demolition derby always gets a little crazy. People get drunk and stupid. They're probably busy dealing with that."

"Too bad for Mickey," Brody said.

"They fought him once, they'll fight him again. I just have to find another way to get the cops here."

"How are you going to do that?"

I shrugged. "Stuckey's is a cop bar. I have to believe my boss will know someone who'll listen."

"You'd do that?"

"It's worth a shot." I looked at him. "I won't bring your name into it. I know you don't want to get into trouble."

Brody reached out and took my hand. "It might be fun, getting into trouble with you. I am a bad boy, after all."

I blushed because he probably had read one of Jacksie's texts to me. And I blushed because his grip felt so warm. I wondered if his fingers could feel my pulse race. "Trust me. I'm an expert at rehabilitating all kinds of lost causes."

BREAKWATER IN THE SUMMER DARK
L LARK

Part I

Though Cody Simmer does not believe in the monster of Oxwater Lake, he is the fifth to see it and the first to photograph it—an out-of-focus cell phone shot that shows the beast's back breaking through a layer of summer-thick algae. This happens during his morning row with the kids from Blue Bear cabin. Afterwards they clutch each other on the lake's bank, pink-faced and screaming, "Did you see it, Cody? Did you see it? Did you see it?"

"No," he'd replies, pocketing the phone and tying the rowboat to the dock without another word.

❖

Cody Simmer is nineteen years old and he is afraid of the dark. He is also afraid of large dogs, old elevators, and the noises that ricochet through his apartment's stairwell at night.

But darkness is the worst. This is why his heart does not slow until well into the afternoon, when he forces himself to gather his laundry and drag it across the camp to the employee facilities. He is not scared of the lake because of the monster, he tells himself. He is scared because the water is deep and black.

Cody has been away from Oxwater for too long to be able to cope with mysteries.

Harris Webb is sitting cross-legged on top of the camp's only washing machine, reading a paperback copy of *The Phantom Tollbooth*. With his teeth buried in the skin of his lower lip, Harris's expression is ambiguous. He does not move when Cody drags his laundry basket into the room, and shoves three loads' worth of clothes into the empty machine. Harris licks his finger, turns a page, and stares at the text as if it were revealing some devastating secret about the universe.

Cody starts a wash cycle. The stillness of the room is put to rest by the tidal whirr of the water pumps and the sound of a quarter tumbling against the machine's walls. Only then does Harris acknowledge Cody with a nod and an impassive smile.

Cody hates when people smile at him, hates the obligation to smile back. He hopes Harris has finally given up trying to talk about what happened last summer.

"My parents said they're not letting anyone swim or go boating in the lake until the monster is dead," Harris says. The vibration of the washing machine makes his voice sound as if he is speaking through spinning fan blades.

"That's crazy. There's no monster."

"Heather Cromley says you saw it this morning."

"Heather Cromley is eight years old."

"She said you took a picture."

Cody's phone remains silent in his pocket. There is no reception at Oxwater, but occasionally he manages to pick up Wi-Fi from the general store two miles down the road. He's avoided even that indulgence for some time now, unable to cope with the reminder that his friends are enjoying their last summer before college in places where buildings have a thirteenth floor and no one carries acorns in their pocket to ward off ghosts.

Harris unfolds his legs and drops one down against the face of the washing machine. He is composed of more protruding angles and lines than he had been last year.

"I don't know what I saw," Cody says. "And it happened too fast. I didn't get a picture."

Harris dog-ears his page and tilts his head. The light slanting in from the window casts his face in silhouette, and Cody has to draw it from memory. Harris has a mouth like a frog, wide and jutting, and eyes that approach every object with the same tremulous concern. Harris is eighteen, one year younger than Cody, but his frame is slight and Cody often confuses him for a camper if he has his back turned.

"Well," Harris says, turning his eyes down to examine his hands. Cody had once felt one of Harris's hangnails snag in the hairs at the base of his neck, but he hasn't thought about that for nine months, and he is not going to start dwelling on that now. "Maybe next time."

There's not going to be a next time, Cody thinks, *because there is no monster*, but he feels his throat constrict because he is not entirely sure can believe the lie.

❖

Camp Oxwater has been nestled between the base of the Pocono Mountains and the dark expanse of Oxwater Lake for thirty years. The air is thick with the scent of pine sap. Cody can feel it coating his lungs. At night, mosquitoes hum outside his cabin. He imagines breathing them in and the way they would become trapped inside his body, struggling against the muck.

Darcy Webb, Harris's mother, had been the maid of honor at his parents' wedding. As a result of this, Cody has spent every summer at Camp Oxwater since the age of eight.

As for Harris, Cody has begun to suspect that he has never left these grounds, even for school. The gulfs in his practical knowledge are frighteningly wide, and three months of each year in Cody's childhood have been spent chasing after Harris to keep him from wedging knives into electrical sockets or tossing rocks at wasp's nests.

This is why Cody does not understand Harris's statement when the boy approaches him the following day.

"Elasmosaurus platyurus," said Harris.

"God bless you."

Cody is the leader of Blue Bear cabin; Harris, Red Rabbit. These children are between eight and ten, Oxwater's youngest campers. Cody knows he has been burdened with this responsibility because of his outward projection of unending patience. Harris—well, he suspects Harris might have trouble communicating with anyone who walked the path of puberty.

Today, Blue Bear and Red Rabbit are scheduled for an arts and crafts activity together. This means that Cody and Harris will proceed to make eighteen macaroni pictures while the campers chase each other throughout the cafeteria, yelping and belching and killing insects in staggering numbers.

"No, *Elasmosaurus platyurus*," Harris repeats, adding the last bit of dried pasta to what appears to be a giant alien scaling the side of the Empire State Building. "Otherwise known as a plesiosaurus. Estimated to have gone extinct over sixty-five million years ago. It's the same dinosaur they suspect the Loch Ness monster to be."

"You're joking."

"You've claimed many times I have no sense of humor."

Cody closes his eyes and thinks of eating Italian ice in Central Park...and of Cynthia Harper, who might finally hook up with him now that she is moving to Boston in the fall. He thinks of how wonderful it will be to sleep in his parent's eighth-floor apartment, where the risk of being eaten by a coyote in the night is negligible enough to ignore.

"Cody…"

"I heard you. I've just chosen not to let this conversation proceed."

Harris stares at him for a long moment, his expression unreadable. Cody tries and tries not to think of the way Harris's mouth had been dry and warm, the way their teeth had clicked together, and the way Harris's neck had smelled of pine and insect repellent and campfire smoke.

❖

That week the monster is sighted for the sixth, seventh, and eighth time, though never more than a curved spine breaching the water's surface or the glimpse of an elongated neck in the distance. At night, Cody stares at the mass of gray skin captured by his cell phone camera with his finger hovering over the delete button.

It could have been anything, really, he tells himself. *Anything.*

But the campers are no longer allowed within forty feet of Oxwater Lake, and yesterday a news van arrived at the camp's entrance. Harris met them at the gate, waving violently, and gave the reporter an enthusiastic tour, ending at Oxwater Lake. Cody had been there when they'd arrived, surrounded by Blue Bear kids who'd begged to go watch the newscast.

"My research has led me to believe that the monster may in fact be the last living species of dinosaur, making it a discovery of great scientific importance," Harris says to the cameras. Both the children and reporters stare at him as if he were the sole source of stability in a rapidly tipping world.

"If I am correct, we have little to worry about. They have

never been known to consume human prey and subsist primarily on small fish and cephalopods."

Later, Harris flops unto the ground next to him uninvited, hair green from the reflection of sunlight on the grass. Cody expects him to speak, but Harris presses his cheek against the soil and inhales. Cody watches his ribs expand and contract, but he's not looking anywhere else, not ever again. Around them, the babble of the children is constant and steady.

Cody misses his early summers at Oxwater—wading shin-deep in the frog ponds and plucking bees from Harris's shoulders. Those days are gone now and must remain gone. Maybe he should write a letter to his parents, complain about the prehistoric animal rearing up out of the black water, ask to go back to New York, and then maybe Cynthia will let him fuck her, and that will forever dispel the memory of wanting to reach across his sleeping bag and move Harris's hair out of his ears.

"I'm so happy," Harris said finally, and knowing Cody will not respond, adds, "About the monster."

"You're crazy."

"No," Harris says, into the earth. "I'm just not afraid."

❖

Cody cannot trust his own memories of The Incident last year. They are uncomfortable but not unpleasant. He wants so badly to wince and cringe and retch dryly into the camp's portable toilets, but he can't.

It had happened like this: Harris was chopping vegetables in the mess hall, Cody watching over him. Harris's cooking privileges had recently been reinstated after a two-year period of forced abstinence following an incident known as The Great Oxwater Kitchen Fire. Now they were alone and Cody was eyeing the knife because Harris's fingers seemed too relaxed to hold a pencil. The knife tipped and wobbled over the cutting board, but it was impossible to tell the moment Harris actually cut himself.

"Cody," Harris said. He was holding the wrist of his right hand. There was a slim cut on his index finger, but his expression seemed to register no pain. He eyed the wound skeptically, as if he had never considered this issue to be within the realm of possibility.

"Idiot," Cody said, but didn't mean it. He fetched the first aid kit from the Blue Bear cabin and bandaged Harris's finger. Blood did not bother him. Next year, he would graduate from high school and study biology at Columbia, then medical school, and then he would never see Harris or his bleeding finger again.

"This next year is my last," he said, without being sure why.

"Yes," Harris continued, watching Cody's hands over his own.

"What are you going to do, Harris? You can't stay here forever."

Harris blinked. Cody watched the words *DOES NOT COMPUTE* flash across Harris's eyes.

"This is my home."

Cody taped the gauze in place and drew back, but Harris's eyes did not leave the place where their hands had been joined.

"Why don't you go to school? You're smart, sometimes. You can get a job. You can do anything you want."

"Anything I want," Harris repeated, his voice flat. His attention shifted to the half-sliced tomato on the countertop. "I like it here."

Cody sighed, picked up the discarded knife, and began slicing.

"I do too, but this isn't real life."

By now, Cody knew that he was Harris's only link to the world beyond. Every year Cody brought pictures and playbills, Japanese candy, American comic books, cell phones, and MP3 players, and loved the way Harris's eyes widened in dumbfounded amazement.

"I like it when you're here," Harris said, disregarding Cody's second statement. He reached out and dabbed up an eyelash from Cody's cheek.

Cody's hand froze mid-motion.

"I like you," Harris said again, his bandaged finger scratching Cody's forearm. After a moment, he pressed the digit into the soft crook of Cody's elbow and left it there. Cody watched his arm lean into Harris's touch, until the pressure of his finger on Cody's veins was too much and his fingertips went slack.

The knife clattered to the countertop. Harris moved closer, and their knees knocked together. It was painful. Cody wanted to move away, but didn't. A group of older campers approached the mess hall and then continued along the path toward Oxwater Lake. When their voices faded, Harris took another step forward.

"Harris," Cody said. "I don't know…what—"

Perhaps it was because Harris had never had any friends aside from Cody, or that he'd never experienced the awkward humiliation of grade school. Maybe he was just so socially crippled that he didn't know to be nervous. Harris reached out, took Cody by the collar, and pulled him in. In the end, Cody could not know who closed the distance between them, only that Harris tasted like honey graham crackers.

It was nothing like kissing Cynthia Harper…or any of the girls from high school, drunk and eager and sloppy. It was not pleasant at first. In fact, it hurt. Harris's teeth scraped across the dry skin of his lower lip, and Cody was sure the sharp edge of the bandage had nicked his cheek.

Harris drew back, as if he had only just realized what was happening, but this time Cody was sure he was the one who lurched forward, recapturing Harris's mouth mid-word. He'd never thought about Harris like this, never, even when they'd spent hours a day swimming naked in the canals that lead to Oxwater Lake, but now that it was happening, it seemed natural.

Cody and Harris, together. Like they'd always been.

"No," Cody said, although he wasn't sure why, since this felt good, and Harris's fingers had moved to his lower back and were pressing in with a force that was more than enough to remind Cody that he was *not* making out with a girl. "Stop."

Harris did, and pulled back, his mouth wet and downturned. He did not speak, but inhaled as if about to begin a sentence. Cody waited, realizing his hands were still bobbing in the air where he had once been clutching Harris's ribs, but he couldn't drop them now without breaking the terrible stillness that stood between what had just happened and its backlash, crouched and ready in the future.

He was unable to suppress the sigh of relief that escaped his mouth when Harris turned away.

"I should have figured," the other boy muttered, "Sorry."

He did not have the chance to respond, and three days later, he was on a train to Manhattan, where he could forget about Harris's warmth beneath the cold shadows of Fifth Avenue.

❖

The next day the newscasters are back because the remains of an eight-foot gar washed up on the shore of Lake Oxwater, and the wounds on its side look exactly like they were made by row after row of giant teeth. Cody only gets to see the fish because Harris wakes him up by tapping frantically on the glass of his cabin at six in the morning.

Cody hates waking up before sunrise. Pre-morning darkness is the worst; in the city, they have gurgling late-night buses, and sirens, and taxis vying for parking space, but here, there is nothing but Harris's arrhythmic breathing.

"You have to see—I just want you to see, so that you…" Harris says, beckoning Cody along. "I want you to believe me."

Cody is struck with a rush of misplaced sympathy, but he's not about to let Harris know that, especially not when he's running on four hours of sleep and he's supposed to take Blue Bear hiking up Mount Oxwater in two hours. The thought of the altitude makes him dizzy. Cody is not entirely afraid of heights, but he used to dream of the mountains, bending forward toward the camp, impossibly large.

Cody smells the fish before he sees it. He feels his stomach seize, but Harris seems unperturbed, so he is too embarrassed to voice his discomfort.

The fish is tipped on its side, mouth open. The rising sun hits its scales at an angle, and Cody is temporarily blinded. He stumbles and reaches out to grasp Harris by the forearm. Harris does not pull away, but continues walking, oblivious.

"Anything could have done that," Cody whispers. He hasn't yet let go of Harris's arm, but the movement would be too obvious now. They remain connected, watching two men in lab coats haul the fish unto a hospital stretcher. The mattress sags under its weight; Cody had not seen the chunk missing from its torso until now.

"They say it was bitten by something much bigger than it is," Harris says, and bends his elbow so that Cody's finger slides into the crook and stays there. Harris does not seem to notice. His eyes are exuberant. "It's amazing."

This time, Cody does not argue.

❖

Cody masturbates unenthusiastically, thighs sore from the day's earlier hike up the mountain. Then he sleeps. Next to him, his uncharged cell phone sits on the nightstand.

He dreams. At first, about New York City, feeling claustrophobic beneath the shadows that fall on his back and shoulders. He dreams about Cynthia Harper's tits, and the frozen lemonade kiosks in Central Park, and then about Lake Oxwater.

In the dream, he is stumbling down the fishing pier with Harris's hand clutching the back of his shirt. He dreams about Harris pressing into him over the black water, Harris's breath warm on the skin behind Cody's ear. The other boy's face is dark. The shadows beneath his brow and chin seem too heavy. Cody leans in, searching for a hint of reflected light in Harris's eyes, but finds none. It's so unsettling that it makes the moment Harris lurches forward and pushes his mouth against Cody's seem mundane in comparison.

It doesn't hurt, like it did in the real world. In fact, Cody feels nothing, aside from the cold wetness of Harris's tongue, and curls of water vapor rising into his clothing and hair.

After a moment, Harris draws back. "You shouldn't be afraid," he says. It's a dream voice, bouncing joyfully between Cody's ears.

"The monster isn't real."

"I'm not talking about the monster," Harris says, but that doesn't matter, because a shape has unfurled out of the water behind him. He does not seem to notice, although the water running off the animal's muzzle showers down onto his hair.

Cody wants to run, take off down the old fishing pier, back to Blue Bear Cabin, where he can fall asleep listening to the long sleep-breaths of the children in the next room. He gains the courage to test his legs, feels his calves tighten in preparation, but Harris's grip on his arms does not falter.

Harris kisses him again. This time it is soft and brief, and over before Cody has a chance to react. The monster tilts its head down to watch, but makes no other motion.

"Don't be afraid," Harris says again.

Cody, for a moment, believes him.

❖

Cody hears the steady tone of the generators in the distance, and a series of intermittent thumps that are too loud to come from the raccoons that come to steal sequins and glitter glue from the storage cabins.

He has been lying in bed, staring at an empty patch of sky through the window. Cody hooks his fingers over the window ledge and pulls himself up. Outside in silhouette is the hunched figure of Harris, dragging behind him the rowboat that had recently been placed into storage.

Cody indulges in a long moment of hesitation. There is no reason to try to stop him, he figures, even though he is already searching beneath his bed for a pair of flip-flops.

There is nothing in the lake, he knows, though an hour of every evening has been spent staring at a grainy photograph on his cell phone screen. Harris will ride around all night, and maybe that will finally quell his obsession with the monster, and life around Oxwater can return to normal.

"I hate you so much," Cody whispers, shutting the cabin door behind him.

Harris doesn't notice him until he is pulling the boat up to the edge of the lake.

"Hello," he says, unexcited, as if he'd known Cody would be there all along.

"Hello," Cody says. Harris's skin is ruddy from too much

sun, but the whites of his eyes are like beacons in the darkness. "I thought you might need help."

"I don't." Harris lifts a cord that's been dangling from his neck. On the other end is the rusted key that Cody knows opens the lock to the storage shed where the boat is kept. "I've been doing this every night, all summer."

Cody helps him to push the boat out regardless. Harris settles into his seat, pulling a paperback book from the waistband of his jeans. It's too dark to read the title, but Cody recognizes the cover. It's *A Wrinkle in Time*—Cody read it in elementary school, but he can't remember anything about it.

Harris makes Cody row, of course, and remains silent until they travel far into the lake. He reaches down, flounders about along the boat's bottom, and emerges with a can of anchovies. Cody watches him drop them one by one into the lake. The cradle of mountains around them amplifies the sound they make as they hit the water.

Cody doesn't bother to ask. He knows he can't grapple with Harris's logic.

"Aren't you my friend anymore?" Harris asks, propping his head against the palm of his hand.

"Of course I am. Don't be ridiculous."

Harris is silent for a long time, staring out at the water's surface. "I was glad about the monster. I thought it would give me an excuse to talk to you again."

"You don't need an excuse."

"Yes, I do," Harris says, with such authority that Cody doesn't bother to question him.

He leans back into the boat and feels it rock as he shifts his weight. He wants to tell Harris to move his foot, to turn the boat around, to crack a genuine smile for the first time all summer, but he *can't*, physically can't. He feels like he's swallowed a mouthful of lake water and now there is algae coating his throat and lungs, and if he tries to speak, it'll just pitter out of his mouth ineffectually.

"Cody," Harris says and leans forward. Cody feels his body respond involuntarily before realizing that Harris's eyes are not fixed on him but on a spot just over his left shoulder. Harris attempts to repeat his name, but it comes out as a mess of vowels.

Cody has the feeling that he shouldn't turn around. He has the feeling that if he turns around, that will be the end of everything he thought he knew about Camp Oxwater and the world, and he's not ready for that.

Across the boat, Harris is grappling with the oar. Cody reaches out for his own, but his grip falters when the boat rises and tips to the side. It takes him a moment to steady himself, and give the boat one powerful heave, but by that time, the water has stilled.

It doesn't matter. They row until the boat lurches against the banks of Lake Oxwater, and then they keep rowing until they realize they've hit the shore, and stumble out of the boat, holding each other by the elbows. Their run is directionless until one of them locks onto a faint sodium light in the distance, and they tumble toward it together, finally collapsing into the grass, muscles spasming in odd syncopation.

"I didn't actually see it," Cody says, once he's evened his breathing. His leg is still wedged beneath Harris's, and he can feel the other boy's calves tense. The sound in his ears reminds him of driving too fast with the windows down.

"I didn't see anything."

For a long time, Harris does not speak. His skin looks sallow in the yellow light, and there is a moth sifting through his hair. Cody wants to take back what he's said, wants to erase the look of betrayal from Harris's eyes, but he's been hurtling down this path for so long, he'd not sure he can turn around.

Harris never replies. Instead, he stands, brushes the dirt from his jeans, and disappears into the unearthly darkness of the camp.

The fear—which he has lived with for so long now, that is seems powerful and alive—crawls back to settle in Cody's throat.

❖

The following morning, Kimberly Stout goes missing.

She is a ten-year-old from Green Goose. Cody can't recall her face—by their second week at Oxwater, every kid resembles the same greasy, devastatingly sunburned creature—but he knows she kept her hair in a braid. She wore pink shoelaces and refused to use a fork.

Peter Bentley is her cabin leader. Cody finds Peter lingering in front of the mess hall, holding a lit flashlight, despite the fact that the sun has fully risen. He looks like he's just witnessed a car accident.

"One of the other girls said she saw Kimberly heading for the lake. You don't think—?" he begins, but interrupts himself to listen to a twig snapping in the distance. Cody knows Darcy Webb led a search party into the woods three hours ago, but the counselors have been ordered to stay at the camp and watch over the children.

"No," Cody says. "That's impossible."

He is lying, but as it turns out, he's right.

Kimberly Stout strolls into the mess hall that evening, interrupting a solemn dinner shared by the campers, parents, and volunteer rescue workers from the town below. She is soaking wet, barefoot, and there is a mint green tendril of duckweed in her bangs. Her skin is faintly blue, but she is smiling.

"That was awesome!" she says, oblivious to the dumbfounded stares of everyone around her. Cody finds Harris's face in the crowd, and sees that he has hooked his index finger over his bottom lip and is also grinningly wildly.

The girl is not given the chance to speak again, because her parents descend on her at that moment. They are weary and smell of liquor and the cheap detergent they use on airline blankets. Cody has met them before. Kimberly's father is in politics. Her mother writes religious novels. Cody does not think they are going to be very happy that their daughter was kidnapped by a monster.

"I saw—" Kimberly begins, but her mother clamps a hand over her mouth.

"Not until we speak to a lawyer," she says, picking a mayfly out of Kimberly's ear. "When we enrolled our daughter into this camp, no one felt the need to mention there was a *creature* living in the lake."

The entire Webb family is visibly rattled, except for Harris. The threat of legal action has done nothing to smother the delight in his eyes. He is staring at Kimberly with what Cody might misinterpret as romantic love if he did not know Harris so well.

"Kimberly," Harris calls as her parents begin to usher her out of the cafeteria.

"It was amazing!" she yells back.

Cody does not understand, but Harris obviously does.

He turns to Cody and raises a fist in victory.

❖

At night, there are noises.
Or wails, more properly.

Oxwater has always had its fair share of strange sounds, but none like this—long and deep and lonely, like a voice from a dream in the moment before waking.

❖

Cody has one of those moments we have all had. It goes like this:

Something bad happens and you move on, because you don't have a choice but to keep on waking up and brushing your teeth and walking out into the sunlight with your hand pulled over your eyes. Something bad happens, and you think you'll feel something, but you don't.

Then one day, you're standing beneath the showerhead, and you feel as though your heart is struggling to restart after years of deep stillness, but by now, the period in which you had to react has come and gone. It's too late to scream and cry and beg, so you just stand there with the water heavy on your hair and shoulders, unable to move.

Somehow, you step out of the shower and into the bathroom. Somehow, you wipe away the steam on the mirror and comb your hair, and then put on a shirt, pants, and a matching pair of shoes. You stumble out into the world, and life proceeds as usual.

But you're not the same, and you can't say why or how.

You might not even be there at all.

As Cody reaches for the doorknob of Red Rabbit Cabin, he is unsure as to whether or not his palm will actually grip the metal or if it will pass through it, useless and intangible. But it's cool and firm beneath his hand.

Cody turns the knob and pushes.

The room seems empty. Cody knows the campers are out on horseback riding lesson, but Harris is not immediately visible. Cody catches the other boy's reflection first, shirtless and barefoot, hair damp from the shower. His spine looks knobby and prehistoric beneath his skin.

"Hey," Cody says before Harris turns around. He knows Harris may be thin, but he's strong. "I think we should go out on the water again," Cody goes on, when Harris refuses to fill the silence. "I want to look for the monster. I lied. I did take a picture of it."

Harris moves out of the bathroom, silently gathering his shirt and shoes. There is an open book on the nightstand, facedown and pressed flat, tension across the wear on the spine. It's *The Lion, the Witch, and the Wardrobe*, which Cody has never read.

"Are you even listening to me?"

Harris bends down to tie his shoes, his hair brushing against Cody's shin.

"I'm confused."

"So am I," Cody mutters, because Harris's forehead is resting on the side of his knee, and neither one of them seems to be making an attempt to move.

Harris stands, his body freckled with rusty water. Cody stares at the mosquitoes trapped in the window screen.

"I'm sorry," he gasps, suddenly forgetting why he came. This is stupid, but Harris's breath is audible and comforting, like rain sliding down an aluminum roof. Cody wonders what it'd be like to press his ear against Harris's chest—wonders if he would hear Harris's heart bellowing against his ear like the monster does in the night, deep and filled with strange longing.

"S'okay," Harris mutters, tugging self-consciously at the towel on his waist. Above them, the cabin's ceiling fan spins on high and Harris's arms are covered in gooseflesh.

"I just wanted to tell you that we should look for the monster again."

Harris takes another step forward. He is close enough to touch

Cody's face, and so he does. His eyes remain flat, as if his hand has acted autonomously and his brain has not had the chance to react. Cody imagines he can still feel the scar on Harris's finger, a slice of sunken skin that will stay with him forever.

He's unsure whether he's about to start sobbing or laughing, so instead he leans forward and presses his mouth against Harris's. It is not a kiss, not really. They remain close-mouthed and awkward, but he can feel Harris's pulse against his bottom lip.

"I thought," Harris begins, without moving. It's good to feel Harris speak against his mouth. He tastes like mint toothpaste.

"Yeah," Cody says.

"So?"

"So."

Harris kisses him properly. Or at least, he attempts to.

"Not so hard."

"Sorry." Harris pulls away.

Cody is left standing with his mouth open, listening to insects slapping against the windowpane.

Harris is still sunburned. There is a strip of skin on his nose, curling back like a white snail, and for a moment, Cody is afraid that this is rejection. That he will never get the satisfaction of peeling away the dried skin from Harris's shoulders.

But Harris's eyes are warm, like they were the first time Cody met him. Back when they'd just been campers and Cody had spent the first week homesick and terrified of the nighttime bear rumbles from the forest. Harris slept on the top bunk, and at night he would let his upper body dangle down and tell Cody that bears mostly ate plants anyway, and there were no monsters out there.

At least, there hadn't been at the time.

"Why now?" Harris mutters.

"I don't know," Cody says, which is the truth. "It's the monster, maybe. Possibly. I want to go look for it again, and we might both get eaten."

"Not eaten. Drowned, potentially and accidentally," Harris clarifies.

Cody kisses him. This time, it feels good.

Harris's chest is damp and bony, and Cody presses his palms flat against it, feeling Harris's heart flit against his skin like a wounded sparrow. He is vaguely aware that Harris's penis is half-hard beneath his towel, but his brain is not entirely certain what to do with this information. It's one thing to kiss another boy, but he hasn't thought beyond that.

He's fooled around with girls before. Sorta. In theory, this should be easier, but he can't seem to make his hands slide any lower. Harris is still kissing him, sloppy and enthusiastic, but his shoulders are stiff and Cody can practically feel the muscles in his back, locked and rigid against his spine.

He hadn't expected Harris to be the reticent one, but now it seems obvious. Of course Harris would force him to take the next step. Harris is a bastard, but Cody is tired of being afraid.

He reaches down to cup Harris's erection in his palm.

"Ah," Harris gasps and jumps back, which was not exactly the reaction Cody had been hoping for. The towel has slipped low on his waist, and Cody's brain settles uselessly on the muscles of Harris's too-narrow hips.

"Sorry, I'm sorry," Cody says, as he watches a swell of terror rise in Harris's face. His stance is hunched and unassertive, water dripping from his bangs to his eyebrows. Cody struggles with a moment of ground-tilting vertigo.

"Let's, uh, let's plan for tonight," Harris says.

Cody feels the world around him creak and moan, sagging under pressure.

❖

Heather Cromley appears an hour later, beating on the door of Red Rabbit cabin with a pink fist. Cody curses into Harris's shoulder because he's finally coaxed the other boy onto the sheets with him, and they're studying a map of Lake Oxwater with their heads leaning against the same bedpost, the smell of oak rubbing off on their hair.

Heather Cromley stumbles into the room and folds over, hands balanced on her knees. Her breath sounds like a door being ripped from its hinges, and her jeans are covered with stinkweed. Heather Cromley's mother sends her to Oxwater with expensive madras shorts and white sunglasses, but by the second week, she's always managed to compile a closet full of clothing borrowed from the boys in the next cabin.

"Mr. Cody," she says, "We've been looking for—did you hear? It's here!"

"What's here?" Cody says, hoping an eight-year-old can't interpret the pink streak across his cheeks and nose. Thankfully, Harris has dressed, but his lips are bruised like he's been eating grape Popsicles.

"The monster! It's here, it's dead, and it's here!"

The muscles in Cody's thighs give out, but he scrambles after Harris, barefoot and blinded by the sunlight.

❖

Cody smells the monster before he sees it.

It is not what he expects, a mixture of brine and rubbery fat, but rather a bitter smell like a blood orange and not entirely unpleasant. By the time he finally catches up to Harris, Cody is scratched and bleeding from the overgrown hedges on the path to Oxwater Lake, and the bottoms of his feet ache from the burning soil.

Harris looks worse for wear. There are grass shavings in his toenails, and he is blinking down at them, rubbing two fingers along his left brow. He does not look up as Cody approaches and drops a hand on his shoulder, which he does more to steady himself than to comfort Harris.

"It's dead," Harris mutters, but Cody can already see that.

The creature alternately heaves and shrivels. There must be bacteria multiplying in its stomach. It is massive and purple, neck spiraled counter-clockwise against its back. Cody does not want to look into its exposed eye; it is circular and lidless, the color of watered-down lemonade.

He turns back to Harris to say, "I think I owe you an apology," but the boy is already gone, lumbering uphill with his hands in his pockets.

Part II

Harris does not return to the lake, not even to watch a group of graduate students haul the monster onto a giant blue tarp and then drag it into a U-Haul truck. In the sun, the monster has pruned and turned a speckled pink. The skies have blackened with crows and vultures, screeching and clobbering each other in midair, while a student waits with a long-handled broom to shoo them off the carcass when they get too close.

Cody, on the other hand, cannot seem to pull himself away from the lake. This is all well and good for the kids in Blue Bear Cabin, who have eschewed all their other activities in favor of a vigil around the monster. Cody has never seen them so quiet. They stand shoulder to shoulder, forming a long row, still and silent.

"What is it?" Heather Cromley asks him, her eyes hidden beneath the shadow of a baseball cap. She sounds older, as if witnessing this spectacle has unleashed some adult understanding that had been cocooned inside her all along.

"I don't know," Cody says, which is the truth.

They fall quiet again, listening to the asthmatic gasps of gasses shifting inside the animal's stomach.

No one knows, and tomorrow, the monster will be gone from Lake Oxwater forever.

❖

Harris does not say anything when Cody follows him into the woods, the light of their campfire trembling in the distance. Harris has never missed a campfire; Cody used to like watching him handle roasted marshmallows with the tips of his fingers.

"Where are you going?" Cody calls out. The woods are dark, and full of bears and snakes and other terrible life forms. All around him, he hears branches creak and snap. "Hey, man! Stop!"

Since the monster's death, Harris has been content enough to offer his mouth up for kissing, but he's refused to speak about Oxwater Lake and shies away whenever Cody's hands wander below his waist. *I really should have figured*, Cody thinks. With his narrow shoulders, and children's books, and the way his eyes wobbled in the sunlight, Harris has always seemed entirely asexual.

Ahead of him, Harris finally comes to a stop and slumps against a tree trunk, pushing his sneakers beneath a pile of last year's fallen leaves. He does not look up when Cody approaches, swinging a branch ahead of him to tear down the cobwebs.

Harris's face is hidden by turquoise shadow.

"I'm sorry," he mutters. His voice does not sound human.

Cody thinks of a wounded dog, grunting and struggling in the dirt. Cody is afraid of big dogs. Cody is afraid of darkness, and car accidents, and earthquakes, but he thinks of the monster now, bloated and bruised on the shoreline, and only feels sad.

"Don't be."

"I just…I think…" Harris begins, but can't finish.

Cody drops his hand down on Harris's neck, cradling the base of his skull. "Don't be," he repeats. "I understand."

❖

It's because he loves the darkness, Cody realizes. This happens late in the night, as his pulse finally falls in line with the rhythm of the croaking frogs outside. Harris loves the mystery. It is why he won't leave this place, with its bottomless lakes and its nightmarish forests, and the monsters that whip and churn beneath the water. He regards the civilization outside in the same way he watches a storm collecting along the horizon—a rush of electricity and light that will cast away the hidden places of the world.

Harris never actually wanted to see the monster, Cody knows. Harris just wanted to know it was there, to feel his heart overflow with desperate happiness, because it meant Camp Oxwater still kept secrets from him.

❖

For the first time in Cody's memory, the campers beg and whine until someone drives into town and picks up a dozen newspapers from the general store. Everyone is desperate for news on the monster—the palm-sized articles that appear on the third page of the local section, detailing the latest scientific findings from the university.

Only the Red Rabbit kids are forbidden to handle this literature. Harris performs regular raids on their cabin when they disappear for archery or horseback riding, scooping them up in one shot and waddling to the Dumpsters. Cody catches him there, standing in repose, as if awaiting instructions.

"What are you doing?" Cody snaps, and watches Harris's spine tilt slowly to the left.

Harris refuses to answer him.

❖

That evening, the monster is spotted for the twelfth time. Cody has to ask Harris's mother to confirm the story three times before he begins to make sense of it. This is what happened:

Peter Bentley and Bree Watts, leaders of Green Goose and Purple Porcupine respectively, had snuck down to the edge of Lake Oxwater to engage in what Darcy Webb had insisted were the most heinous of activities.

"He had his hand on her breasts," she hisses, and Cody decides not to mention that he's been trying to get into her son's pants for the last two weeks. "The thing rears up out of the water behind them in one swoop. Bree had my husband's camera with her, and she managed to snap a photo. Here."

Cody takes the Polaroid. He does not mention that this is not the first photograph of the monster in existence. It is better than his, showing the long neck of the monster parallel to the tree line. Harris will be so pleased.

"You know what I think?" Darcy says, reaching out to take Cody's wrist in her hand. Her hands are calloused from years of gardening gloves, and firewood, and glue.

"I think there's a lot of monsters out there in the lake. I never told anyone this, not even Harris, but—I swear, sometimes, I hear them call out to each other in the night. They are lonely sounds, and lately louder and more desperate. I think they know one of them is missing. I think they're looking for him."

Cody pushes the Polaroid back into Darcy's hand and folds her fingers over it. Cody can remember when Darcy Webb looked like a supermodel from the sixties, tanning topless on the dock in a pair of oversized white-rimmed sunglasses. Now her clothes are bleached from insect repellent and Cody is certain that she has forgotten how to apply mascara, but he wishes he could keep his hands suspended over hers for just a moment longer.

"Oh, Cody," she says. Her breath is cold against his cheek. "Please make sure Harris doesn't go out on the lake at night. You're the only one he'll listen to."

Cody thinks of the bronze key, still dangling from Harris's throat. "Sure thing," he lies.

❖

"We're breaking out of here," Cody whispers through the screen. Harris is staring up at him from beneath the comforter, a cloth mask pushed up on his forehead. When they'd shared a cabin, Harris couldn't sleep with the lights on, but Cody was too terrified to leave them off. Harris had worn the mask in compromise.

"Grab your shoes."

Cody watches Harris stumble out of his bed and feel for his sandals in the dark. The camp has been in chaos since the latest monster sighting, and they have not spoken all day. From outside the cabin, Cody cannot tell whether or not the curve to Harris's lips is a grin or a scowl. It doesn't matter. By the time he appears outside, shrugging on a white T-shirt, Cody has covered Harris's mouth with his own.

"You seem optimistic," Harris mutters.

Cody doesn't quite understand, but he's enjoying the kissing and the way Harris's eyes seem to retain the reflection of his lantern, even after he's turned away. "I thought you'd be happy." Cody's hand travels down Harris's breastplate. The key is there, heart-warmed and heavy. "You were so upset when you thought it had died."

"It *did* die," Harris says, which Cody supposes is true. "Of course there are more out there. They must mate, Cody. They must reproduce in some way."

Cody knows this. He's going to study biology at Columbia. He wouldn't even believe in monsters if he had not seen them for himself.

"Then, what—?"

Harris kisses him to shut him up. It's not fair play, but Cody lets it happen. He takes Harris by the wrist and tugs him in the direction of the storage cabinet. Together, they pull the boat down toward Oxwater Lake, switching off at intervals.

It is an unusually cool night. The scent of pine, crisp and antiseptic, fills Cody with complete gratification. Even the sky is winter-clear. He was to squint against the stars whenever he looks up.

The lake is flat. Harris rolls his jeans to the knee and drags the boat in. For a moment, watching water creep up the fraying strands of Harris's pants, Cody thinks he will never be able to leave this place. Not if this boy is here, reading and dreaming and sneaking out in the middle of the night to search for monsters he has always known were there.

"Let's go," Harris says, and they do.

The sky is reflected perfectly on the surface of the lake. Cody has to fight a wave of vertigo, hand heavy on Harris's knee. It feels like they are encased in a shell of stars and infinite nothingness.

"Don't be afraid," Harris says, not for the first time.

"I'm not," Cody says and means it.

❖

They do not spot the monster that night or the next. It doesn't matter. After their third excursion, they haul the boat back into the storage shed, and Harris takes Cody's hands. For a long time, he does nothing, staring down at the places where their calluses rub together and flake off into the soil below.

"Do you hear that?" Harris says quietly. Cody's nose brushes against his cheek.

It takes him a moment, and he feels it first—a low-frequency vibration in his jaw and eardrums. Cody thinks of the electrical wiring outside his window in New York, or the potential energy suspended in the air a moment before lightning hits.

"Is it them?" he whispers. The sound burrows into the valves of his heart, deep and lonely. Darcy Webb was right. This is a mourning call, an expression of grief. He has never heard it before, but it must be embedded deeply into his genetic code, his most primitive of memories.

Harris says instead, "I'm not ready to leave this place," and punctuates the sentence by kissing the crook of Cody's mouth. "But I may be, one day."

Cody understands. He doesn't think he's quite interested in summer courses, anyway.

They walk without speaking, stepping carefully over luminescent white stones and crickets and candy bar wrappers. Owls watch from overhead, faces flat and cruel and beautiful. Harris's hair is damp beneath Cody's fingers.

They come to the edge of the forest, and then Harris kisses him in earnest, placing his palms on Cody's stomach. After a moment, Harris tugs the shirt off him and flattens it against the ground. He allows himself to be guided down, feeling dried grass crackle beneath them. Harris's mouth finds the untouched places behind his ears, along his jawline, his Adam's apple.

Cody Simmer and Harris Webb are not afraid because they are together, clinging to one another in the darkness, while the voice of a lonely monster winds its way through the woods around them.

BRASS
MARGUERITE CROFT & CHRISTOPHER REYNAGA

His name is Ben, and he plays the tuba. This means he marches at the back of the marching band. I play the trumpet, which means I march in the middle. I wish tubas marched in the middle and trumpets marched at the back so I could watch Ben march all day long.

Ben is a waver, which is probably how surfers would dress if there were beaches anywhere near southern Idaho. He pegs his cotton pants, wears long-sleeved button-down shirts untucked, and has a swept-back crown of *Running on Empty* River Phoenix hair.

I'd like to watch him ride the waves of Los Angeles or San Francisco or whatever big city he's talking about lighting out for this month. I'm not even sure he surfs, but waves aren't the only thing missing in this small town. Half the storefronts we passed on Oakley Street are empty, and though I can hear the crowd on Main Street cheering, the people of this town are still slipping away.

Ben isn't wearing waver clothes today. His broad arms are flexing in the red jacket with the heavy gold piping, and the Romanesque helmet with the Legionnaire symbol on the sides. Not even Ben can make that uniform look good, but as the sun shines off his skin as we round the corner, he tries without even realizing it.

My uniform is insufferable under the Fourth of July sun. We're playing "Mony Mony" for the gazillionith time. In my head I hear Mr. Turner chanting, "Left. Left. Left right left," just as he has all summer back on the football field.

Sweat has made a dam along the interior of my helmet. My back is damp, my crotch is catching up. My armpits would be slick if I hadn't stuck a couple of my sister's maxi-pads under my arms. There's a party after the parade, and I don't want to stink when I talk to Ben.

The drums roll and we jump from "Mony Mony" into "Day-O," another song I never want to hear again after this long, hot summer is over.

I can hear Ben's oom-pah-pahs behind me. I think about how our feet are marching together, at the same pace. His left foot strikes the ground in perfect tandem with mine. Never getting closer or farther away.

I first met Ben in the seventh grade, just before he came out. Our last names are the same until the fourth letter, so we've always had to sit together when our teachers assign seats alphabetically, him just behind me. We talked often enough and probably would have been better friends if I'd been more into alternative rock bands, like R.E.M., and he'd been more into watching *Doctor Who* reruns. I saw Ben all the time, but I didn't *notice* Ben until last January when he showed up to band practice, just after Christmas break. Somehow he'd gotten taller, his buzzed hair had grown, his shoulders had broadened, his smile was less crooked. Suddenly he was less of a geek for playing the tuba. His long fingers and wide shoulders were perfect for handling the giant brass instrument that had once seemed ridiculously big in his hands. I wondered about the muscles hiding under his shirt, and I remembered how Mr. Turner joked that band geeks were the best kissers because we had awesome embouchure.

The class always cracked up at that, and I'd steal glances at

Ben to see if he laughed nervously too, but he never did. I never knew who Ben might have kissed, though I suspected Knox or Tommy Costas from the way I'd seen them talking in the hall, their faces close enough to make me blush as I hurried past.

I'd close my eyes and wish he'd talk to me like that.

When we talked it was just about things like movies we'd seen the previous weekend, or the places he wanted to go. Places I longed to go with him, but never had the guts to say.

I couldn't remember all the conversations we'd had, but I did remember the important ones. I remembered the time I baked a cake for a history project. The cake fell and the frosting melted from sitting next to the classroom heater all morning. Everyone laughed, but Ben said those things didn't matter—he said all that mattered was how sweet the cake tasted, as he popped a bite into his mouth. There was the time I had been sick for a month and Ben called to find out where I'd moved to, and when he found out I hadn't escaped town, said that he hoped I got better soon. And then there was last year when I came out, and some of the guys in the band completely shunned me. I hadn't expected it to hurt this much—Ben made it look so brave years ago, even though he got pushed around. Ben had come up behind me as I emptied the water keys on my trumpet and packed it away. He told me to forget those guys and this whole town if that's what it took; he understood. He put his hand on my shoulder for a second and it was hot like the sun.

We play "Mony Mony" one more time and stop at the end of the parade line, just below the faded red marquee of the Empire Theater. We'd held band fund-raisers there for new uniforms. This year we'd watched a screening of *Young Einstein* with Yahoo Serious. I'd sat with Ben, and for the whole movie I thought about how hot Yahoo Serious looked, and how ridiculous his hair was, and what would it feel like if Ben reached over and took my hand on the velvet armrest.

Ben, who secretly folded his lab notes into origami in class. Ben, who was so talented, he could jam the melody line on the tuba better than the flutes and clarinets. Ben who had the guts to do whatever he wanted—even if what he wanted was to get the hell out of this town and never look back.

Our hands stayed apart—the fingers of Ben's left hand softly drumming his knee, my right hand curled beneath my thigh to hide the chapped red skin from my dishwashing job.

I hear the final shrill bleat of Mr. Turner's whistle and the perfectly formed rows of marching legionnaires break against the end of Main Street like a wave. The others spread outward, tucking away their instruments, pulling open the buttons of their jackets. I turn and turn and can't find Ben until I catch sight of him far down the street, lugging his tuba toward the cars.

I never took track in school, but I make it look like I might try out.

❖

"Thanks for ditching the party early to give me a ride to work," Ben says.

We sit in the front seat of the blue station wagon that's technically my mother's but that I like to pretend is mine when I get to drive it. We're in the back parking lot of Grocery Outlet, where Ben works as a stock boy, pulled close to a stack of splintered pallets. The windows of Breyer's Shoe Store next door are boarded up neatly, but there's already a bit of graffiti scrawled across one window. Clouds move across the moon, and the car is illuminated only by the store's rainbow sign.

Ben's fingers pull against the busted door handle, which does nothing most even numbered days. "Kind of a junker, isn't it?" He laughs.

"It's not my car," I say. I reach across Ben, our faces almost touching, and yank the door handle, but nothing happens. I yank again and realize that I can smell the salt of his sweat from the march. I realize if I don't make happen what I want to happen, the rest of the summer will be an empty waste. If I can't try to start having something with him tonight, it will never happen.

"Let it be," he says, "I've got ten minutes to kill before my shift starts." He rolls down the window and yawns as he looks up at the moon. As he exhales, he blows the strands of hair away from his eyes. "Now that marching band is over, I'm going to sleep in for the rest of the summer," Ben says. He starts picking the label off his Snapple lemonade bottle.

"Yeah," I say. "Me too."

"Man, I can't wait to graduate. Get out of this town. My cousin's got an auto shop in Boise. It's not what I want, but it's a start."

"What do you want?" I ask. What I want is to kiss him. My mind is running a movie reel of everything I know about kissing, which isn't a lot. I only know I've kissed my grandmother on the cheek, and the dog once when I was five, and myself in my bedroom mirror. I watch Ben's lips move as he yawns again, remembering their color, like raspberries.

"Not this," he says, staring at the moon. "I'd better get inside."

I take a deep breath. "Right," I say.

Ben reaches for the door handle again. Quickly, I lean over and yank it and kiss his lips, and then jerk away. His door swings open and rocks on its hinges and I'm backed up, pressed hard against mine.

Ben grabs my hand and pulls me back toward the gearshift. His lips are on mine and I can taste that perfect raspberry color and when his hand slides down and grips my shoulder, I can feel the sun burning me up all over again.

He pulls away. We both step out of the car. I walk around to the front, and Ben meets me there. He puts his arm around me and hugs me. "Whoa," he says. He shakes his head. "Why didn't you do that at the beginning of band season?"

"You were going to move away anyways."

"Well yeah, but maybe not if I'd known you would trap me in a car and kiss me like that."

"I think it would take more to keep you here, even for just a summer."

"You'd be surprised. You certainly *do* surprise. I've been flirting with you since I first met you. You sure took your time."

"Flirting? All you've ever talked about is getting out of this place. What about the big-city talk, or the job with your cousin's auto shop in Boise?"

"I've wanted to move someplace bigger, to find someone. Not just someone to kiss. Someone I *want* to kiss." Ben touches his lips to mine, and this time I completely throw myself into it.

Ben quickly pulls back and chuckles, but not unkindly. He smiles and says, "Hey, I'm not a trumpet." He wraps his hands around my hips. "Relax. Remember what Mr. Turner said about leaning into a song. Becoming it." And then Ben shows me. He leans in, and his lips brush against mine, and the sweet taste of him fills me faster than the racing tempo of my heart, and he presses into me, making it music. I suddenly see what Mr. Turner means about embouchure through Ben's strong, sure lips. As we kiss, we move together, our hands, our bodies, our mouths, as if we're playing a song, playing off one another, yet completely in synch. And then Ben gently breaks away.

"Really good," he murmurs. He smiles at me. "But I think we should set up regular practice dates."

I nod, and lean closer to him. I don't say anything. I just breathe him in, my forehead against his, focusing on the scent of his sweat and how light-headed I feel.

Ben whispers, "Thanks. For that."

"Sure," I say.

"Do you want to pick me up when I get off at eleven?"

"Abso-fucking-lutely."

I get back into my car, sink into the seat, and smile. It's true. We band geeks really do make the best kissers.

SUMMER'S LAST STAND
AIMEE PAYNE

Corey hid from his sister Emily's bad mood in the hayloft of the barn behind their grandmother's house. His sister's book of fairy tales—the old-style ones that had stories with toes cut off and eyes gouged out—lay open on a bristled hay bale, forgotten for the moment, while Corey stared up at a sliver of blazing sky he could see through a crack between sheets of the corrugated steel roof. Brittle hay jabbed through his shirt, making him itch. The book had belonged to their mother; she had read it to them for bedtime stories and never skipped over the grisly stuff. Emily would kill him if she knew he brought it out here to read. He didn't care. He was allowed to miss Mom, too.

Though summer was nearly over, the days remained hot. Too hot for lazing around the hayloft, but nights had cooled enough for jeans and sweatshirts. Corey closed the book. He had hoped reading it would make him feel bad about leaving town for university. He should be guilty about living far away from the only family he had left, but inside all he felt was the need to escape.

"Cor-ey!" Gran yelled from the house, her voice lifting on the last syllable.

He brushed hay off the book cover and tucked it into the waistband of his pants. No reason to piss Emily off any more than she already was. The whole summer, everything he did caused one of her tantrums. Fine if she didn't want him around…she'd get what she wanted. He hadn't told Gran yet, but he planned on getting a job as soon as he got to Columbus. By the time summer rolled around again he'd have enough money saved up for an apartment. Or at least to share one. Gran and Emily could come down to visit, but he'd be out of this dead-end town for good.

"Corey!"

He climbed down the ladder. Out in the farmyard, Gran stood with her hand shielding her eyes against the sun. When she saw him coming out of the barn, she shook her head.

"You're going to fall to your death messing around in that hayloft."

He shrugged, heading toward the house. She poked him as he went by. "Lisa called." Her gray eyebrows gave a wiggle.

Corey kept walking. While Gran knew he was gay—and was one of the few folk around here who didn't care a lick about it—she did still enjoy teasing him about girls. Especially when it came to his best friend, Lees (no one had called her Lisa in ages).

"That girl has nice birthing hips," Gran called after him. She laughed.

Corey pulled the back door open a little harder than he meant, and it smacked against the siding. The cool air from the window unit in the living room blasted his sweat to ice. He pulled off his soaked shirt and wiped himself down. Then he went to the fridge for the two-liter of Barq's Gran bought special for him. He did feel a little bad about leaving Gran. She had held the family together through every disaster: Dad leaving for parts unknown right after Emily was born; after Mom got real sick.

He took his pop and sat at the table. The kitchen hadn't been part of the original farmhouse. Gramps tacked it on sometime in the '50s. It held him at arm's length while the other rooms seemed to hug him close. These days he hung out there as much as possible. It made leaving easier.

Emily walked in. She wore a pair of sport shorts and a baggy T-shirt that might have been Corey's about a million years ago. She smirked when she saw him. "Well, aren't you the most disgusting thing in the room."

He shrugged, but her tone stung. Two could play that game. "Nice to see you, too. Going to church?"

She stopped, her hand reaching for his root beer, and shot him a questioning look.

"You aren't dressed like a baby prostitute, so I thought... church." His hand tightened on the bottle. Let her get her own damned drink.

Her lip trembled. For a second, Corey thought he might have gone too far, but then she rolled her eyes and said, "Jerk." She took a carton of orange juice out of the refrigerator and poured herself a drink.

They used to be close. After Mom died, they'd even slept in the same room. He came home from school one day and found his mattress on the floor of Emily's bedroom. But Emily's nightmares grew so bad, Gran had to take her to a shrink, who put her on anxiety meds. Corey could then move back into his room. For the past two years, Emily had been better...until this past June.

Emily hoisted herself up onto the counter, her bare heels thumping against the wood. Corey ignored her. Brat. "So, when are you checking into the dorm?"

"Monday." He didn't look up.

Her heels stopped. "I thought it was Friday."

"Look on it as an early birthday present."

Emily's frown deepened. She fixed him with a hard glare. Or maybe she just was trying not to cry.

Corey softened. "Em—"

She slammed her empty glass down on the counter. Corey winced at the crack that raced up one side near her fingers. She jumped down. "Don't worry about it," she said, her voice colder than the air. "I don't need any special good-byes."

As Gran came in, carrying a bag full of green beans fresh from the garden, Emily stomped down the hall and up the stairs. A few seconds later, Corey heard her door slam and music start.

Gran whistled. "That girl's temper is shorter than Christmas night."

"All I did was tell her when I was leaving."

Gran nodded as she poured beans into a large plastic bowl, then ran water over them. "She's taking it hard."

Corey pushed back from the table. "I don't think so. She hasn't even spoken to me in two weeks, and that was to yell at me for hogging the bathroom."

Gran brought the bowl to the table and started snapping the beans for supper. "You spend a lot of time shaving."

"Gran!"

She waved her hand at him. "All right. Don't get your panties in a bunch." She paused. "You and me are all the family that girl has. Don't you think maybe she's a little scared you aren't ever coming back?"

Corey didn't have a ready answer. Gran wasn't stupid. Emily wasn't either. They knew it wasn't easy for him here, being who he was. Most people pretended they didn't know. Sort of a community Don't Ask, Don't Tell. But they *did* know, and some weren't so good at pretending…and some were downright mean.

Gran raised her eyebrows.

Emily had been extra bratty lately, but she was his sister. He didn't want her to be scared. He could try to make things okay before he left. He stood. "All right, I'm going."

Gran wrinkled her nose. "It wouldn't hurt you to take a shower while you're up there."

"Ha ha."

The second floor hummed with the sound of window fans trying to drown out Emily's whiny indie-girl music. Gran's theory of thermodynamics required the fans upstairs to blow hot air out of the house during the day and the cool air in at night. It was kind of telling that Gran slept downstairs on the couch with the AC going full blast.

He stopped in front of Emily's door. "Em? Can I come in?"

The music cut out. The door clicked open. Emily walked back to the bed and flopped down. "What do you want?" she said, picking up a beat-up copy of *Cosmo*.

Corey shook his head. That's how they were playing it, then. Fine. She wanted to be mad. Usually when she was like that, the best thing to do was leave her be. He didn't have time for that, though. He sat on the edge of the bed. "I thought you knew when I was leaving."

He was just about to apologize—for nothing—when the phone rang.

"Oh, hell, that's probably Lees. You mind?" He pointed at her phone, an antique with a working rotary dial.

"I'm not home." She disappeared behind the magazine again.

Corey sighed. He answered the phone.

Sure enough, it was Lees's voice on the other end. "Do you want to go to the bonfire tonight?"

"Bonfire?" Corey said. Emily pretended to turn a page in her magazine.

"At some abandoned house in the woods off 33. Which means no supervision, which means the perfect end-of-summer-get-on-with-your-life-already party."

Corey put his hand over the receiver. "Em, you want to go to a bonfire tonight?"

Emily shook her head, still pretending fascination with "5 Ways to Set Your Man On Fire."

Whatever. "Yeah, Lees. I'll go. Em's not interested."

They said good-bye. When he hung up the phone, Emily rattled the magazine, pretending to turn another page.

"So you're going," she said, a little too cool.

Corey shrugged. "There's going to be fireworks."

"It's just—I mean, it could be dangerous out in the woods."

Corey smiled. Dangerous? When was their corner of Ohio ever dangerous? "No more so than any other time beer and fireworks are involved."

She frowned. "I don't think you should go messing around that abandoned house."

"How did you know where the party was?"

Emily's face flushed. He thought she might say something, but she shook her head again. "I heard. Have fun."

"If there's something you want to tell me…"

Her fierce look stopped him. "Shut the door behind you."

"Fine." He did as she asked. That's all he ever did.

❖

Corey spent the rest of the afternoon napping. He came downstairs for supper: Gran's green beans, potatoes, and ham. Emily didn't show. Dealing with her snit would have to wait until tomorrow.

But when Lees pulled into the driveway and honked her horn, Emily was at the bottom of the stairs, her head poking through the dark gray hoodie she was pulling over a plain white T-shirt and faded blue jeans. She stuck out her chin. "I'm coming along."

That was all he needed, a spoiled brat pouting at him while he was trying to have fun. He grabbed a jacket and said good-bye to Gran. Emily followed.

Lees waved. She had recently given up her uniform of cat T-shirts and jumper dresses and was now in the clutches of a new phase: black skinny jeans, long gray shirt, black vest, and a gray fedora sporting a red feather.

As she drove, Lees launched into a rapid chatter about her new job as a library page. From the way she spoke, it mostly involved gossiping over who spent a little too much time in the erotica section and the stupid things patrons asked her to find.

Corey would miss Lees. He doubted he'd ever find at Columbus anyone who liked Baz Luhrmann movies and '80s hair bands as much as she did. And who else wanted to stay up all night eating cherry licorice and learning the dance routines in old Britney Spears videos? They'd been doing that since seventh grade. Just last week they got all the way through "Oops...I Did It Again" without any mistakes. It took so long because Lees's Britney impersonation made him laugh until his head ached.

Lees turned off the paved road onto a rough gravel one marked TR 33. Someone had spray-painted 1/3 next to the number. In the back, Emily groaned when they turned onto an even rougher road. Hardly a road, even. It was two tracks with grass tall enough to brush the underside of the car. The headlights picked out the glint of broken glass up ahead. They passed a few cars parked in the grass. Firelight silhouetted the house so that it looked not only deserted but derelict. It didn't get any better when they turned and their headlights revealed the front. If the house had ever been painted, the color was gone now, the boards weathered to a dull gray, the windows gaping an empty black. The thump-thump of a stereo out back sounded like a heartbeat.

Lees parked the car and hopped out. "Come on," she said, taking off toward the house. She was keyed up about something.

Emily got out and plodded after.

Corey followed. As he did, he realized he was already *over* this party. He'd graduated. He was past the whole high school thing. Next week he'd be in college with college parties and college guys. He didn't need this, and the idea of spending any more time with his former schoolmates left him cold.

Corey and Emily walked around the house. The bonfire was more of a campfire. A few kids from his school—make that his ex-school—gathered around a keg. A few stray firecrackers popped in the dark.

Lees headed straight for the house's rickety back porch. A boy pushed away from where he had been leaning against the side of the house. That's what she's so excited about, Corey thought. Go Lees.

The boy was cute. Not just any old cute, either. This boy was exactly the kind of cute that Corey liked. Floppy hair, slight scruff, but not too "done." Corey had to admit he was actually sort of jealous.

"Ritchie!" Lees ran the last few feet and launched herself at the boy. He caught her and swung her around.

"I get it." Emily stood next to Corey. "She's setting you up."

"What? You don't know that."

"Yes, I do. He's her cousin from Cleveland."

"He's just a kid."

"Not anymore," Emily said, then walked over to Lees and Ritchie.

Corey groaned. Just what he needed: a set-up.

Lees broke away from the boy and gestured for Corey to come over. "Guys, this is Ritchie Crilow. He's my cousin."

Emily shot Corey an I-told-you-so look. All right. She'd earned that. She was still a brat.

The boy took Corey's offered hand. "It's Rich. Only Lisa and my mom call me Ritchie." Rich's grip was strong.

Corey thought of Gran's comment about Lees's birthing hips and wondered what she'd say about Rich's handshake. He blushed. "I'm Corey, and this is my brat Emily."

Lees went to the keg and returned with bright red cups of beer for all of them. Like usual, Lees did most of the talking. Corey half listened, letting the beer seep into his brain. Every so often he found himself staring at Rich. So cute. Maybe they didn't have to leave so soon.

Emily sat on the porch floor with her back against the house. Her beer cup sat next to her, untouched. She laughed at Rich's jokes, but every so often she'd stop and scan the growing crowd. Probably looking for one of her juvie friends so she could run off. Whatever. Corey didn't need her shit. He edged closer to Rich. He had better things to think about.

"Hey, faggots! The party can start!"

Corey froze, his cup halfway to his mouth. Three guys rounded the corner of the house. Ray, Mike, and Jason. He didn't bother with last names. Assholes don't usually formally introduce themselves when they are slamming your head into a locker. Corey hadn't had any serious run-ins with them, just the stupid stuff in the hall. He had made it his business to steer clear of them.

The three made for the keg, and Corey lowered himself next to Emily. Lees noticed him on the floor and raised an eyebrow. Corey nodded toward the keg. Her eyes widened. "Shit," she muttered.

"What?" Rich turned to look. "Who are they?"

"Homophobic assholes," Corey said.

Emily let out a strangled noise.

"Em?" Corey touched his sister's shoulder. She flinched away.

Lees knelt next to Emily. "Are you all right?"

She wasn't. She hadn't been the life of the party before, but now she was almost catatonic. Her back had stiffened and she'd pulled the hood of her sweatshirt down over her face. Before the meds, she used to do the same thing right before freaking out.

"I think we should go," Rich said.

The three guys had taken over the keg and were spraying beer from the hose and spigot into each other's mouths. They probably had started drinking hours ago. One of them, Jason, kept throwing glances in their direction.

When Corey stood up, to lead the way back to Lees's car, Jason smirked and smacked one of the other guys.

"Oh, hell." Corey gauged the distance from the porch to the corner of the house. They'd never make it to the car. They'd have to go through the house. He glanced at the back door at the other end of the porch.

Rich caught Corey's glance toward the door. "If they turn back to the keg for a fill-up, head for the door."

Corey smiled at Rich. That boy had just earned a good-night kiss if he wanted it.

He eased Emily to her feet. Lees sprang after them. They moved toward the door. Jason and his friends weren't coming toward the porch. Maybe they didn't want a fight. Or they weren't so drunk to forget that football practice had already started for the year; the coach ran a clean team with a zero tolerance policy, so if the boys got caught fighting, they'd get benched.

Jason swiped the tap and started to fill his cup. As soon as his eyes were off them, Corey nodded at Rich. They hustled Emily and Lees across the back porch. Corey twisted the doorknob. The door opened about three inches, then stopped.

Fireworks crack-popped behind them. Jason let out a yelp. One of surprise, not pain. Corey and Rich threw themselves against the door. It scraped across the warped floorboards.

Corey pushed Emily and Lees through the opening, then

squeezed through after them. Rich came in last, pushing the door closed after him. He locked the ancient slide bolt.

"If they figure out where we went, that will hold them for a few minutes."

They stood in a room bare except for the rotted cabinet with an old iron hand pump rusting on top. Probably a kitchen. Opposite the back door was another door leading to a hallway.

"Here's Johnny," Rich said, leaning through.

Corey grabbed his hand and pulled him away from the door. "Let's not be here if they get in."

They filed out of the kitchen and into the hallway. The house was silent. Another hour and the party would trickle inside, two by groping two.

Lees closed the door behind them, cutting out any light from the fire.

"I can't see anything," Emily said.

Corey nudged her forward, very aware that he still held Rich's hand. He felt warm and jittery. He would get his sister out of this. "Just follow the hall. The front door is at the far end."

They crept forward. The air stank of a hundred years of mold. It felt heavy, like they had to swim through it instead of walk.

Corey's eyes adjusted to the dark but not enough to make out more than the faint edges of the stair railing and the outlines of a door with a boarded window in front of them. They shuffled forward, all in a group.

At the foot of the stairs, Emily stopped. Corey bumped into her, then Rich bumped him. He tripped over some broken splinters of stair rail. Rich reached out to steady him, and his breath caught. Just a quick squeeze, he told himself. It doesn't mean anything.

"Something's wrong," Emily said.

"The door's right there," Corey said. His palm started to

sweat. Rich dropped his hand. He probably thinks I'm a gross pig, Corey thought. He wiped his hands on his jeans.

Emily inched forward. "Did you hear that? Like an echo?"

Corey listened. The house creaked around them. The sound of fireworks came from out back, more like popcorn than gunshots now. He shook his head. "I don't hear anything."

"Corey—"

"Stop being such a baby." The words came out harder than he meant, but he didn't have time for her brat act. "We have to get out of here or those guys are going to beat me to a bloody puddle."

Emily rounded on him. "That's right, Corey. Everything's about you."

And here was the freak-out. At least they'd get it over with before Corey got his face broken. "Who else would it be about? I've been ducking a game of Smear the Queer with those guys for two years."

"And being your baby sister is so easy." She gestured toward the back of the house. "Listening to the comments assholes like that make about you is *so* much fun."

Corey's mouth opened. Even when she'd still talked to him, they'd kept their distance at school. They moved in different circles. Her with popular party kids, and him with Lees.

"I don't need you to protect me." He meant that he could take care of himself. Only, it came out like he didn't need her... which, in a way, was exactly what he'd been telling himself for that past three months.

Emily's eyes narrowed. "Fine. I won't." She turned and marched toward the door. She only took a few steps before Corey saw why she'd heard an echo. There was a hole the size of a truck tire right in the middle of the hall.

"Emily!"

It was too late. Her foot caught the lip of the hole. If she hadn't been angry, she might have been able to hop forward. But she'd put her foot down too hard. Her arms slammed into the floor as she caught herself before going all the way through.

Corey lunged forward, but Rich caught his arm and pulled him back. "You don't need to fall, too." He nodded toward the floor.

"You don't know how stable the rest of it is." Corey took a deep breath. "Emily? Are you okay?"

"Of course I'm not okay. I'm hanging by my armpits in a *hole*!"

Corey would have laughed if it wouldn't have made him look like a jackass. If Em was acting like a brat, chances were she wasn't hurt too bad. Gran was still going to kill him, but she wouldn't kill him too dead.

Rich pulled out his lighter. Corey looked at it, then up at Rich's face. "You had that the whole time?"

Rich gave him a sheepish grin. "I'm sorry. Everything happened so fast." He lit it and held it up.

Now that he could see the hole, he couldn't believe they'd missed it. Well, Em hadn't.

Lees rolled her eyes. "You guys are useless." She scooted around the hole and lay flat on the floor. She clamped her hands over Emily's wrists and pulled. Emily shifted maybe a half inch. The floor creaked. Lees scowled up at Corey and Rich. "You think you two could give me a hand instead of standing there like a couple of idiots?"

"I saw a door that might go to the basement," Rich said. "We can try to push her up…or catch her." He held up the lighter. A door was set at the back of the stairs.

"We'll get you, Em," Corey called. He smacked Rich on the shoulder and headed for the door. As soon as Corey opened the door, the moldy smell multiplied by a factor of ten. He coughed. Definitely the basement.

"That reeks," Rich said. "And those stairs could be just as rotten as the floor."

Corey eased himself onto the first step. "It seems solid enough."

Rich tensed, handing Corey the lighter.

"What?" Corey said.

He turned toward the kitchen. "I haven't heard the back door explode into kindling."

Where was the asshole brigade? "Maybe they didn't see where we went. I'll worry about that when I've saved my little sister from breaking her neck."

Rich shrugged and started to follow Corey down the steps.

Corey held up a hand. "Maybe you should wait until I'm all the way down." Corey tested each step with his foot, feeling them bow beneath his weight.

When he reached the bottom of the stairs in one piece, he motioned Rich to follow but he didn't wait. "Em, I'm coming!" He made his way to the spot where he thought Emily should be. He held up the lighter. He saw the hole, but Emily's legs were gone. "Emily!"

Her face appeared in the hole. "What?"

"What happened?"

"I climbed up. In case you haven't noticed, Corey, I'm not actually a baby."

"You better hurry," said Lees from above. "Those guys are out by my car."

Corey ran for the steps and ran smack into Rich. They fell in a tangle of arms and legs with Corey on top. The darkness settled around them. Before Corey could push up, Rich's lips brushed against his. He tasted like mint gum.

For a second, Corey relaxed. He stopped thinking about Emily and the guys outside. He stopped thinking about leaving.

It only lasted a second.

Corey pulled away.

Rich's breath whuffed out. "What's wrong?"

"I've never had a boyfriend," said Corey.

"It's just a kiss."

Just a kiss, thought Corey. Just? He'd read all the stories. A kiss always meant something. They brought girls back to life. They turned frogs into princes. They made heroes forget.

"We're not picking out china patterns. I'm just kissing a cute boy."

Just, again. The kiss freaked Corey out, and Rich's way-too-cool reaction to it kind of hurt. He didn't expect Prince Charming to sweep him up on a white horse or anything, but he'd wanted his first kiss to be special.

Rich backed away. "I didn't mean to upset you."

The stairs creaked as he climbed up to the first floor. Corey sat in the dark. It smelled like the inside of last summer's cooler, but it was a lot better than going upstairs. He put his head in his hands. What had he been thinking? Just brush off his best friend? His family? All because he didn't like living here.

"Hey, Corey?" Lees called down through the hole. "You might want to come up here."

Corey picked his way up the stairs as fast as he could. Lees, Rich, and Emily huddled around the door's window. Lees had cleared a small hole near one corner and was looking out.

Something crashed against the door, and all three jumped back. "Beer bottle?" Corey said.

Lees glanced at him. "The Three Stooges are on the front porch. I think they popped my front tire with a hunting knife."

Rich wouldn't look at Corey. Emily did, though.

"They want to kill me," she said. Another beer bottle hit the door. She flinched.

Corey stared at her. "You?"

She stared right back. "I was at a party graduation night."

Not mine, Corey thought.

"I'd had a couple of beers. Jason and his goons stumbled in, already plastered. Jason said, 'Hey look, it's the fag's sister.' I told him to shut up, but he kept calling you a fag. It pissed me off, so I punched him." Her hand curled into a fist, as if fondly remembering the act.

Corey looked down. The spokes from the stair rail lay on the floor next to his feet. "You shouldn't have done that."

"I couldn't just stand there and listen to that shit."

"It's not fair, I know. Things will be better when I'm not around."

She wiped her hand across her face. "You're my brother, Corey."

"You sure haven't acted like it for the last three months."

There it was…the real reason he wanted out of this place so badly. He could take people pretending he was just like everyone else. He could even take the occasional run-ins with jerks like Jason. What he couldn't take was his sister acting like a stranger.

"Come out, little girl," someone—Corey guessed Jason—called in a singsong. "Let's see how you do in a fair fight."

Emily looked down at her feet. "So you're going to leave?" Her voice wobbled, and the sound stabbed straight into Corey's gut because that's exactly what he had planned.

He'd called it "moving on," but it was really running away. But not anymore.

She'd punched a guy for him. He almost laughed. Who needed a knight on a horse when his baby sister was around? And there were Rich and Lees, peeking out the window at the very guy. They probably could have just walked around the house… especially Rich. But they didn't. They stuck with him.

Something heavy hit the door. The lock held, but the old wood around it split. Lees, Emily, and Rich picked their way around the hole. Another couple of hits like that and the thugs would be inside.

Corey stepped back and almost tripped over the stair rail spokes. Something hit the door again. This time, Corey could see the door outlined in light. Someone's pointed their headlights at the front of the house, he thought.

He picked up one of the stair rail spokes. It was heavy, oak maybe, about the length of a baseball bat. He gave it an experimental swing. He hadn't been in a lot of fights, but he figured it would be worth something.

"How far away are you parked?" he asked Rich.

Rich picked up another one of the posts. "Just at the end of the drive."

"You mind giving us a lift?"

Emily picked up her own makeshift club. Lees bent to get one, but Rich stopped her. He held out his keys and motioned toward the back of the house. "You go around back and head for the car."

Emily took the keys. She turned to go, but Corey grabbed her elbow.

"We are going to have a long talk when this is over." He had to tell her how much she meant to him, that he wouldn't just abandon her.

"Great," she said with a grin.

Corey turned to Lees. "Stay out of the light."

She nodded.

They slipped back down the hall. Corey heard the back door creak open. At least they'd be safe.

Rich flashed him a half smile. "This is one hell of a first date."

Corey lifted his post, hiding a grin. Maybe he hadn't completely blown it. "So, take a couple of swings, then run?"

Rich laughed. "Oh hell, yeah. Don't leave me behind."

"I won't."

He couldn't even if it had been just a kiss. Sometimes you stood and fought. Sometimes you ran. Either way, there were some people you knew you could stick with.

MOST LIKELY
STEVE BERMAN

Gray sky, gray surf, dim house with gray floorboards— summer should be golden, not dismal, thought Roque as he peered out the window of the darkened rental at the empty beach. The scenery would be ideal viewed as a black-and-white photograph, but experienced live it was a disappointment. Sheets of rain fell upon the sand and the air inside felt like gelatin, thick with moisture. Beads of sweat made his tank top cling to his skin on his back and sides. His swim trunks were dry.

Lying on the couch, one foot kicking pillows, the other wedged beneath the surviving upholstery, his younger sister, Leonia, moaned because the power was out, so no television, no telephone. Nothing that modern man had invented worked. Except the toilet. Not that Roque minded peeing outdoors, even in the pouring rain. "I'm bored," she called out.

"Read a book, Leo," Roque said without turning away from the view of the beach. Could the white froth of the churning waves mesmerize away a dull afternoon? Doubtful.

She lifted up the cold washcloth spread over her forehead. "Three days after school ended and you want me to read something? *Raro.*"

"Then get ready for cosmetology school." It was a cruel blow, Roque knew. Back in their old neighborhood in North

Jersey, girls didn't go to college but did hair. And gossip. Maple Shade offered new opportunities. Leo wasn't dumb. Just sixteen, so annoying beyond belief.

"I can't even call my friends!"

Her cell phone had been charging when a surge struck the house. Or the house next door. However electricity liked to travel. It fried her phone and everything else attached to that outlet. She then borrowed Roque's phone last night—without asking!—and drained it near death after ninety-some minutes of bitching to her friends back in Patterson.

He left the room because otherwise he'd start yelling at her, which would only annoy their parents, who'd blame him. Now that he was eighteen and out of high school, he had to be an "adult." When did someone hand him a pamphlet on How to Be a Grown-Up? Did that mean he should fret over money, like his mother, who had already bitten her fingernails down to the bloody quick because their vacation at Sea Isle City was a disaster thanks to ever-present storm clouds? Or should he be like his father and Uncle Manny and drink glass after glass of beer and lemonade until he couldn't see what cards he was dealt, so he started to lose hand after hand of Texas Hold 'em?

He went to the bedroom—shared with Leo, unfortunately— and unzipped his backpack. He was the one in the family who liked to read. Thank you, Lita Sancia, he thought. Her eyes were bad, so when she had baby-sat Roque she'd asked him to read to her. He could never refuse her, especially knowing how she would praise him for being "such a smart boy" and then offer him a piece of hard candy she'd hidden in a pocket.

As he began pulling out dog-eared paperbacks, his fingers found something hard and heavy and slick at the bottom of his backpack. His high school yearbook. He didn't remember packing it...and shrugged off the mystery.

He flipped through it to find the page with his senior photo. He had spent a week agonizing over how to style his hair and taken to the salon three pages torn out of *GQ*. His best friend Charles always got a close shave. As the stylist hovered behind him in the chair, like a massive mosquito complete with buzzing from her razor, Roque chose a razored crop.

He smiled down at his photo, then frowned at the writing beneath. His own handwriting in his favorite purple ink. *Gregg, I'll miss seeing you every day in class. And thinking about you every night in bed. I wanted to ask you out but could never find the nerve. Xoxox Roque.* He rubbed the ink. It smudged a little.

Gregg. Gregg Lehman. He had spent every year of high school mooning over the boy. And every night imagining what it would be like to hold his hand, caress his neck, kiss his lips…and other, sweatier pursuits across Gregg's lanky landscape.

But he had not written this. Why would he pen something so revealing in his own yearbook? If Leo opened it—and one day she'd surely be so bored that she would—he'd never hear the end of her teasing. *Lehmann? He's Jewish. They chop off the ends of their bicho.*

He opened the book to the endpapers, covered in signatures and sentiments. All made out to Gregg Lehman. He had the wrong book. They had traded yearbooks to sign right after English, but he remembered Gregg handing his back, had read what Gregg wrote—*Never stop developing.* Too short and referencing their brief stint together as partners in Photography class. Roque had wanted Gregg to admit his undying love and desperation at being parted with the start of summer. Or to ask for a kiss. But no, the guy had just smiled and said his good-bye.

So how could Roque be holding Gregg's book? A book with a message he never wrote. Roque began reading the sentiments from his classmates:

I thought you were kinda weird but know I'm grateful you loaned me a hundred dollars to get my fake ID. Thanks for helping me get wasted often!

I stared at you. A lot. All through Geometry. Why don't you like blond girls? Everyone likes blond girls. TV tells us so.

Dude, I don't even know who you are.

None sounded the least bit like something you would write in another person's yearbook. Not to a friend. He flipped to Gregg's photo. He wore glasses with round frames dipped down his nose so you could see his eyes. The photographer had caught him in mid-wink with a hint of a smile. Roque sighed, and then laughed at himself. Was he that lonely? No. Did he want a summer fling? Maybe. With Gregg? Definitely. And it needn't just be a fling; nearly every kid from their high school was destined for Rutgers University because it was cheap.

Gregg's photo moved. Moved as if it was a few seconds of video trapped on paper. He dropped the book onto the floor. Pages flipped. The weak light from the sole window in the room must have tricked his eyes.

The yearbook lay open to pictures of the underclassmen. Juniors maybe. A drawn red ink heart surrounded one girl's photo. Roque knelt down to read what was written beside it.

Sharon Cohen, who *owned* her frizzy hair and cat's-eye glasses. *I'm proud* (underlined a lot) *to be your only girlfriend. So what if it was back in 9th grade. We rocked!!!* (The base of each exclamation point was a tiny, perfect heart.) *Now go kiss a boy and try not to think of me.*

A notion tingled inside Roque's head. Maybe Sharon was

teasing Gregg. Maybe…Gregg never ever mentioned a girlfriend. He'd gone to prom stag like Roque. But Gregg was a quiet guy, the sort that frustrated gaydar. There had been umpteen mental checklists trying to figure him out. Dresses preppy (√). Oblivious when he spills ketchup on shirt (X). Artistic—photography class (√). Takes photos mostly of girls (X). Doesn't know how hot he is (X). Borrows my music (√).

He flipped through more pages. Every salutation, every acknowledgment written by another student or teacher was just too personal. Mrs. Groolesky's *I wish you had an uncle. An uncle who had your looks. An uncle who had your looks and was a divorce attorney* made him laugh but Mr. Trall's *I gave you a B-because you're a heathen. Mark 23:37-38* left him ready to spit on the Latin teacher's photo.

Roque turned to all the various student clubs and activities, where the unpopular kids banded together for mutual understanding if not protection and the school's darlings gathered in shallow pools to reinforce their saturated popularity. In the photo of the Astronomy Club huddled around a telescope, Gregg knelt on the grass. Next to him sat Duncan Hall, the most notorious gay kid at Maple Shade High. Duncan, whose favorite class was Gossip. A fresh tattoo on his arm, a string of numbers in blue ink tattoo that bit into the glossy page that could only be his phone number. And below the photo: *Now that you've dumped that Cherry Hill brat, time to give me a call.*

Roque put the yearbook on the bed and began pacing the room, which seemed to have shrunk until its walls confined worse than any cage.

There was no reason to be jealous. Gregg was straight and Duncan was just being Duncan, all forward and flirty with any guy that moved. And Duncan *knew* how Roque felt about Gregg; he had told Roque not to obsess over near beer, whatever that meant.

Roque walked back into the living room. He felt like his spine was a lit roman candle, that sparks would fly out of his fingers if he didn't clench them into a fist. His sister peered up at him from a book, a guide to winning poker, and then tossed the paperback onto the floor.

"What?" she asked. "So now if I want to read, I'm not allowed?"

"No. I mean…yes. Just don't talk to me."

"You're *raro*," she called after him as he went into the kitchen. But he couldn't open the fridge. With the power off, he'd let the cold air escape and his mother would howl if she even suspected something might spoil and food money be wasted.

He opened the door onto the beachside porch and stood at the edge of the wooden planks so raindrops would strike him now and then as he paced. He just had cabin fever. If you could have that in summer on the beach. Cabana fever?

Roque held a hand out to collect rainfall in his palm. Even the sensation of the cooling drops striking and pooling above his wrist, where blood rushed to and fro beneath the skin, could not distract him from thoughts of Gregg calling Duncan up, Duncan suggesting they take a ride into New Hope with all its cute shops and hipsters, Duncan faux laughing in the jeep on the highway, Duncan draping an arm over Gregg's shoulder and, with his fingers, adjusting Gregg's shirt collar. Then he'd stop laughing and lean in close…

Roque could feel a scream of frustration building inside his chest.

What he needed was to hear Gregg's voice. That would mean the difference between a weekend of complete misery and…well, something better than misery. He had kept his crush on his friend hidden and managed to remain non-miserable all though senior year.

Maybe the neighbors would let him use their cell phone.

Roque was somewhat confident he remembered all of Gregg's digits. 7-9-6-2-1-0-6. Or 2-0-1-6.

He ran through raindrops, crossing the space between cabins. The screen door rattled when he knocked against the metal frame. The interior was as dim as the one he'd left. A couple minutes later, a pair of round heads appeared in the doorway. Frowning round heads, one with shaggy brown hair, the other black and spiked with way too much product.

The teens blinked at him, as if suddenly awakened. A pair of "What?"'s followed.

"Um, hey. I was wondering—our power is out also—could I borrow a cell phone?" He realized the request sounded lame, so decided to add an "It's an emergency" to the end.

Spikey, the shorter of the boys behind the door, looked to and fro, as if expecting the flashing lights of a police car or ambulance just at the periphery of his vision. Spittle struck the rusty metal screen and Shaggy said, "No."

"Please?"

Spikey muttered something to the boy, who then asked, "You the brother of the girl who's staying next door?"

"Uh, yeah, why—"

"Rican girls are hot. So if she had asked…" Shaggy said. Both boys laughed, showing braces, as they shut the flimsy wooden door beyond the screen in his face.

❖

Roque collapsed on the floor near where Leo read. "If it ever does stop raining, don't even think about wandering that way," he said and gestured toward the next cabin.

"Oh?"

"They're *gilipollas*." And he told her what had happened. Nothing about the yearbook or Gregg, though.

Leo giggled. "Rican girls are also trouble when we're bored." She dropped the book. "I have an idea. Grab a deck of cards and follow me."

Seeing Leo with him, the boys let them inside. But their smirks faded when she started demanding they clear space on the living room floor and bring over some candles.

"I'm not into any voodoo shit," Spikey said.

Shaggy, who might have been a year older, nudged his friend in the stomach. "Cards is tarot, not voodoo."

"Relax." Leo took the top card from the deck of cards Roque held. Jack of hearts. "Just regular old playing cards. I thought we'd play some strip poker."

Every guy in the room—Roque included—let loose a "What?!"

"Well, not traditional strip. You still have to ante up. That means money, boys. But if you win the pot, the losers also drop trou." She grinned. "Eventually."

Roque shook his head and held out the cards to her. "I am not going to sit here and play strip poker with my sister—"

"Of course not." She shoved the deck of cards against at his chest. "You're the dealer."

"But…"

"Confía en mí," she said. *Trust me.*

She stretched a moment, and the two brothers stared longingly at her. Then she sat down on the bare floor. Roque sat beside her, then the other boys.

"Texas Hold 'em is the game." She cracked her knuckles.

Leo pulled out a wad of dollar bills from the pocket of her shorts. She unfolded one and tossed it onto their midst. The brothers did likewise.

She didn't need to explain the rules. Cable television taught kids everything they needed to know to survive adolescence.

She won the first hand. The boys shucked their sneakers. Overpriced sneakers, Roque noted.

She lost the second hand and did not hesitate to remove her T-shirt. Her bra was peach and lacy at the edges. The boys' jaws dropped, as if the rubber bands attached to their braces had snapped. Roque looked at the hand she had folded. A pair of nines. It would have beat theirs.

After that…she never lost. A half hour later, the boys were pale and doughy and down to their underwear, ironically tighty-whities for both. Roque estimated they had lost at least fifty dollars, plus however much Spikey's sports watch might be worth.

"So," Leo said, "I'd be willing to use this"—she held up her winnings—"to rent a cell for the night."

Spikey groaned and reached into the pocket of the shorts lying next to him. Shaggy scowled. "How do we know you'll give it back?"

She rolled her eyes. "You've seen my wanted posters? I'll tell you what, I'll give you both what you really want," she fingered the bottom fringe of her bra, "a long look—"

"All right!" Spikey shouted.

"If—and only if—you lend us your phone." Then her lips turned into a grin Roque had never witnessed before. "And you kiss each other."

"Kiss?!"

"With tongue."

"No way no way no way," Shaggy said, but Spikey was paying more attention to Leo's hands slipping behind her back to reach the latch of her bra.

Roque stayed quiet because he was sure he had someone stepped into some crazy television show and was waiting for the laugh track to commence. Or a commercial break.

"I want to see them," Spikey said.

"Dude, there's better on the 'net."

"No. Nothing's better than real life." And Spikey leaned over before Shaggy could escape. With one hand he grabbed a handful of brown hair at the back of Shaggy's head, securing the way for their lips to meet. Shaggy's cheeks puffed out, as if he were playing the trumpet and not kissing another guy.

Leo laughed. Roque slapped a hand over his eyes because he knew what she'd do next. He heard gasps, though whether that was from the effect of a first boy-on-boy kiss, seeing his sister's bare breasts, or C) all of the above, he didn't know. Or want to.

❖

On the walk back through the rain, Roque stayed a few steps behind his sister, who had pulled back on her T-shirt but cradled her bra in one hand and the phone in another like a pair of trophies.

He was still in awe. "You learned to do all that after one read?"

"Don't be an idiot. *Papi* taught me how to play ages ago."

Roque handed her a towel to dry her hair.

"Here." She pressed the cell phone into his hand. "You have ten minutes to speak to the *mariposa* that has you stir-crazy. The rest of the battery belongs to me."

❖

Roque retreated to the bedroom to make the call. On the third ring, a voice answered. Not Gregg's. No, it was pitchy, unmistakably Duncan's: "Speak to me."

Why the hell would Duncan have Gregg's phone? Roque's

insides trembled. As if he were on the edge of the flu. "Where's Gregg?"

"Roque Prieto! How's the surf?" A giggle. Everyone in the area knew of the torrential rainfall.

"Just put Gregg on."

"Still all moist after that one?"

"Duncan. Please."

"If I could, I would, hon. But he's not here right now. After sharing a fabulous breakfast together—well, you know how I leave men *crazy*—he drove off forgetting his phone. But don't fret—"

Roque hung up. He didn't want to hear details.

The weird yearbook lay open in his lap. But Gregg's photograph was now empty, as if he had ducked when the photographer clicked the camera. Or he was hiding from Roque. The caption of *Most Likely to Hack into the Smithsonian* had changed to *When I take a drink I become another person, and the other person wants a drink too.*

He tossed the book across the room and was satisfied at the thud it made, at the plaster it cracked on the wall.

Back in the living room, he dropped the phone on the sofa by Leo, who watched him move to the front door and struggle with the latch. She asked him where he was going, but Roque didn't answer.

He started running through the rain. He often fell to his hands and knees onto the chilled, dark sand, but picked himself up again and again. The beach was deserted and he was determined to reach the farthest end he could. And then? Then he'd just sit in the rain until he got pneumonia. Or the rain, which fell so hard it stung, would erode him into tiny pieces that would wash away into the frothy Atlantic.

He reached a line of rocks jutting out of the sand,

perpendicular to the shore. Before he could climb over them, a car horn startled him. He looked over his shoulder. A Jeep drove over the dune grass, its headlights trained on him. He stepped aside.

It stopped inches away. The driver's side door opened. Gregg leaned out. "You're not supposed to swim *on* the beach." Raindrops began to spatter Gregg's glasses.

"What are you doing here?"

"Looking for you."

"Liar."

Gregg's forehead furrowed. "I drive through a storm to find you and I'm rewarded with attitude?"

"I'm not the one that had breakfast with Duncan! Was that his treat after you treated him to dinner?"

Gregg shook his head. "Get inside and we'll talk."

"No. I'd rather swim."

"You know I could get arrested for driving on the beach."

"Really?" Roque glanced up and down the beach.

"Honest. And I promise to be honest with you."

Roque walked around to the passenger side. He was thankful to get out of the rain, though he couldn't be more soaked if he had dived headfirst into the surf.

"When you're wet your eyelashes look huge," Gregg said.

"Duncan. Tell me now."

Gregg sighed. "Yes, I did go to Duncan's house this morning. And he cooked me breakfast. But I went there just to talk."

"'Bout what?"

"You. I needed a neutral party to talk to—like Switzerland."

"Duncan's not Switzerland. He's more like…like Hannibal Lecter crossing the Alps."

"That makes no sense."

"Nothing this day makes sense. I think I have your yearbook—"

"I'm not interested in Duncan. But he's been out for ages. You're out. And...and I'm not quite there yet."

"Wait...what?"

"I've always thought you were cute. Since we met. I was kinda hoping you'd ask me out some time. I couldn't because...I mean, do two guys go to movies together? Hold hands? What are the rules? But then, you never seemed interested in me *that* way, so I just buried my feelings and was sorta content to be friends."

Gregg reached out and pressed his hand on Roque's shoulder. "And then, when you signed my yearbook, I realized high school is over and I won't be seeing you like every day. Even if we're both at Rutgers, that place is huge. And all I wanted to do was ask you out, but I thought you'd say no."

"No. I mean—I wouldn't have."

Gregg smiled. "Duncan told me that you sweated me."

"He did?" Roque leaned closer to Gregg.

"Yeah. He encouraged me to go after you, told me he overheard you telling folks you'd be down the shore this weekend."

Roque mentally groaned at being such an idiot, such a jealous idiot, with Duncan.

"And here you are."

"And here I am. I want—"

Roque leaned forward and kissed him.

Gregg blushed. "Uh, yes, I wanted a kiss, too, but I was going to say, 'I want that date.'"

"I'm here in your car. You can take me anywhere."

Gregg was the one who started the next kiss.

"You really have my yearbook?" he asked.

"Buy me a drink and it's yours."

"A drink?"

Roque nodded. "I think you'd be a very different person hammered." He regretted saying it moments after it escaped his mouth. He didn't want a different Gregg but the very one that risked the rain for him.

"At one time," Gregg said. "But I'm really more of a coffee drinker these days." He reached into the cup holder and shook the paper cup a little. "It's not as hot as it used to be."

Roque wiped water dripping from his forehead into his eyes and looked out the streaked windows. "There's gotta be a pier somewhere close. We could share."

Gregg smiled and put the Jeep in gear. "Would you believe this is sort of how I pictured our first date would be?"

"Most likely, I would believe anything you did, anything you told me." Roque's hand reached for the cup and found the heat of Gregg's fingers instead.

Leap
'Nathan Burgoine

After three hours crammed in the back of the car, the last thing I was going to do was unpack. I'd thrown my stuff into the small room in the cabin that would be mine for the next three weeks—this time we had cabin four, because we'd been the last to call in our reservation—and had immediately set off down the dirt path to the lake. My dad was still unloading the car, and my mom was arranging the kitchen. Both of them had been smiling and had waved me off, saying they didn't need any help. They were in a great mood—I knew they looked forward to this every year. We'd been renting a cabin for the last weeks of August as a family for as long as I could remember.

I closed my eyes, let the sun hit my face, and relaxed. *Finally.* I started down the familiar path, listened to the birds, and enjoyed the sound of the wind through the leaves—it had always reminded me of the water rushing over the dam at Hog's Back.

At the top of the rise, there was a path that went farther up, to an outcropping. I thought about heading straight up there. You could take a running leap from the top and launch yourself out into the lake. It was gorgeous out. The water would be warm.

Then I heard laughter from down below, and I went down to the lake instead. When I came out of the trees, two familiar faces were waiting for me at the usual spot at the end of the small wooden dock.

"Ryan!" Angie grinned, getting up from her blanket and running up the dock. She was wearing a bikini, and had more than enough curves to fill one. Beside her, Barb put down the book she was reading and got up, too—her swimsuit was a one-piece, and flattered her lean build.

"You cut your hair!" I said, and grabbed Angie in a big hug, picking her up and swinging her in a circle. She laughed, kicking her feet. I put her down.

"Do you like it?" she asked, touching the short auburn bob.

"Very chic," I said.

"I keep telling her it makes her eyes pop," Barb said, walking up and giving me a much more sedate hug. "But she never listens to me."

"Gay boys are better at that stuff," Angie said, giving Barb a snooty smile. "Besides, you've been wearing a ponytail for, what, eleven years?"

"It's functional," Barb said, and rolled her eyes.

"If I had her cheekbones, I'd go for a ponytail, too," I said.

"Eww." Angie wrinkled her nose. "Long hair on boys is gross."

"I almost did the leap it's so nice out, but I thought I'd come find you guys first."

Barb smiled. "We haven't jumped yet either." Every year since we'd been old enough to finally dare each other into action, we'd jumped off the ledge and into the lake with loud screams and lots of laughter.

"And not in this swimsuit," Angie added, motioning to the bikini.

I laughed, and the three of us made our way back to the dock. I unfolded my towel, pulled off my shirt, and lay back, sighing comfortably as the two girls sat down. I rolled my head to the side, looking at Barb.

"Okay," I said. "So why do I find out you're an award-winning writer on Facebook?"

Barb had the grace to look abashed. "The newspaper story contest? I won second place. Sorry. I've been really busy."

"And she had a boyfriend, but she dumped him," Angie said.

"I didn't dump him," Barb sighed. This was obviously a discussion they'd had before. "We just sort of put it on hold."

"Pictures or it didn't happen," I said.

Angie picked up her phone and started thumbing through her photos while Barb rolled her eyes at us. Angie held out her phone. I sat up. A boy with blond hair and a great smile was beaming out of the phone at me. "Very cute. I approve. How come Angie knows about this dumped boyfriend, and this is the first I've heard about him?"

"Like I said, it's been busy…My mom and Stuart are doing that puppy love thing all over the place, and they keep taking me out places and having 'family nights.' I think my mom wants me to feel secure that he's not like my dad was. Anyway, Angie only knows because we go to the same school." Barb shook her head. "It wasn't anything serious. John and I had four dates in March and April, but he was going on kibbutz for the summer, so we put it on hold until he gets back."

"They've arranged their schedules to share a few classes," Angie added.

"Really?" I raised an eyebrow, grinning. Barb and Angie weren't especially close to each other, I knew, except for August when we were all here at the cabins. They moved in different circles even though they went to the same school. Angie was a cheerleader and was looking forward to joining her mother's sorority, Barb was more likely to join a writing group and only cheered when there was some sort of breaking news she cared about. I'd known them for what felt like forever. Our mothers had all been friends since grade school.

"I refuse to answer that," Barb said, but she was blushing, and her lips were twitching.

"I assume you and Chris are still the thing? Any major breaking news there?" I asked, looking at Angie.

"Nothing serious," Angie said haughtily, doing a perfect Barb impression.

Angie and I burst out laughing, and Barb stuck her tongue out at us.

"Oh my God, though," Angie said. "My parents are thinking about giving me the car."

I sat up. "Excuse me?" I hoped I didn't sound as jealous as I felt.

She waved her painted fingernails, excited. "So you know how my sister got married, right? Well, a couple of weeks after that, she announced they've gotten lucky and are pregnant right away—no one bought that for a second, but we're all pretending—and so now my folks are head-over-heels about the impending baby."

I stared at her. "And why does that mean you get a car?"

"My parents are gonna give me my mom's Mazda. Apparently the baby seat they've bought wouldn't fit in it, so my dad got her an Element and I get the hand-me-down." She grinned.

"Nice hand-me-down," I muttered. She smiled at me. Barb made a noise I agreed with—something between a groan and a sigh.

"Hey, I'll need wheels when I go to university," Angie said.

I took a breath. "I worked at the gas station all summer—which, let me tell you, gives you a whole new perspective on your fellow man—and I don't get a car. Life is unfair."

"Completely," Barb said.

Angie stuck her tongue out, but laughed. "Cars make you lazy. Don't you prefer running?"

I rolled my eyes. "I shaved almost an entire minute off my five-K run this year," I said, proud. "I think I've got a real shot at bringing home the gold."

"And the hunt for a boyfriend?" Angie asked. Barb looked up at this as well.

"I'm the only out guy in my school," I reminded them. "So that's a big ol' 'no.'"

"What about that Skype guy?" Angie asked.

"James?" I lay back on the dock, sighing. "He lives three hours away. Also, he found a boyfriend of his very own."

"Ouch."

"Yeah," I agreed. James and I had met online when he'd admitted his giant Jake Shears crush on a Scissor Sisters blog. A follow-up comment from me praising his taste had turned into an e-mail, then a couple of Facebook chats, and then Skype. He was cute—French Canadian, he had a great accent, and my attempts at high school French had made him laugh. We shared music with each other, sent stupid texts back and forth, and it had been what I'd thought could have turned serious, right up until the "I met this guy" text had come in, and then he'd pretty much vanished.

Boom. Back to being the only out gay guy in my school.

"How was this year?" Barb asked.

"It was a lot better," I admitted. The first year I'd come out had been bumpy. There'd been a kid in another school, Brady Adams, who'd come out on his fifteenth birthday and made the news with his blog about the day-to-day life of being the only gay kid in his school. Some idiots had started sending him nasty messages when the news story aired, but a lot of support poured in, too. The good outweighed the bad, and I'd seen so many messages on his blog from adults telling him about how much better it would get, but there hadn't been any other teenagers. After one of his posts where he'd talked over and over about how much it sucked to be alone, I'd posted my first reply to him.

You aren't alone. Three words, but it changed everything for me.

I'd known I was gay since eighth grade, but when I'd read Brady's blog I'd decided to come out. My mom—she was a elementary school teacher—had been fantastic about the whole thing and had always been outspoken about her opinions on the subject, so I'd known she'd be okay when I finally got up the nerve to tell her. My dad had taken a little longer not being awkward around me—he was a quiet guy, and when he'd finally told me "it doesn't matter, you're my son," it had taken a lot of effort not to burst into tears.

School had been a bigger step than my folks, but I kept thinking about Brady, and that got me through it. I wasn't worried too much about bullies—I wasn't exactly popular, but the track team had my back, and nobody wants to piss off one of the yearbook photographers. I wasn't a social outcast. I figured I could hold my own, and if nothing else, three years of cross-country pretty much gave me all the training I needed in the "run away" department. But it hadn't been like that. I'd started small—my friends and the team had been mostly okay with it, though one or two of them had kind of faded away over the year. My track coach, Ms. Fletch, had been amazing and she'd steered me toward PFLAG and other stuff like that, and even asked me if I wanted to set up a Gay-Straight Alliance next year, which I was thinking of doing.

Sure, there were jerks—most notably Chad Donovan—and boy did those jerks manage to make some days pretty rough, but for the most part it had only gotten better over the last year. Chad had graduated now, too, so I wouldn't see him again. I liked myself more now—it had taken a lot of effort to be someone I wasn't. Then I'd met James, and things seemed to be going in a much better direction.

Until he met someone.

"You're totally gonna get scooped up the minute you get to university, Ryan," Angie said. "Mark my words."

"If Brady doesn't get you first," Barb said.

I groaned. I'd eventually met up with Brady Adams at a coffee shop, only to learn that he thought we were on a date. I'd thought we were just going to hang out. He was tiny—and fifteen, for crying out loud!—and it was really awkward. He liked Lady Gaga. He'd sent me messages and written poems about me on his blog. It was humiliating.

"Bite your tongue," I said. "Besides, I think even he has managed to find someone now. Or at least, there's no poetry about my dimples anymore."

They laughed.

"Anyone show up for cabin three yet?" I asked, changing the subject.

"Not yet," Barb said. There were four cabins in the group, and last year, the fourth family had been a young couple with twin four-year-olds. They were cute, but we were all sort of hoping they'd take a pass this year. They'd pretty much lived at the dock, and we'd always felt like it was our space. Our parents liked the large yard that the four cabins shared, pulling picnic tables together and playing games and laughing the day away, the men barbecuing and talking sports while the women shared stories.

We settled back, letting the sun warm our skin and talking about movies and books and the bits and pieces of the last year, until the sun started to dip and the mosquitoes came out.

❖

The sound of a car door closing woke me, and I sat up and looked through the small screened window in my room to see that there was now a car outside of cabin three. A couple of figures moved about in the moonlight, and I peered, trying to see if there were any shadows the right size for the twin boys. There weren't. In fact, it looked like there were only three people there at all, and all of them were too tall to be children. Their voices were muffled—they were obviously trying to be as quiet as they could, aware it was quite late, and I watched for a little while as they unloaded a cooler and a few bags from the car, then went into the cabin. I lay back, smiling to myself that there'd be no children yelling and splashing in the water, and that the dock was once again our domain.

The next morning while the sun rose I went for a run around the road that led into the cabins. Even without the sun beating down, it was hot, and I was soon sweating and swiping away some lingering mosquitoes. I did a full set of laps, and then headed back for the yard the cabins shared. I could hear laughter as I made my way around the last bend. Everyone was already outside, the picnic tables once again rearranged into the cluster the way our mothers did every year, with a jug of milk and boxes of cereal over one of them. Angie's mom and Stuart were sitting at one table with Barb's folks, and my parents were at another with a couple I didn't know. I made a beeline for the food and grabbed a bowl and a spoon from the breakfast table.

"That's our son, Ryan," Mom said, shaking her head. She turned to the couple, who seemed to be about the same age as my folks. "He does have manners, but he's in a growing spurt again and eats three times his weight after a run." Then she looked back at me. "Ryan, this is Mr. and Mrs. Sullivan. They've got cabin three this year."

I smiled and said hello. They smiled back. Mrs. Sullivan was very pretty, with dark hair and dark eyes. She had her hair back in a scrunchie, but you could tell she'd still taken time to do her makeup and put on a nice blouse. Her husband seemed more relaxed—he looked like he'd probably played hockey or something when he was younger—he was a big guy. He was either bald or shaved his head—probably a mix of the two—and seemed to fit in more in his comfortable shirt and cut-offs.

I started pouring some cereal. I scanned for Barb and Angie, but they'd probably already headed down to the dock.

"Our son is still asleep," Mrs. Sullivan said. "He's growing, too. He'd sleep all day, if I let him—but we got in pretty late." She and my mom shared a laugh over us boys.

"I'm up," came a voice, and we all turned.

The guy coming out of cabin three was tall and dark-haired and looked rumpled and out of it. He rubbed his eyes with the palm of one hand, then looked around. When he looked at me, I shivered. *Hi, there.*

"This is Will," his mother said. She introduced him to my parents, and he said hello. He was wearing an Arcade Fire T-shirt—*hello, good taste!*—and a pair of tan cargo shorts, which I could forgive since he had great legs, and wide shoulders.

I was suddenly very aware that I was sweating like a pig and probably smelled foul.

"Ryan," my mother said. "Show Will where the cereal is."

I looked at the table in front of me where the cereal was in plain view of anyone with even one half-functional eyeball. I pointed at it. "Cereal," I said.

He smiled—a crooked smile, which was really hot—and I saw my mother roll her eyes at me. Will joined me at the table, and I cleared my throat. "Bowls. Spoons." I pointed at each.

"All right, smart-aleck," my mother called, but Will laughed. He had a deep laugh.

"I'm Ryan," I said. *I'm gross and sweaty and you're tall and cute.*

"Will." He nodded. He poured some flakes into his bowl and grabbed the jug. His T-shirt was tight, and that was a good thing. He obviously hit the gym. I pressed my own arms against my side, holding my bowl against my chest. Could he smell me?

"Nice to meet you. Grab your spoon, and I'll show you where we go to escape the old people." *And where I can get into the lake and clean off my stink.*

❖

"Ladies," I said, carrying my bowl in front of me and leading the way while Will walked behind me. "You will notice that I am not accompanied by five-year-old twins."

Barb and Angie held their hands over their eyes as we approached the dock. Angie had a much more modest swimsuit on today, I noticed, though it definitely still worked her curves.

"Thank God!" she said.

"Hi," Barb said, rising, and offering her hand. "I'm Barb. She's Angie."

"Will," Will said. He looked at the dock, and the lake. "This is pretty nice."

The dock wasn't the only thing that was nice. Will's eyes, for one thing, were the colour of dark chocolate. I dropped my towel and spread it out awkwardly with one hand, still cradling my breakfast with the other.

"Did you just get up?" Angie asked me.

"I went on a run," I said. "Some of us work and train our butts off all summer and don't get hand-me-down cars we don't pay for."

"Please." She smirked. "You worked in a gas station. What ride are you gonna buy, a bike?"

"Don't mind them," Barb said. "They're not used to guests."

Will laughed, sitting down beside me. I scooched over to give him some room and to try to stay downwind. He took a spoonful of his cereal and chewed. He had a great jawline.

"So what school do you go to?" Angie asked.

Will swallowed. "We just moved from Toronto. Next year I'm going to Ottawa Central. It's my last year."

"That's my school," I said, and Will looked at me, interested.

"What's it like?"

My brain went blank. "It's a high school," I said.

He pointed at his bowl. "Cereal."

I laughed. The girls regarded us like we were idiots.

"We thought we'd do the leap today," Angie said. "You're welcome to join us."

Will was eating, so he shook his head and raised an eyebrow. I'd always wanted to be able to do that one-eyebrow thing. I'd trade in my dimples for knowing how to do the one-eyebrow thing in a heartbeat.

"Our mothers are all friends," Barb explained. "We come here every summer. There's a path that takes you to that outcropping." She pointed, and Will craned his neck to look at it. "We jump in the lake every year. It's like a tradition."

Will swallowed again. "That looks pretty high."

"It's terrifying," Angie said. "But it's totally fun."

"I'm not good with heights," Will said. He was still looking. In profile, you really noticed his eyelashes. I looked up. He was right, the outcropping was a good forty feet high, and the face was nothing but rock. You had to really hoof yourself over the edge when you jumped. One year Angie had ended up with stitches in her foot from not quite clearing the rocks at the bottom. From up at the top, looking down it felt more like eighty feet. I think it was the way the sky reflected in the water.

"Don't worry about it," I said. "It's an epic jump. It took us years to get up the nerve." I was racing through my cereal, and done a few moments later. When I put my bowl down, Angie rose.

Barb looked at Will. "You sure you don't want to give it a try?"

He nodded. "Very."

She got up, and I followed suit, tugging my shirt off and avoiding looking at Will. No matter how hard I tried, I was always a little embarrassed when a guy was looking at me without my shirt on. I hoped the breeze was covering my reek.

"We'll be up there in a little bit." Barb smiled at him. "And then we'll swim back here right after."

"Maybe I'll take the bowls back and then come back down here to watch." He shivered, obviously uncomfortable. "Enjoy."

❖

"I wouldn't have pegged him for a wuss," Angie said.

I rolled my eyes, following the girls as they climbed the steep path. "He's not a wuss. He just doesn't like heights. May I remind you that we basically had to throw you off the top the first time you did it?"

Angie laughed. "Legit."

Barb said, "He seems nice."

"Yeah," I said. "He does."

The two girls looked at each other, and I felt my face turning red. They laughed, and I sighed.

"So you should ask him out," Angie said.

"Right," I said, nodding. "Because straight guys love that, and it won't make the next three weeks awkward at all."

"You think he's straight?" Angie said.

"You don't?" I said. I hoped my voice had come out more even than it had sounded to me.

"Wager on it?" she asked.

"First bottle?" I said.

"Deal." We shook. For the past few years, we'd made a game out of sneaking a bottle of beer here and there from our parents. So far, they hadn't noticed.

When we were at the top of the path. Angie paused, looking at me. Barb pointed towards the edge.

"On three?" she asked.

Angie nodded. I smiled.

"One," she said.

"Two," I said.

"Three!" Barb said, and the three of us ran off down the path, towards the edge. I jumped our as far as I could, and for just a second it felt like I was surrounded by nothing but sunlight. There's a moment when you're in the air, and you look down and see the water and you're just hanging. Then gravity reminds you who's boss and you go down, laughing and screaming, toward the lake.

I gripped my legs, cannonballing, and hit the water with a huge splash. It felt awesome—the water was just cool enough, and I let myself float under the surface for a couple of seconds before kicking off. Everything was blue, and I swam back up into the light.

I broke the water and yelled in triumph. The girls were already at the surface, and laughing. I was grinning like an idiot as we swam back to the dock, showing off a little on the way with some butterfly strokes.

It didn't hurt that I saw Will was watching from the dock.

❖

"You're all crazy," Will said as we swam up. He was standing and had his arms crossed. He stepped back as we started to climb up onto the dock, splashing water everywhere. We grabbed our towels and wiped ourselves down.

"The best thing about short hair is drying it," Angie said, rubbing her head vigorously and grinning at Barb, who was squeezing her long hair out and rubbing it with her towel.

"The water was so nice," I said, grinning. It's amazing how much more confident you feel when you don't smell like ripe gym socks.

"I'll change into trunks later," Will said. "And walk out from the shore like a normal person. You guys are crazy," he repeated. Somehow, I liked the way he was saying it. He crouched back down again and sat down on the edge of the dock, letting his feet dangle in the water.

I shrugged back into my shirt and sat on my towel, letting the sun hit my face. I glanced at Will, who was looking out at the water. His eyelashes were so long. I glanced away, and Angie winked at me. I tried to ignore her grin as my face turned red.

"So what's up for tonight?" Barb said.

I looked at the sky. "Not many clouds so far—we might have a good night for stars."

"Toasting marshmallows?" Angie suggested.

"Do people really do that?" Will asked.

Angie leaned back. "Holy crap. You *are* from Toronto, aren't you?"

Will raised one eyebrow again. God, that was cute. "Nobody's perfect."

Angie laughed. "I like you. You can stay." He shook his head, but smiled. "Seriously, though," she said. "We do roast marshmallows. And we tell stories around the campfire, too. Or, well, Barb does, because she's good at it. She's our resident writer."

"You write?" Will asked.

"I'd like to," Barb admitted.

"She won a fiction contest in the newspaper," I added.

Will seemed impressed. "That's cool. What was it about?"

It occurred to me I didn't know. "You know, you never did send it to me," I said.

"She didn't?" Angie said. She smacked Barb's shoulder. "Naughty girl."

I frowned. Barb looked at me, blushing. "I used your name for one of the characters."

"That's really cool," I said. "What was it about?"

"It was a love story," Angie said. "Except you died at the end."

"Harsh. Wait." I looked at her. "You read it?"

Barb put her hands over her face. "They read it over the school P.A."

Angie was giggling. "You're quite the kisser," she said to me.

"Really?" I looked at Barb. "That's good to know. Did I use tongue?"

"Ryan's kiss took her by surprise," Barb was quoting, I gathered. "Cassie hadn't expected it, but the moment she felt his hands on her shoulders, she knew she wanted it." Will and Angie were both laughing, and Barb was shaking her head at my expression. "I just sort of put your name in as a place-holder, but then I got used to it…"

"And then killed me off." I crossed my arms and frowned. "So you don't think I'm a good kisser?"

"We've never kissed!" Barb laughed. "And we're not really likely to, are we?"

I saw Will blink and saw Barb jolt when she realized what she'd said. I felt myself tense up, and my face was burning.

Angie leapt in for the rescue.

"Oh my God!" she said. "Did I tell you guys Chris got his braces stuck in my earring?"

As Angie told her story, I watched Will out of the corner of my eye. He was an attentive listener, and laughed as Angie mimicked her boyfriend trying to explain things to his orthodontist. He'd pulled up his knees and wrapped his arms around them—they were great arms. Will absolutely made time for the gym. He glanced at me and caught me looking, and I looked away, feeling my face burn. Well, this was what I wanted, right? This was being out?

I looked at Will again, and wondered what his favourite Arcade Fire song was.

❖

I built the fire on the beach, making a kind of tepee out of the logs and filling the underneath with kindling. It caught on my second attempt, and I poked it into a decent blaze. On the shore of the lake, the wind was just enough to work with the smoke to keep most of the bugs at bay. I'd still worn a hoodie and sweatpants, just in case. Our "sitting log" from last summer was still there, and I dragged it closer to the fire.

"I am so sorry," Barb said, coming down the path. She had a red sweater on, and jeans.

I smiled at her. "It's okay. I'm out—that's sort of the point." I looked behind her. "Angie not with you?"

"She was playing Scrabble with her folks—she said she'd be down once she won." She looked up. "You were right about the stars."

I looked up. It was a gorgeous night. The moon wasn't up yet, and the stars were incredible. I moved over a bit on the log and Barb sat beside me. She leaned her head on my shoulder.

"So that was the first time I ever outed anyone," she said.

"As a journalist, I expect you to hone your skills on closeted conservatives."

She laughed. "I really am sorry."

I put my arm around her. "Honestly, it's fine. And hey—it's not like he bugged out or anything. He was cool."

"Do you think he'll come?" she asked.

I looked at the marshmallows. "I hope so. Because otherwise, I'm going to eat that whole bag."

"If I have to, I will eat half. It will be a tough punishment, but I will endure it," Barb said solemnly.

We grinned.

"Did you bring sticks for them?" she asked.

"I found the unfolded coat-hangers from last year." I pointed.

"Excellent." Barb took one, and I opened the bag.

"Triple 'queen' for the win!"

We both turned. Angie strode out onto the beach, one fist in the air.

"There's only two of us queens here," I said.

"Ha and ha again," Angie said, coming to the log and sitting. "I tripled 'queen' at Scrabble."

"And I'm sure you did so with reserved grace," I said.

"Pft." She smirked. "I danced the 'take that' dance." Angie rose and did a kind of taunting touchdown dance that had Barb and I laughing and holding our stomachs.

"You look like a drunk belly dancer," I gasped out.

She stuck her tongue out at me and joined us on the log. "Mallow me."

Barb passed her the marshmallow she'd already speared on the wire.

"If you have to do the dance before you get a marshmallow, I think I'll skip out on this."

We all turned. Will was just at the edge of the trees, and

though it was hard to see by the light of the campfire, I was pretty sure he was smiling. I felt myself relax a notch.

"No dancing required," Barb said.

The only space left on the log was beside me, and I tried not to react when Will sat down. I speared a mallow on one of the wires and handed it to him. He watched as Angie and Barb put theirs over the flame, then followed suit. He was still wearing his T-shirt, but he'd put on a pair of faded gray sweatpants—they looked well worn. I wondered if he played any sports. Maybe we could go for a run. I got another mallow ready and put it over the fire.

"You want to wait until it's just a little brown all around the outside," I said, turning my marshmallow around slowly. "And then you can peel off the skin and get a second go at it."

He looked at me, but nodded, and tried to mimic what I was doing.

When we pulled our marshmallows out of the fire, he watched me skin mine—the browned portion came off in a caramelized layer—and then he skinned his own. I ate mine.

"Now it feels like summer," Barb said, licking her fingers.

"Okay," Will said, chewing. "That is good."

"Tomorrow night, spider dogs," Angie declared.

Will leaned forward slightly, and said. "What's a spider dog?"

"Oh my God, Toronto is like…so out of touch." Angie shook her head.

"It's a hot dog," I said. "But you sort of slice it, and it curls up and looks like a spider."

"So you jump off cliffs and eat spiders." Will shook his head. "You guys are brave."

"Doing the leap was nothing after Chad Donovan," I said, and then caught myself.

"Who?" he asked.

"Just a jerk at school," I said.

"He was a complete asshole," Barb said, surprising me. "He treated Ryan like crap, said stuff, posted on his wall—it got pretty ugly for a while. Generally just a miserable human being."

Will was quiet for a while. "He still around?"

"He graduated," I said. "I think he's recruiting for the conservatives now. Or a clown. One of those."

Will laughed, and again it struck me how deep his laugh was. I smiled at him.

"You're flaming," Angie said. I flushed, looking at her— *just because I'm smiling at Will, it doesn't mean I'm—oh.* My marshmallow was on fire. I tugged it out and blew on it until it went out, then ate the gooey mess, blackened parts and all. Will managed to skin his again, then ate the lump that was left on his third run through.

"So tell us about you," Barb said. Will looked at her, surprised.

"Barb's going to be a journalist," I said.

Will smiled. "What do you want to know?"

I bit my tongue.

"What are you into?" Barb asked.

"Music," Will said, without even taking a second to think about it.

"Epic band," I said, pointing at his shirt.

"The best." He nodded.

"And?" Barb leaned forward.

Will laughed. "I don't know. I went to an arts school, so I got to do a lot more music stuff than I could do in a regular high school. And art. I like sculpting, but I suck at painting." He sighed. "I'm going to miss my crew. We had this great little group." He grew more animated as he talked, and started moving his hands. "We had a band, and played for the assemblies and stuff. There were art shows, and writing groups." He nodded at Barb. "It was a cool school."

"You are *not* trading up," I said. He flashed that crooked grin again.

"Mallow," Angie said, and I handed her another marshmallow.

We roasted half the bag, mostly quiet, though every now and then Angie would break the silence with "Oh my God, I forgot to tell you guys…" and go off on another story about Chris. It was obvious from how much he embarrassed her in public that she adored him. Or at least that was the way it seemed to me.

Will didn't add much often, but when he did, we were all rapt. He had a way of talking that was somehow confident—like, when he said something was cool, you knew that it was absolutely cool. When it got a little cooler, he worked on the fire, asking us what to do and listening to our advice. He wasn't all macho and didn't assume he knew anything.

He was awesome.

Barb turned in first, and Angie went next, doing her "take that" dance all the way back up to the path. Will chuckled beside me, and I watched the flames of the fire, now growing low. It wasn't an awkward quiet, just the two of us, and I was glad. Will was cool with the whole gay thing—which made sense if he'd been at an art school.

"Are there many gay guys at your school?"

It was like he was reading my mind. "No. Or, well, probably. But I'm the only out guy. I'm going to start a GSA next year, though. My track coach, Ms. Fletch, is going to sponsor one."

"You run track?" It came out a little surprised.

"In between redecorating rooms and designing ball gowns, yeah."

He laughed. "I didn't mean it like that."

"I'm just kidding," I said. "I like to joke about it. People seem to handle it better that way."

"Except for Chad Donovan?"

I was surprised he remembered the name. "Yeah, well. Except for him. Hence the GSA."

"There are some plusses to being at an art school," he said, and reached over and took my hand.

"I bet," I said, distracted by the feel of his fingers squeezing mine. His fingers were rougher than mine, which surprised me, and made my stomach do little flips. I looked down, convinced I was turning red and glad for the fire. Will was being really cool. There aren't many straight guys confident enough to give a supportive hand squeeze to a gay guy spilling his guts. Except it wasn't a hand squeeze. Seconds were passing. It was moving past hand-squeezing and into hand-holding. I looked up at him, and he raised one eyebrow.

I clued in. "Oh!"

He laughed. "Yeah."

My stomach was in free fall. His hand was very warm. I realized I was sitting perfectly still—I felt like if I moved, something would break. He might shift. He might let go. I didn't have the slightest idea if I should be saying something. I hoped I shouldn't, because right now all I wanted to do was tell him his hand felt awesome, and that would probably ruin the moment.

"Ryan?" Will said.

"Yeah?"

"Thanks for the marshmallows."

He let go of my hand—I tried not to make any whimpering noises—but then he wrapped his arm around me. I leaned against him. Will started telling me about his old school, his group of friends, the bands and music they'd play and what it was like to tell his folks their only kid was gay. I listened, then told him my own stories and about Brady's blog and James, feeling the heat from Will's arm around my shoulder and trying to memorize everything. Will liked the Scissor Sisters, too. My stomach refused to stop flipping, but my hands slowly stopped shaking. We talked, mostly about nothing important, and I felt normal for the first time in a very long while.

We watched the fire until it died.

❖

Running the loop the next morning, I replayed the evening. Was I supposed to have offered him a turn leaning on me? I hadn't, and now I was pretty sure that made me look needy or clingy or something. Or maybe just neurotic. I was muttering to myself as I was running, and I wasn't really focusing on the run. It took a lot longer than it should have, and I was barely out of breath when I got back to the cabins.

Had I really told him about chatting online with James? And that coffee thing with Brady? Why had I told him I'd gone on a date with a fifteen-year-old? I had to be mental. It was the only explanation.

I wasn't sure if or what Will would do the next time we were all together, so I tried to be casual when I went down to the dock with my cereal. The three of them were already there, and the only space was beside Will. I managed not to barf when I sat down beside him. Will bumped shoulders with me and smiled, and I grinned back, all my worries draining out of me in a rush.

God, he was cute.

Angie was grinning at me, smug.

"I'll bring you the bottle later," I said, when Will and Barb were talking.

After that, the four of us settled into the same routine the three of us had always had, except it was four of us now. We swam a lot, and Will watched us do the leap a couple of times, still convinced we were all a little crazy. At night, we'd light campfires, and we introduced Will to spider dogs and s'mores. Barb told a great ghost story that made Angie swear she wouldn't sleep at night, and Will brought out his guitar and playing for us, while we sang along very, very badly. He had a good voice on his own, though.

❖

On the first rainy morning we had, I went for a miserable run, dried off, and made myself an omelette for breakfast before my parents got up. On rainy mornings the parents generally gathered in cabin two—Barb's cabin this year—and we'd hang out in one of the other cabins. My mother had sleepily offered to do the dishes if I made omelettes for her and my dad. They were on the couch having coffee in their robes while I stood at the stove.

"Ryan seems to getting on well with Will," my mother said.

I turned to look at them. They did realize I was in the same room, right?

My father glanced at my mother over his mug. "He is?"

"You know," she said, "I thought having a boy meant I'd be spared that anxiety of my child getting their first boyfriend."

"Oh Jesus," my father said. He took a swallow of coffee. "Are they dating?"

"I'm standing right here," I said. "I can hear you."

"Will seems to tell his parents a lot more than our son does," she said. "Lorraine tells me he's very open with her and Martin. That'd be lovely, don't you think?"

"Okay, enough," I said, embarrassed. I sliced the first omelette in half and flipped it onto two plates, bringing them over to my parents. "We're just hanging out."

"Uh-huh." My mother's eyes sparkled.

"You guys do know I'm seventeen, right?"

"Honey, we were seventeen once," my mother said, and smiled at my father. "Remember what we were like at seventeen?"

"Oh Jesus," my father said again, grinning at her. Then he pointed at me with his fork. "You're being careful, right?" He frowned. "Wait." Watching him realize that no one was going to end up pregnant was painful. Also, humiliating.

"I am not having this conversation with you two," I said.

"Will's parents are very nice," my mother said. "She said I shouldn't worry. Ryan is in good hands."

"Oh my God," I said. "I'm going to Angie's."

"Have fun, honey," my mother said. I snuck a bottle of my dad's beer from the fridge to pay Angie and pretended I couldn't hear my parents laughing as I jogged across to her family's cabin.

❖

It didn't stop raining, so we spent the day in Angie's cabin and played Scrabble and cards, and eventually, Barb and Will teamed up to do the "take that" dance when they beat Angie and me at euchre. Will taught us Texas Hold 'em, and he came up with using the Scrabble tiles as poker chips, which was pretty smart. After losing all my tiles round after round, I had to admit I couldn't bluff to save my life.

"It's a good trait," Barb said. "Means you're honest."

"Or a sucker," Angie added, raking the large pile of tiles toward herself. She'd taken the beer without comment—thankfully—and tucked it in her backpack.

Will turned to me and said, "My parents have been talking to your parents."

I nodded. "I know. Apparently I have a lot to learn from you."

Will raised an eyebrow, and I realized what I'd just said. Angie and Barb burst out laughing. Will was grinning. If I was lucky, maybe the earth would open up and swallow me whole.

"I meant my mom thinks you're better about sharing stuff with your folks," I said, while the girls calmed down. Will's grin quirked. "She thinks I need to tell them more."

On the couch, Angie wiped tears from her eyes and said, "My mother thinks you're both adorable."

"So does Stuart," Barb added, shuffling the cards.

"Oh Jesus," I said, echoing my father.

Will laughed and wrapped one arm around me. I leaned back on his chest. He kissed the top of my head, and my entire body shivered.

"That's probably why," Angie said, holding up her phone and snapping a picture of us before we could protest. We both laughed when she turned the phone around and showed us, and Barb dealt another round.

This time, I won.

❖

We were swimming in the lake the next morning when Will caught me treading water, just watching him. His dark hair was wet, and his tanned arms were strong as he stroked his way through the water.

"What?" he asked.

"You're hot."

He laughed and splashed me. I splashed back, and we got into a water fight. When he grabbed me and dunked me, I managed to get my arms around him and push off from the bottom enough to toss him away from me, where he made a huge splash and went under. He came up sputtering and laughing, and we bobbed in the water together.

He leaned in and kissed me. It was sudden and awkward—both of us treading water, and neither of us steady—but his lips hit mine and we were kissing. I had no time to prepare, and that whole thing about time slowing down turned out to be complete bull. His lips were soft, but the kiss itself had some pressure to it. By the time I realized I was having my first kiss—my first kiss!—it was over, and I was bobbing in the water and staring at him with my jaw open like some sort of yokel. I hoped I wasn't drooling.

When I didn't say anything, he raised one eyebrow. He looked a little nervous.

"You taste like coffee," I blurted.

"Sorry." He smiled. "You taste like toothpaste."

Was toothpaste bad? I didn't know. My heart was pounding—did that just happen? I couldn't look away from him.

"It turns out I like coffee," I said, and kissed him. His tongue slipped between my lips, just a little, and I struggled to stay in place in the water. It lasted a bit longer, and when it ended, we were very close to each other. His eyes were so dark.

"You okay?" Will asked.

"I am having the best day of my life," I said.

He laughed. It was true what they said—the third time really is the charm. My tongue even had some courage, it turned out, and although keeping us both afloat and maintaining the kiss took a bit of effort, the challenge was worth it. He was good at this, I decided, feeling my body sort of loosen and tighten up all at the same time. I put one hand on his chest—he felt solid, and warm, even in the water.

"Oh Lord." Angie's voice was loud from the dock. "They're being adorable again."

I jumped and tried to push back, but Will wrapped both arms around me and tugged me back against his chest.

"Nuh-uh," he said. "You're not going anywhere."

Oh wow. It was a good thing we were in the water, because I was pretty sure my knees weren't capable of working properly. I waved at the dock, then looked back at Will.

"More coffee?" I asked.

He laughed.

Days passed like that. Mostly, we hung out, and laughed, and then—at night when the girls had gone to bed—Will and I would lean on each other and look at the stars, making out a little bit. Whenever we got particularly energetic, Will would always stop and ask me if I was okay. It was perfect. I never wanted it to end.

So, of course, it did.

❖

"We leave tomorrow, later in the morning," Will said. He poked at the dying fire. "That way my dad says we can miss some of the traffic."

I nodded. That was pretty much the same story for us, too. We always drove back on Labour Day.

"At least I'll see you at school on Tuesday," I said. "It's only one day." I wasn't convincing myself. Otherwise, why would I be so miserable?

He nodded. I knew him well enough now to know he was worried.

"It'll be fine," I said.

"It's not like at my old school," he said. "I mean...Chad Donovan."

"He graduated," I reminded him. It was weird to see Will act nervous.

"At my old school, we had a group. At your school, there's just you."

"I like to think I can fill a room all by myself."

He smiled. "You know what I mean."

"Yeah." I nodded. "But you're forgetting someone. You." I leaned forward. "So at my school, by my count, that makes two."

He put down the stick and opened his arms. I smiled and slid over. He wrapped himself around me and squeezed, shaking me. He needed to never stop doing that. "You? Awesome," he said. He kissed the top of my head.

"I'm also told I'm adorable."

❖

I ran early on the last day and went down to the dock to watch the sun while I walked it off. Dragonflies were zooming about, and the day promised to be warm and clear.

"Hey."

I turned. Will smiled at me from the edge of the trees. "You're up early," I said.

"You, too."

I nodded. "Went running. It occurred to me that next year I'll be getting ready for university. This might be my last year here—or maybe next year."

"Next year," he said, firmly.

I looked at him. He was smiling, but he looked nervous.

"So, come on," he said, gesturing.

I started up the dock. "Where are we going?"

"You'll see."

He led me up the path toward the cabins but veered off at the trail that led up to the outcropping. He started dragging his heels a little after that, looking ahead with a tight expression on his face. He was tapping his fingers against his thumbs.

"You need to say something," he said.

"What?"

"Distract me."

Easily done. I kissed him, and we spent a few moments against a tree. His hands were a little shaky. When I pushed away, he made a grab for my shoulders, but I took a few steps farther up the path. He sighed and started walking again. I didn't say anything, just following, until we got to the rise. He lingered a few steps behind me. I turned and saw him peering out over the outcrop, arms crossed.

"It's pretty freaking high," he said.

"Yep." I was grinning. I held out my hand.

He laughed—that wonderful deep laugh—and then closed his eyes, taking a deep breath. He tugged his shirt over his head and dropped it on the trail. I would never get tired of that particular view—tanned and smooth, except for a little bit of hair on his stomach, Will was so much fun to look at. He breathed again, opening his eyes and looking at me. I walked back down the trail to him, taking my shirt off and adding it to the pile. I kicked off my shoes and pulled off my socks. Will slid out of his sandals.

Then he took my hand, and squeezed.

"On three?" I said.

He gave a shaky laugh, but nodded.

I counted down, letting go of his hand, and then we ran. His long legs ate up the short path, and I actually had to put a bit of effort into keeping up with him. He started yelling before we even made it to the edge, and I joined him, laughing and feeling the familiar drop in my stomach as the edge approached.

At the edge, Will launched himself off with a bellow, arms pinwheeling, and I cleared the edge a half second later, pushing myself off to the left. His yell echoed over the lake, and the sun and the sky had us both for that heartbeat. Then we dropped downward. I heard his splash moments before I hit the water, and when I came up, he was already bobbing in the lake, his hair wet and grinning from ear to ear. He was breathing heavily.

The water was warm. Will swam toward me with strong strokes that drove him through the water. I waited for him.

"See?" I said. "Epic."

"Holy crap," he said.

I looked at him. There were beads of water on his face and shoulder, and the morning sun made them glow with little bursts of light. My chest felt tight.

"Thanks," I said.

He shook his head, sending spray everywhere. "Well, I figure…If I can do that…" He shrugged.

"Yeah," I said.

"I gotta go pack," he said, but he didn't move.

"Me too," I said.

"Ryan?" he said.

I looked at him. "Yeah?"

"Will this be okay, at school tomorrow?" He kissed me. I wrapped my arms around him and he did the same, both of us kicking to keep afloat. Then we tipped our foreheads together while we treaded water.

I smiled. "It will be great," I said. "Promise."

BARK IF YOU LIKE BOYS
SAM CAMERON

S ean Garrity: millionaire jet-setter, world's most eligible
gay teen, regularly voted Sexiest Sixteen-Year-Old on
the Planet. Here he stood in the crowded stacks of the Florida
Keys Bookmine, shelving historical romances not because he
needed the money but because he was a nice guy with a good
heart. Charity work. *Noblesse oblige.* Every teenage millionaire
had a charity cause to fill their Saturday afternoons—

An elbow poked him in the ribs.

"Stop daydreaming," said Robin McGee, his compadre in
shelving. She wiped her dusty hand on the hem of her black
T-shirt and frowned at the smudges. "You're getting your Ps in
your Qs."

"Am not," he said automatically, but there was the proof:
Rosamunde Pilcher wedged between Amanda Quick and Julia
Quinn.

Robin gave the book in her hand a disgusted look. "Look at
these abs! Definitely Photoshopped. Completely sexist. Don't you
get angry when some publisher's marketing division perpetuates
ridiculous masculine stereotypes?"

Sean glanced at the shirtless model. Another historical
romance set in the Scottish highlands, so of course the guy had
long hair, a flawless body, and improbably perfect shining teeth.
Inside the book, the hero fit every single cliché of romance

writing: dark, brooding, courageous, tormented, and absolutely ferocious in bed. Sean knew that for sure because he'd read every previous book in the series and substituted his own name for the vapid heroine's.

"Yes, I'm completely furious," Sean said, and made a note to grab the book when Robin wasn't looking.

A middle-aged tourist with a floppy straw hat stopped in the aisle. She asked, "Can you tell me where to find the NASCAR romance section?"

NASCAR romance. Where the cars went fast but the sex was strictly G rated. Sean refrained from scoffing out loud and showed her the way. The Bookmine was the only decent-sized bookstore between Miami and Key West. And it was more than decent: Mrs. Anderson, the owner, had linked three separate buildings on the Overseas Highway and connected them with corridors, courtyards, and gazebos. According to the computer inventory, they had almost half a million books crammed into the shelves. Sean thought they probably had twice that many if you counted the stuff in boxes or in the warehouse out back. Tourists stopped by all the time, sometimes looking for stuff easy to find, other times on a treasure hunt.

Sean was on his own treasure hunt, every single day, but sadly frustrated. Fisher Key was a tropical paradise but it had a severe shortage of cute gay boys. Of gay boys at all, actually. Counting himself and Mrs. Anderson's son Denny, there were two. Total. And Denny was so far into the closet he couldn't even find the doorknob.

Sean Garrity: Only Gay Kid in Town.

El Solo Gay-o.

Lone Twee in the jungle.

And usually he could deal with it, he could totally cope and pretend that it didn't matter, but last night his sister Louanne had brought home a whole new boyfriend, a cute guy named John

Love (no kidding) who lived down in Marathon. How fair was that? She batted her big blue eyes and boys flocked to her like seagulls to bread crumbs. Sean could throw crumbs all day, and all he'd get was bird crap on his head while the birds flew on by overhead.

Worse than John Love was that Monday was the first day of the new school year. It was sad enough to be going back to school before the end of August. It was positively tragic to be returning without a single anecdote of romantic kisses, groping in the moonlight, or making out on the beach while the pounding surf rolled over the boy of his dreams.

"Sean," Mrs. Anderson said from the front counter, where she was bagging a customer's purchases. She was a short woman, dressed as always in bright tropical dress with her dark hair piled on her head. "Will you check out the bathrooms? Something smells fishy."

Another glamorous part of his job: bathroom duty. And "fishy" wasn't quite the word for what he found there. "Hazardous toxic waste dump" was more like it. Honestly, did some people just save it up for days so they could deliver a big, nasty gift to the book-loving world? Sean donned plastic gloves and the paint mask he kept for especially maladorous situations. He averted his eyes as best he could and pretended he was a famous teen actor sentenced to community service for too many speeding tickets in his Ferrari. As soon as he left the building he'd be swarmed by fans, paparazzi, and handsome boys who wanted to take him home…

The toxic waste eradicated, his hands thoroughly disinfected, Sean stopped by the community bulletin board near the bathrooms. One corner was reserved for the business cards of local dive shops, real estate agents, handymen, and computer geeks. Another had postings for yard sales and the big flea market up in Islamorada. Three local girls had notices up for baby-sitting, someone else was selling a man's bicycle, the church was having a bake sale on Saturday, and in the middle of it all was Sean's own notice:

Free to Good Home, 3 puppies, mixed breed, good health, need love.

He'd printed out a photo of Huey, Dewey, and Louis in their basket and put his home phone on tags along the bottom. It had been three days since he'd posted, and no one had taken his number.

"Oh, that smells much better," Mrs. Anderson said, walking past with a pile of books in her hands. "No takers yet on your puppies, eh?"

"I wish I could keep them," Sean said. Because all three were adorable, and he hated the thought of them being split up or taken in by people who wouldn't love them. Too bad his mom was allergic to dogs. She broke into sneezing fits whenever he took them into the house.

Mrs. Anderson elbowed open the door to her office. "Whoever left them in that Dumpster should be arrested for animal cruelty."

Louanne had found them after her shift one day at the Li'l Conch Cafe. Three small, trembling animals in a soggy cardboard box. Now, a month later, they had somehow become Sean's responsibility to feed, play with, and find new homes for. Which was unfair, but that was just the way things went when you were a jet-setting teen heartthrob.

Robin called for help from the front counter, where one of their local customers had brought in a box of books to sell. After that, things got really busy. Sean didn't have time to check his notice again until just before closing time. No one had ripped off his phone number, but someone had left a yellow sticky tacked to the side of it.

"Whoever said you can't buy happiness forgot little puppies."—G. Hill.

Sean was perplexed. Hadn't he put the word FREE in a big, bold font? He underlined the word with a pen and threw the sticky note away. It was time to go home, feed the dogs, and pretend he had a social life like every other kid on the island.

❖

The next day, Sunday, was his day off. He was supposed to be doing his summer biography on Ernest Hemingway but decided to procrastinate even more than he already had. He walked the puppies down to Beaker's Point, where no one cared if you let them off their leashes to play in the white sand and clear blue water. It was well past eighty degrees and he stripped off his T-shirt to get some sun. For the umpteenth time he vowed to start bench-pressing and working out. Being gay didn't mean he had to be scrawny, after all.

He started to do some push-ups right there in the sand, but they were too tiring. Soon he was throwing sticks for Huey, pulling stinky seaweed from Dewey's mouth, and rescuing poor frightened Louis from some tiny sand crabs. All three puppies piled on him and rewarded him with sloppy kisses.

"Yes, I know," he said. "I'm a god among dogs."

"I was looking for a local deity," said a dry voice behind him. "Good thing I found you."

Sean sat up and squinted against the sun. A teenage boy his own age was perched on a battered blue bicycle. Not just any teenage boy. This one was tall and thin, with curly blond hair and a suntanned face. He wore jeans and a Rush T-shirt and was definitely a tourist, because Sean had never seen anyone in the Florida Keys with eyes that green and alluring.

"I'm available for baptisms, weddings, and bar mitzvahs," Sean replied, feeling a flush in his cheeks. "But mostly I pick up dog poop and get my shoes chewed up."

The kid cocked his head. "Cute puppies."

Sean brushed sand from his elbows. "They're not mine. I mean, right now they're kind of mine, but I have to give them away. Want them?"

For a moment, longing flashed in the other boy's eyes. Sean knew that feeling: wanting what you couldn't have. Wanting it so keenly that it was a like a knife, stabbing quick and ruthlessly. But the gleam was gone as fast as it had appeared.

"Can't," the boy said. "We're just passing through. I'm Rob."

"I'm Sean. Passing through to where?"

"Good question," Rob said. "No good answers. That's why a deity would come in handy. I was going to sacrifice a rubber chicken or get my palm read."

Sean pretended to consider the matter seriously. "Deities don't read palms. We delegate it to fortunetellers and carnival workers. But I have a friend who does tarot card readings. How about that?"

Huey barked. Dewey peed on a piece of driftwood. Louis, who'd scampered off at Rob's appearance, poked his head out from behind a palm frond and eyed the situation with trepidation.

"Tarot card sounds cool," Rob said. "When and where?"

Sean was surprised. And delighted. But not foolish enough to start gushing about it, for fear he'd scare him off. "There's an ice cream place at the end of the island called the Dreamette. How about high noon?"

A woman's voice called out from the campground park behind the trees: "Rob-ert! Rob-ert!" She sounded shrill, maybe kind of desperate.

Rob grimaced. "I'm supposed to help my mom today. How about six o'clock?"

"Okay," Sean said. "Sure."

With a nod and a last longing look toward the puppies, Rob mounted his bike and pedaled off on the concrete path.

Sean watched him until he disappeared around the bend and then grabbed his phone. His boring Sunday suddenly seemed a lot brighter. Supernova bright: bright enough to blot out the sun and make him feel warm from head to toe. All he had to do now was find someone who could read tarot cards.

❖

"This is stupid," Robin said from her side of the picnic table. "What if he actually knows something about these things? I'm going to look like an idiot."

Sean studied the ornate, colorful cards spread on the worn wood. They'd borrowed a deck from the Bookmine and had been practicing for two hours, but there were seventy-eight cards and nowhere near enough time for Robin to memorize them all. She'd already told him how much she detested superstition, astrology, witchcraft, and any kind of magical thinking. He'd had to promise to take her down to Key West for a foreign film series just to get her out of her house, where she'd been Skyping with friends on how to overthrow student government this year.

"He doesn't know anything about them," Sean promised. Which was probably true. Maybe true. "Keep practicing."

Just before six o'clock, Rob pedaled up on his old blue bike. He wasn't alone, though. "This is my brother, Andrew," he said, as Andrew parked his own rusty bike at the end of the bench. Andrew had the same curly hair and lanky build but was a little shorter, his hair an inch longer.

"Are you twins?" Robin asked.

Andrew plopped down on the bench. "Irish twins."

"I'm Irish and I don't know what that means," Sean said.

"Born nine months apart," Robin said mischievously. "Your parents were busy bees."

"Nine and a half." Rob sat down and eyed the cards curiously. "So, Colman-Smith, huh? I haven't seen one of these decks in a while."

Robin kicked at Sean's leg under the table.

Sean ignored her. He was busy noticing the bruise on Rob's face. It was long and pink, right cross his cheekbone. It hadn't been there before. "What happened?" he asked.

Rob put a hand to his face in embarrassment. "Fell off the stupid ladder."

"Because he wasn't watching where he was going," Andrew added. He eyed the Dreamette shack, where a cluster of kids from the middle school were buying scoops and sundaes. The old-fashioned sign from the 1950s glinted in the sunlight. "How's the ice cream here?"

"Best in the Keys," Sean said.

Andrew glanced at Rob, who shook his head. Sean had seen the Anderson twins do that kind of silent communication before. It was sometimes fun to watch, and sometimes a little creepy. Andrew said, "Be right back," and headed to the counter.

Robin scooped up the cards and shuffled them. "So, did Sean tell you? Ten dollars for a reading."

Sean glared at her. "Five."

"Inflation," Robin said.

"How about seven?" Rob asked.

With the price agreed upon, Robin banished Sean from the table. "I do all my work in private," she insisted. Sean was forced to relocate to a bench closer to the water's edge, where he could see traffic crossing the modern bridge and watch fishermen on Flagler's old, outmoded bridge. The salty breeze off the Atlantic was nice enough but chilly for this time of year. He wished he'd brought a sweatshirt, or a blanket, or a blanket that he could share with Rob under the stars.

"Butter pecan," Andrew announced, returning with a scoop nestled in a chocolate waffle cone. He sat down opposite Sean. Now that Sean was really paying attention, he could see that Andrew's face was fuller than Rob's, and he had more freckles sprinkled on his nose. Andrew asked, "You live here all the time?"

Sean replied, "Since forever. Where are you from?"

"North Carolina. Near Raleigh. But we haven't been there in a while. Mom's a travel writer. She's always driving us all over America, chasing stories."

"What about school?" Sean asked. "We start tomorrow."

Andrew took a big lick from his ice cream. "Homeschooled. Works out pretty good. I'm sort of in eleventh grade, and Rob's taking his GED next month."

Sean glanced over at Rob, who was studying the tarot cards in front of him with an intent expression. It was hard for Sean to tell if the reading was going well or not. "Don't you miss it?"

"Nah. I always hated school. Too many rules. You like it?"

"It's okay." And most days it was, except around Valentine's Day, or around prom time, or anytime there was a party that Sean had to go to alone or with Robin because there weren't any alternatives. He liked English class and history, too, because they were full of stories. Math was like torture, though. And this year he was scheduled for physics, and he thought he might have to prop his eyes open with paper clips to keep from falling asleep.

Andrew licked more ice cream. His tongue was long and pink. "What grade are you in?"

"Starting eleventh."

"So if we stayed here permanently, you could show me all around," Andrew said with a smile.

"It's not that big of a school," Sean said. Then he sat up a little straighter, because that smile wasn't maybe just an ordinary smile. Maybe it was an I-want-to-get-to-know you smile, which meant Sean had been focusing on the wrong brother. Where was his gaydar when he really needed it? "Are you staying here?"

A trace of wistfulness appeared in Andrew's voice. "Probably not. But this is the nicest place we've been in a while. Trust me, the suburbs of Atlanta are not as exciting as they sound."

They didn't sound exciting at all, actually, and Andrew had several funny stories to tell about how desperately bored he'd been while his mother wrote her last book. Sean laughed out loud more than once, earning him a sideways glare from Robin as she tried to concentrate. But Andrew was very witty, and he kept licking his ice cream cone with that quick tongue, and Sean was almost annoyed when Robin and Rob finished their session and joined them at the water's edge.

"How'd it go?" Sean asked, hoping Robin hadn't totally screwed it up.

"Totally worth seven dollars," Rob said.

Robin actually blushed. Which was so rare that Sean almost snapped a picture. "I think it's on the house. You know a lot more than I do."

Rob didn't argue. He knocked his elbow against his brother's shoulder. "We should get going."

"There's no place we have to be," Andrew replied, his voice firm.

Sean studied them both. That silent communication thing was going on again, and Sean couldn't decipher what was being said. Rob's gaze shifted from his brother to the ocean and the flat white clouds darkening in the east.

"Get some ice cream," Andrew suggested, and after a moment of contemplation Rob wandered off to the counter.

Robin got herself a milkshake, and Sean finally caved in to get himself a double scoop of chocolate fudge. The four of them lingered on the picnic bench as the sun went down. Andrew told more stories about Atlanta and Knoxville and Tallahassee. Robin offered up scathing satires of Fisher Key High. Sean tried to compete with stories from the Bookmine—the crazy customers, the horrible bathroom messes—but he felt entirely outmatched and in danger of just sounding silly.

Rob was the quietest of them all. His eyes stayed on his ice cream or the ocean. Sean noticed that he didn't have a cell phone to fidget with, or else was too well-mannered to haul it out and start tapping like everyone else would.

Eventually the sun went down. The kids around them drifted home, everyone either excited about school tomorrow or dreading it with all their hearts. Andrew and Rob had to bike back to the campground in the darkness. Sean worried about the traffic on the highway. A lot of drivers weren't safe around bikes.

"We're used to danger," Andrew said, flicking on a safety light on his rear bumper. "See you around."

Rob just nodded and followed his brother across the conch shell divider toward the road.

Sean swung around to Robin. "What did you guys talk about? He's hardly said a word since you did it."

"Client-attorney privilege," Robin said. "Or is that priest and penitent? Anyway, I can't breathe a word."

And she was serious about it, too, stubborn as a rock. Sean wouldn't be able to crack her open even with sticks of dynamite. He changed subjects.

"Do you think he's gay?" Sean asked.

"Which one?"

"Rob," Sean said. "Or Andrew. I don't know."

"I don't know, either. Maybe they don't know." Robin watched the bikes recede and made her voice low and ominous. "Maybe only the tarot cards know."

"You're no help at all," Sean said, and snatched the deck from her hands.

❖

Sean stayed up past midnight to finish his report on Hemingway. By the end of it, he was completely sick of Papa and bullfighting and fishing in Cuba. In the morning he turned his cell phone alarm off twice before staggering out into the cool morning to free Huey, Dewey, and Louis from their temporary kennel in the yard. He walked them around the community baseball field and bought himself a giant cup of coffee at the Gas'n'Go.

"You don't know how lucky a dog's life is," he told the puppies.

Huey sniffed at the coffee cup, Dewey rolled over to have his stomach rubbed, and Louis cringed as a motorcycle rode by.

The first day of school was full of sound and fury, signifying nothing. Sean saw the same old faces he saw every year, plus one or two new kids who looked ridiculously heterosexual. He desperately missed his bed and pillows. As he dragged himself from class to class he envied Rob and Andrew. How nice it must be for them to sleep in, set their own schedule, and live a life unencumbered by bells and teachers and a cafeteria that served unidentifiable lumps of alleged food.

"I hear you made some new friends," said Denny Anderson as he poked his fork at burned squares that were supposed to be chicken nuggets.

"Rumors of my improved social life are greatly exaggerated,"

Sean replied, though he was secretly pleased to be the subject of even the tiniest amount of gossip. He picked disgusting pepperoni off his pizza slice. "What did Robin say?"

"That maybe one of them is gay."

"And?"

Denny chewed one of the so-called nuggets. "And one of them is kind of New Age-y and flaky."

"Flaky!" Sean said. "Not at all. There is no flakiness."

"He likes tarot cards. He knew more about them than Robin did."

"Everyone knows more about tarot cards than Robin."

"Not me." Denny gave up on the inedible chicken nugget and spat it into a napkin. "Is the flaky one gay or is it the other one?"

"The jury's still out," Sean said. He wished Denny would just come out and admit that he was gay, too, and maybe he could add in that he'd had a lifelong secret crush on Sean, and hey, they could be boyfriends for the rest of their high school careers. Because that would be the culmination of years of Sean's daydreams.

"Why are you staring at me?" Denny asked, eyebrows lifted.

"Nothing," Sean said.

It was a miracle that Sean made it through the rest of the day without a heavy-duty nap. After school let out, he wanted only to go home and sleep forever in a nice soft bed. Unfortunately he was scheduled to work three hours at the Bookmine. No one had taken a tag for the puppies but another yellow sticky was clinging to the notice.

"Money will buy you a pretty good dog, but it won't buy the wag of his tail"—J. Billings.

Sean scowled. He took it to the counter, where Mrs. Anderson was trying to replace the receipt roll in the cash register.

"I don't think this person understands the dogs are free," he said.

She read it carefully. "I think someone's flirting with you."

"What? No." Sean studied it. "Really?"

"Really," she said, jamming the paper roll into place.

With her help, Sean made his own sticky note and put it up:

"All knowledge, the totality of all questions and all answers is contained in the dog."—*F. Kafka.*

For three hours he kept watch on the bulletin board, hoping to catch his canine correspondent. No one even looked at it. The next day Sean wasn't scheduled to work at all, but he swung by just in case there was a response. His sticky hadn't been disturbed at all. Maybe he'd been trying to sound too erudite. On the bright side, two of the phone tags were missing.

Mrs. Anderson said, "I think Principal Bradshaw took one," and Sean almost shuddered. Principal Bradshaw ruled Fisher Key High like a despot. He'd probably kick any dog he owned, or keep it imprisoned in a crate, or use it for lab experiments in his continuing quest for world domination.

Mrs. Anderson laughed. "Don't make that face, Sean. He's the sweetest man on this island."

"You say that because you only know the Jekyll part of his ferocious split personality," Sean grumbled.

With plenty of light still left in the day, he took the puppies to Beaker's Point and into the Sunset Harbor campground. Only a dozen or so campers were parked under the scrappy palm trees. In the farthest lot from the entrance was a rusty trailer that was probably twice as old as Sean. A picnic table and some old plastic chairs sat out under a green canopy. Rob was perched atop the table, stringing fishing line in a rod.

Sean admired him for a full moment—the curve of his neck, the deft movement of his fingers, even his long legs under jean shorts. The puppies were unnaturally quiet, their heads tilted as if the fishing pole were the most fascinating thing on the planet.

"So I hear this is the place for tarot cards," Sean finally said, when it seemed likely Rob wouldn't notice him anytime soon.

That brought Rob's head up. His somber expression brightened at the sight of Sean. Or maybe that was the puppies that cheered him up, because now they were yapping on their leashes, eager to make a new friend. Rob didn't move off the table, though. He seemed to be deliberately holding himself back.

"I don't read the cards," he said. "Just get them read to me."

Sean asked, "Did they tell you to go fishing?"

"If I can find a good spot. Know any, oh wise deity?"

Sean never fished, but he knew that Denny and his brother Steven liked a place near Jeffers Bridge. "I can show you one, sure. Where's Andrew?"

Rob slid off the table and grabbed a fishing box. "He said he was running away to join the circus, but I think he's at the bookstore."

"Oh," Sean said, and his heart jumped at the idea that Andrew was over there right now, leaving him a note. That Andrew, with his big smile and hearty sense of humor, was interested in Sean in the same way that Louanne's friend John Love was interested in her. Even if it was just a temporary thing, even if Andrew and Rob's mother loaded them up and drove off at the end of the week, any romantic development at all in Sean's life was an improvement over the current gaping void of nothingness.

Rob added, "He's probably shoplifting manga."

"What?" Sean asked, jolted from his happy thoughts. People really did shoplift from the store, and it drove Mrs. Anderson nuts. "Would he really?"

"Nah, not really," Rob said. "Probably not."

And then Rob smiled, a little secret smile, the first that Sean had seen out of him. All thoughts of Andrew flew away. Sean fervently wished it was Rob leaving him the notes. Rob, with his deep green eyes and ridiculously short hair and the patient way he'd been fixing the fishing line. The mark on his face had faded but there were new bruises on his right arm, just a few inches above his wrist. Some of them looked like fingerprints.

"Never wrestle your brother over the last of the Lucky Charms," Rob said when he saw Sean's focus. His smile faded. "Come on. Show me this lucky spot."

Sitting in the shadow of Jeffers Bridge with his knees pulled up in the tall grass, Sean watched as Rob cast his line into the slow-moving creek. Rob didn't seem inclined to talk. Sean's natural tendency was to fill the silence any way possible, so he chattered on about the first days of school and how he already had a week's worth of homework and how it sucked that summer was over. The puppies dozed in the sunlight, piled on each other like a stack of brown potato bags.

"Summer's not over until the equinox in September," Rob pointed out, once Sean had stopped for breath.

"It feels over," Sean said, trying not to sound too morose. "Everyone's hooking up and pairing off and next thing you know, I'm everybody's third wheel."

Rob reeled in his line. Hooked on the end was a plastic bag. He got it loose and put it aside. "You're not dating anyone?"

Sean hesitated. It was always kind of risky, saying stuff aloud to people you didn't really know yet. "I'm the only gay kid in the school. Well, the only gay kid who will admit it."

Rob cast his line again. He didn't seem surprised or upset. "There are others who won't say it?"

Thinking of Denny Anderson, Sean said, "Maybe."

"It's lonely being unique," Rob said. It could have sounded mocking but it didn't. It might also have referred to Rob himself, but Sean wasn't quite sure.

"What about you?" Sean was glad his voice didn't squeak with nervousness. "Dating anyone?"

"We're always moving around," Rob reminded him. "I think in a past life my mother must have grown up and lived in the same small town all her life. Maybe she was trapped there by marriage. Because in this life, ever since she and my dad divorced, all she wants to do is wander from town to town."

In the puppy pile, Louis whined from an unhappy dream. Dewey shifted a paw, stilling him. Huey snorted and started to snore.

"You believe in past lives?" Sean asked. He'd never given it much thought, really, though if you got to pick your future lives, he'd opt for something with a mansion and a cabana boy.

Rob shrugged one shoulder. "I believe in karma. You get what you earn, in this life or the next one."

"So what does this life hold for you? College somewhere, after you pass the GED?"

"College sounds kind of boring." Rob's line jerked. He jiggled it and stepped back on the bank, keeping the tension. "I was thinking of going to a Buddhist monastery one day."

Sean cringed. "Like where they shave your head and make you be celibate?"

"Or maybe an Indian ashram." Rob started to reel in his catch. "Or I could do a Sufi khalwa. You lock yourself away for forty days and only come out once in a while to talk to your teacher."

"No TV or Internet? I'd go crazy."

"I think it would be fun," Rob replied. "Spirituality is cool."

Denny Anderson in his closet and Rob locked in a monastery. It was a shame and maybe a crime and just Sean's rotten luck that the cute boys he knew were determined to avoid the pleasures of the world.

Or run away from it, maybe. Denny certainly was. But what was Rob fleeing from, if he was fleeing at all?

"I think you can be spiritual wherever you are," Sean said, and Rob shrugged.

When the sun started to go down they walked back to the campground, two small fish slung over Rob's shoulder. Sean was worried that Rob was going to gut and fry them right away. Fish blood always made Sean barf. But when they reached Sunset Harbor, Andrew was riding his bike in dusty circles in front of their trailer. He gave Rob a silent look and Rob turned to Sean.

"You should go home and do that report for Western Civ due next week," Rob said.

Sean was surprised that Rob even remembered that part. He was also taken aback at what sounded like a pretty firm dismissal. Andrew rode his bike in another circle, pedaling with unnecessary force, and the noise of it made Sean pause. He didn't understand exactly what was going on, but it wasn't about homework. Even the puppies seemed uneasy. Louis whined and rubbed up against Rob's leg.

"Is everything okay?" Sean asked.

"Perfectly fine," Andrew bit out.

Rob reached down and petted Louis for the first and only time that day. "It's okay. Go on home."

The door to their trailer opened. Sean couldn't see clearly because of the darkness, but a woman in a long nightgown appeared in the doorway. She was thin and unsteady, her voice as shrill as he remembered.

"What are you boys doing out so damn early?" she demanded. "It's not even dawn!"

Andrew stopped his bike. "It's eight o'clock at night, Mom."

Their mother's voice rose. "It is not. Stop lying."

"I brought fish for dinner." Rob moved to her and took her arm. "Come on, aren't you hungry?"

"I'm not!" she snapped, pulling away. "Stop pushing me around!"

She slapped him, then. Hard and fast, across the face, with a crack like sudden thunder. Sean cringed and took a half step forward in outrage, but Andrew blocked him.

"Mom, stop," Andrew pleaded. "We've got company."

Three heads all turned to Sean. He didn't know what to say: *Hello, stop hitting your son* seemed inadequate. He wanted to protect Rob, but that was ridiculous. Rob was taller than his mother, and stronger, too. Sean wished he hadn't seen this, and that Rob and Andrew didn't have to live it.

"Who are you?" their mother asked. He couldn't clearly see her face, but he imagined her expression all twisted up and ugly.

"He's just a friend," Rob said, but he didn't sound friendly at all now. He sounded wrecked and ashamed. "Good-bye, Sean."

Andrew echoed, "Yeah. Good-bye."

Sean walked home as fast as he could, resisting the urge to call Robin and tell her what he'd seen. The bruise across Rob's face made sense now. The fingerprints on his arms. How he didn't want to go away to college. Sean would have run like mad, but then Andrew would be all alone. He wondered if Rob's mother was really any kind of travel writer at all, or if she just carted her sons around the country in chase of the next bottle of booze, the next place where she could hit her son.

At home, Louanne and John Love were making out on the sofa.

"Why so sad looking?" Louanne asked, making a half-hearted effort at disentangling herself.

"Nothing," Sean said. "Where's Mom and Dad?"

John Love kissed the side of Louanne's neck. She squirmed and giggled and said, "Out to dinner. They said there's pizza in the freezer and do your homework."

Louanne didn't have the curse of homework. She'd graduated two years ago to embark on her spectacular career as a waitress. Sean threw the French loaf pizza in the toaster oven and collapsed on his bed. He should call Denny. His father was the local sheriff. Would getting the police involved help or hurt Rob? Even now, his mom might be trying to pack them all up, get them on the road to somewhere new.

He didn't even know their last names. Didn't have a picture of Andrew or Rob on his cell phone, or have any way to reach them if they left.

Louanne yelled out from the living room. "Your pizza's burning!" And then she shrieked with laughter in response to John Love's hands or mouth or who knew what else.

Sean pulled the pillow over his head. He didn't care if the whole house burned down. He wished he really was a teenage movie star, with the power and money to send Rob's mother to rehab and get Rob and Andrew a home without wheels on it. If he were any kind of deity at all, he'd wave his hands and make all their problems go away. Rob would never have a bruise again, and Andrew would never have to stand by helplessly.

Being a powerless normal kid really, truly sucked.

The next morning he made it all the way through second period but couldn't wait any longer. He rode his bike to the Bookmine. Mrs. Anderson was surprised to see him.

"Are you skipping school already?" she asked. "It's only the first week!"

He tapped impatiently on the counter. "Kind of, but for a

good reason. There's a travel writer in an RV at Sunset Harbor. I'm trying to find out her name, find her books."

"Oh, sure. Susan Turner. Her sons come in here every day." Mrs. Anderson gave him a conspiratorial smile. "I think one of them might be your secret pen pal. There's a new note up."

Sean went and checked. The green sticky said:

"Dogs are better than human beings, because they know but do not tell."—E. Dickinson.

"Do you know which one left this note?" Sean asked Mrs. Anderson. "Rob or Andrew?"

"I'm not sure. You can't really tell them apart, unless they're standing together. But one of them is back in the dog section right now—"

Sean hurried back to aisle seven before she could finish. It was empty. He scoured the nearby aisles as well, suddenly hating the maze of stacks that offered up a hundred different hiding places. Finally, in aisle seventeen, he found Rob sitting cross-legged on the floor. He was skimming a coffee table book about Sufism. More books were piled beside him.

"Hi," Sean said, trying not to sound out of breath or too eager or too worried.

Rob didn't look up. "There's a Sufi center for learning in Charlottesville. We drove all over Virginia last summer, and I never even heard of it."

"I don't know what Sufism is," Sean admitted.

"You ever see videos of guys in white dresses swirling around and around? They call them whirling dervishes." Rob closed the book in his lap and picked up another. "That's kind of like me, spinning in circles."

Sean sat down beside him. He rarely got the chance to sit while working. It was odd, this new perspective, with shelves towering all around them. Billions of words waiting to be read. All those stories ready to be told and mysteries hoping to be solved.

"I thought maybe you'd be gone this morning," he admitted.

"We're paid up until tomorrow." Rob raised his face. His cheek had a tiny cut on it, up high, where his mother's ring had cut into the skin. "Then we're driving up to Key Largo."

Sean touched Rob's knee. It was a bold move, unprecedented, and he was glad that Rob didn't jerk away. "She's not going to stop. It's not right."

"I know," Rob said softly. "But I can live with it as long as she leaves Andrew alone."

"What does Andrew say?"

Rob snorted. "He says we should run away. I told him maybe Mom will get better. She'll wake up one day and realize that everything's gone wrong. But if she doesn't, we'll both leave when he turns eighteen. They can't make you come back if you're eighteen."

"Come back here," Sean urged. He leaned forward, both hands on Rob's legs now. He tried to sound calm and sincere, not like a crazy person, but everything was so damn unfair. "When you're both eighteen. You can come here and get an apartment and get a dog or two or three. Don't tell me you don't want a dog."

"And where will you be then?" Rob asked skeptically. "Are you going to live on Fisher Key forever? Because no one knows where they'll be next month, or next year, or whenever, even when you think the future is set in stone."

"I don't plan on leaving anytime soon," Sean replied. "And if I do, that's what cell phones are for."

Rob's mouth quirked. Sean desperately wanted to taste his soft-looking lips. It occurred to him for the very first time that instead of waiting, he could actually make the first move. If he dared. If he wanted to risk everything. But what if he mashed noses, and how far should he tilt his head, and what if he was totally wrong and Rob punched him in the face?

He moved his head forward slowly. Instead of pulling back or running away, Rob met him halfway. His hands gripped Sean's shoulders to pull him closer. The touches of his fingers were tiny sizzles of pleasure. Tiny sizzles turned to bigger joy as their mouths came together, the warm sweetness of shared breath, and maybe Sean made a faint noise of relief and happiness.

His first kiss. Right there on the floor of aisle seventeen, surrounded by books.

Tomorrow Rob would be leaving. That would suck. Summer was slowly ending, and that would suck, too. And there was no end to the suckiness that would come when he had to give up Huey, Dewey, and Louis to new owners. But this first kiss was better than being a jet-setting movie star, better than being a god among dogs.

Rob eased back first, his eyes wide and happy. "I'm glad you did that."

"I'm glad I did that, too," Sean answered. He couldn't stop grinning. "I think we should do it again. And then some more. Maybe somewhere else besides this floor, though. Or where my boss won't find us."

Rob stood up. "Don't you have to go back to school?"

"I'm officially skipping the rest of the day," Sean said, getting to his feet. "Do you have to go home?"

"Not until tonight," Rob said. "I say we do everything possible to make this the absolute best day ever."

"It already is," Sean said, and kissed him again to prove it.

WHEAT, BARLEY, LETTUCE, FENNEL, SALT FOR SORROW, BLOOD FOR JOY
ALEX JEFFERS

When Luke wakes with the dawn, he's pretty well sure where he is. Not his house in Berkeley, California—his bed at home doesn't rock except during earthquakes. He's aboard a big sailboat, the *Esin*, a Turkish gulet, which his dad chartered for a two-week cruise along the Aegean coast. But he's not in the bunk of his cramped little cabin that smells faintly bad, mouldy, musty—sour, as if some earlier passenger had given in to seasickness before reaching the head and residue still festers between the planks of the floor. He opens his eyes. The gulet's two masts go up and up into a cloudless sky blanching toward blue. He fell asleep on the foredeck, on one of the sunbeds. Somebody, Perla or his dad, threw a blanket over him before going below. The blanket and the bits of the sunbed that weren't covered—and his hair!—are damp with dew. The air smells so good, so salty and crisp. He inhales thirstily, pushes the blanket off, sits up.

Freezes.

Somebody lies sleeping on the other sunbed.

Not *somebody*. Levent. The deckhand. The beautiful, beautiful deckhand. Luke swallows hard. When he saw Levent the first time, boarding the *Esin* two days ago, he hadn't been able to think for a full thirty seconds. The thought that finally bubbled up was *Damn!* Then, *I'm going to kiss you if it's the last thing I do.* Levent was still wearing a shirt then.

Not now. Now he's pretty close to stark naked, no blanket or sheet, just the little scarlet swim trunks he wore all day yesterday grappling the sails and whatever incomprehensible sailory duties as the *Esin* skipped down the coast, stretching and flexing so Luke hardly dared look at him or he'd start drooling.

He wants to look now—gaze, ogle, devour Levent with his eyes—but the sun coming up over the mainland hills puts Levent in shade. He's lying on his side so the light plates his upper shoulder, cocked hip, the length of one thigh in liquid gold, makes a brilliant halo of the dew clinging to his curly black hair. Shadow and his crooked arm hide the amazing belly and spectacular chest and Luke can't really make out his face. That face.

Luke's dreaming, soppy romantic dreams, swimming together through languid warm waters to a deserted beach where they recline in the shallows kissing and hugging and…when he realizes one of Levent's eyes is open. That Levent is staring at him. Him, sitting hunched over on the very edge of the sunbed with elbows on his knees and one fist covering his mouth as if to stifle a moan: him staring at Levent. Who's staring at Luke.

"Günaydın!" Luke chirps, one of three Turkish words he remembers, dropping his hands to where his dick yearns to burst through his boardies' Velcro fly.

"Good morning." Sitting up, Levent stretches and yawns. It's even harder to make anything out with him blocking the sun entirely, just a glowy nimbus around the Levent-shaped shadow. "Your father decided not to wake you. It is pleasant to sleep under open sky and stars—yes? Would you like coffee?"

"I don't think anybody else is up." Luke means Altan Efendi's, the captain's, wife, who served him coffee yesterday morning. Luke means he doesn't want Levent to disappear into the galley, though it would be wonderful if he moved just enough so Luke could see him properly.

Stretching again, Levent stands. Luke half imagines he can make out something stiff making interesting folds in the stretchy fabric of Levent's trunks. "Roisin Hanım is happy for me to make my own coffee," Levent says, turning toward the stern. Luke is even more sure of Levent's morning wood when he casually adjusts it with his big left hand. Sunlight catches the tattoos on the inside of his forearm, making the blossoms glisten like fresh paint. "You prefer it without sugar, I remember," Levent says and starts away.

Luke watches him go—that ass! Red fabric straining to contain the lush muscularity of it. "Teşekkür ederim!" Luke gasps.

Looking back, Levent grins broadly, sun glinting on wet teeth. "No problem," he says like an American, and keeps going.

Luke imagines himself saying *Augh!* as he collapses facedown on the sunbed, but really he doesn't utter a sound. He's touched a few nice asses. Well, two. Wanted to do more. Four months ago he thought Douglas was working up to suggesting they do more, but what he was really working up to was breaking up. Breaking Luke's heart.

Not really. Bruising it a bit.

Luke's dad thought Luke's heart was broken. At least that's the only reason Luke can think of why Sam insisted his seventeen-year-old son come along on this trip, this Blue Voyage. Luke hadn't been at all sure about a two-week Turkish vacation with his dad and new stepmom, but he wasn't offered a choice. It would have to be better than the alternative: staying with his mom and her prick of a husband. He wonders if Perla had a choice. She's far from a wicked stepmother, and as best he can tell likes him almost as much as he likes her, but it *is* pretty much her honeymoon.

They're down below him right now, in the master cabin, his dad and Perla. Sleeping or…not sleeping. Which isn't anywhere Luke wants to go.

When he abruptly sits up, he thinks he hears water running—splashing. Standing, he looks aft past the mainmast, through the wide windows and open door of the deckhouse. Levent's standing at the taffrail, standing tall and stalwart on the cushioned bench with his back to Luke, right hand on hip, left hidden. After a moment the splashing stops and Luke vividly imagines him shaking himself off, tucking himself in, tying up the drawstring of his trunks. Before he can turn around, Luke looks away.

No way *he's* brave enough to piss over the side but now the thought's in his head, the need pressing at his bladder. When he gets to the deckhouse door, Levent's already inside, hovering over the galley stove. He flashes another big grin as Luke edges past and down the companionway.

In the tiny head next to his cabin, Luke does what he needs to do, brushes his teeth, washes his face. No shower, but he swipes deodorant under his arms. Before he can stop himself, he spritzes himself with the really expensive French cologne Douglas gave him for Christmas, when they were still boyfriends. It's too much. He knows it. *If* Levent's gay (he probably isn't), *if* he's the least bit attracted to Luke (how could he be?), *if* Luke can muster the nerve to make a move (like that's going to happen), how do they manage to get up to anything interesting on a sixty-foot boat under the eyes of Levent's bosses and Sam and Perla? Plus, while sex would have to be fantastic with a guy as handsome as Levent, there's no chance of any kind of relationship. Luke's going home to California in less than two weeks.

He climbs back up the companionway. The coffee must be done because Levent isn't in the upper cabin. On the stern deck under the canvas awning, a tray sits on the bench below the taffrail, just where Levent stood to piss. But no Levent.

Then Luke hears footsteps overhead. He ducks through the door, looks up. Crouched on the deckhouse roof, Levent beams down at him. "Coffee is served, sir. I will be down momentarily." He's holding a pitcher, watering a clay pot of something as green as the foliage painted under the skin of his left arm.

"What's that?"

Levent inspects the shrubby plant as if he has no idea. "Keklikotu. Cooking herb. In English, I think...oregano? Good luck for sailors: earth and herb from Efendi's garden to ensure we return home safe. Also Hanım uses it in the excellent meals she prepares."

Pointing behind Levent toward the flying bridge, Luke asks, "What about those?"

Levent glances over his shoulder. On either side of the bridge stand two old olive-oil tins overflowing with fiercely red geraniums. "Just flowers, for beauty. Those I irrigated first."

"And that?"

That is a round, shallow, closely woven basket perched on the edge of the roof two steps from the keklikotu. The first evening aboard, returning from a trip to the head, Luke saw Roisin Hanım up there, carefully scooping dirt from a bucket into the basket. She was murmuring something Luke couldn't hear—he had more trouble anyway with her Irish brogue than her husband's or Levent's accents, and maybe she was speaking Turkish. Or Gaelic. As he watched, she sprinkled water over the soil, then scattered seeds from four different packets. She seemed completely intent on what she was doing, entirely oblivious of anything but earth, water, seeds. Feeling obscurely nervous, Luke didn't say anything and moved away before she looked up, joining his dad and Perla on the foredeck. With Sam's amused permission, Perla poured Luke a glass of Turkish white wine.

"That"—Levent doesn't even look, his expression blank, his voice flat—"is woman's business. Hanım's business." He jerks his chin up and back, a quick gesture Luke's already learned means the same in Turkey as an American headshake. "I am not to know. Not to inquire. Not to touch."

"Oh." Weird.

But Levent shrugs off whatever disturbs him and smiles again, crinkling the fine skin around his eyes. "Coffee?" Setting the pitcher aside, he swings nimbly down the ladder rungs bolted to the bulkhead. Somehow he misses the last step and staggers onto the deck, crashing one shoulder into Luke's chest. Startled, Luke grabs hold to steady him, then doesn't want to let go. He'd thought Levent was taller but it must have been an illusion of his beauty: they're the same height.

"Pardon my clumsiness!"

"No—" Luke doesn't want to let go. The warmth of Levent's flesh, slightly greasy with sweat and yesterday's sunscreen, sears his skin. He thinks he can feel Levent's heart beating. He *knows* he can feel a woody working up in his own shorts. He lets go. "No problem."

Grasping his hand warmly, Levent leads him to the bench, sits him down, sits himself down really close, hips and thighs touching. Dumbly, Luke wishes his boardies were as short as Levent's trunks so it would be naked thigh to naked thigh. Levent releases his hand, but it's only to reach over Luke's lap to the tray. "Coffee! I remembered: no sugar. I hope you like it."

Luke can't taste anything but the sweat-sunscreen-saltwater fragrance of Levent fighting with his own cologne, but he sips from the little cup and says, "Very nice."

"Excellent." Holding his own cup with his right hand, Levent lays the left on Luke's leg, just above the knee. The visible fragments of tattoo look as bright as the hibiscus blossoms printed on Luke's boardies. "Are you enjoying your Blue Voyage, Luke Bey?"

Before they left California, Perla had sat Luke down for a

little talk. She knows the Turkish Aegean coast well—her mother is an archaeologist specializing in the Bronze Age Lycian city-states, so Perla had spent pretty much every childhood summer in Muğla province. It wasn't archaeology she wanted to talk about, though. It was Turkish men. "They're really friendly," she said, "really affectionate and touchy-feely among themselves. So you'll see lots of very handsome men holding hands and hugging, but you absolutely can't assume they're gay. It's a different culture. If you get friendly with some kid he'll want to touch you, be close to you, but it's never about wanting to be your boyfriend or anything like that. Okay? It's different social norms, different conceptions of personal space."

So Luke knows he shouldn't make any inferences out of Levent getting so close. God, how he wants to, though. Throat tight, he says, "I'm having a great time."

"That is good. This morning, I believe, we will sail a few more kilometers down the coast to a protected cove with a pleasant beach. No hotels and package tourists like here—" Levent waves his coffee cup vaguely toward shore, where rows of green canvas parasols and folded sunbeds mar golden sand, waiting for tourists from the hotels above the beach to descend. "Tomorrow, Perla Hanım and Sam Bey plan an excursion to ancient ruins a little inland."

"Perla's mother is working at those ruins, I think."

They're having a conversation, Levent and Luke, which is somehow astonishing until it's just a conversation. Before Roisin Hanım comes up from crew quarters below the stern deck, Luke learns that Levent isn't from Didim, the *Esin*'s home port, but his father is and Levent's known Altan all his life, crewed for him on the gulet every summer since he turned thirteen. The rest of the year, he lives with his family in İzmir. His English is so good because, except for Turkish literature and history, all instruction at his high school was in English. He graduated a month ago—

he's just a year older than Luke. They laugh, amazed, when they figure out they share the same birthday.

Luke remembers only now and then that he's totally infatuated. When Levent's face falls into brief repose, his features as classically regular and handsome as an ancient marble bust of Adonis. Or when he leaps up to make more coffee and half turns to beckon for Luke to come with him, the torsion and symmetry of his nearly nude body as elegant as the Diskobolos, but alive and human. When the sun hits his eyes at the right angle and Luke sees the opaque black rings around his irises, gleaming, lucent caramel brown bleeding into golden green mandalas around the pupils. Sees sun glistening on thick black stubble rising through the flushed gold skin of his cheeks, chin, above his finely molded lips. Beautiful.

Levent interrupts his latest reverie with a question and Luke explains he's lived with his dad the last four years because he doesn't get along with his mother's husband. He doesn't say that Roger (he won't call the man his stepfather) is a homophobic born-again asshole and he despises the woman his mother's turned into since she married Roger.

"Have you thought about college?" Levent asks out of nowhere.

"Not really. Not yet. Why?"

"Because…" Levent looks away. Luke's struck dumb by the impression his profile makes against pale blue sky, then dumber when Levent squeezes his hand and goes on, "Because this autumn I will be attending the University of California at Berkeley."

Half a minute of utter shock later, Luke blurts, "That's half a mile from my house. I mean—less than a kilometer."

"I know." Still gazing out to sea, Levent smiles very slowly. "Not that it was so very close, that is, but that you live in Berkeley.

It would be lovely for me to have a friend nearby when I go to live in your country. Shall we be friends, Luke Bey?"

There's no hope of throttling down the insane hope pounding in Luke's chest. "Yes."

Levent squeezes his hand even harder. "Of course, I would wish to be your friend for this short time that you are aboard *Esin*, but perhaps in California we may become very good friends."

"I think that would be…excellent, Levent Bey."

Chuckling at the Turkish honorific, Levent turns the full force of his grin on Luke. "And then, you see, it would be quite sad for me if after a year my good friend were to go away to Princeton or Yale."

Brain racing, Luke's been thinking the same thing. Not Princeton or Yale, his SATs and grades aren't that stellar, but the little he's ever contemplated college has always involved running far far away from the Bay Area. *Maybe* he can get into Berkeley. San Francisco State for one safety school and, and…and he's *almost* certain Levent is just about to kiss him.

"Good morning, boys."

Roisin Hanım's cheery greeting makes Luke flinch and he wants to think he hears dismay in Levent's "Günaydın, Hanım."

"Levent made coffee for you, Luke? Lovely. Did you sleep well?"

"V-very well, thank you."

And then Levent's jumping up to help Roisin with breakfast—"Turkish breakfast or Irish breakfast?" she asks of the air. And then Altan Efendi is pacing around checking out every square millimeter of his beloved gulet—he clucks with mild disapproval over the dew-damp blanket Luke left crumpled on his sunbed and hangs it over the foremast's boom to dry. And then, slightly bleary-looking, Luke's dad appears from below, plops down on the bench next to his son—not as close as Levent—

and asks earnestly if it was okay for him not to wake Luke last night and insist he go below. Luke assures him it was just fine. He'll probably want to sleep on deck every night it doesn't rain. Then Perla, carrying a book, radiating calm pleasantness. Then breakfast, which Luke assumes must be Turkish because he can't imagine olives being part of an Irish breakfast.

It's a jolly meal, full of plans for the day, though Luke never says much of anything and realizes after a bit that he goes perceptibly blank every time he looks at Levent. So with a certain amount of conscious effort he stops doing it. He was never so moony over Douglas.

But Douglas had been loudly out since seventh grade, so there was never the same kind of doubt. He waited to pursue Luke until after Luke came out years later, so no doubt there either. And Douglas was, is, merely cute, not as beautiful as a demigod.

Luke catches Perla peering at him, wonders if she's guessed he's doing what she warned him not to. Wonders if she'd been on the *Esin* before and Levent is exactly who she was warning him about.

That's a horrible thought. He won't allow it toehold in his brain. He wants to be Levent's friend. More would be awesome but you don't turn down an offer of friendship just because the guy isn't interested in messing around. Luke and Douglas are still friends.

Sort of.

Into a moment of silence, he says, "Will there be time for a swim before we set sail?"

Altan appears about to hem and haw, but Roisin says something in Turkish, then, "We're in no hurry, surely. But the cove where we plan to stop for lunch is much more pleasant"— she gestures toward the now crowded beach—"so perhaps just a quick dip. I won't need help, Levent, why don't you join Luke? Refresh yourself before my husband puts you to work."

Levent offers her the intoxicating splendor of his smile. "Teşekkür ederim, Roisin Hanım."

Half a minute later, both boys tumble over the side, crash into the deep blue water. When Luke surfaces, ears ringing, he hears a jocular "Watch out for sharks!" from the railing far above and flips his dad a cheerful bird.

Then something grabs hold of his ankles and he's going under again. He knows it has to be Levent, so he doesn't panic, but his mouth was open and his lungs empty, so he does panic when salt water floods his sinuses. Looking up when Luke starts to thrash, Levent goes wide-eyed. He lets go immediately. One powerful frog kick later, his arms are around Luke's chest, two, and both heads break the surface again and Luke's coughing on his shoulder.

"I'm sorry!" Levent bleats, sounding really frightened. "I'm sorry! Are you all right?"

"I'll—" Luke coughs again. "I'll be fine in a minute."

"I'm so sorry. I won't let you go."

Luke knows he ought to put his hands on Levent's head and push *him* under, that's what a roughhousing straight boy would do, but he's queer and though his throat feels flayed it's just so lovely to be safe in Levent's embrace. "I'll be fine," he grumbles again, "you just surprised me," and turns his head to rest his cheek in the crook of Levent's shoulder.

Levent murmurs something. Luke catches his name but the rest is Turkish garble. "What?"

"Nothing, really."

Lifting his head to catch Levent's eyes, Luke demands, "No, what did you say?"

Levent blinks. "I said, it is my very great pleasure to hold you like this, my friend." And then Levent lets go.

❖

He isn't convinced he actually fell asleep, but what he remembers was awful. He was thirsty, so thirsty, in a place where there was no water, just dust. An endless ocean of sepia dust broken only by distant outcroppings that might be isolated mountains, might be stupendous buildings. The air was so thick and sere, the oppressive brown sky so low, he couldn't really see, but he felt that if he could reach one of them he'd find something to drink. Eternal ripples and waves of dust brushed over his ankles as he slogged, billowed up to his knees. He couldn't see his feet. It shouldn't be a surprise that he would eventually trip, but it was a dream so it was a surprise.

He stumbled and fell headlong on top of something that wasn't dust, but dust puffed up all around, choking. Voices like sandpaper whistled, *We mourn. We mourn him, cut down in youth and beauty.* The fall knocked tears from his gritty eyes, though he felt certain he was too parched even to spit. He tried to lift his head so the tears would run into his mouth, but the springs were already stopped up again. Desperate, he was ready to search with his tongue for damp residue in the soil or wet spots on stone, but he hadn't fallen on soil or stone. He'd tripped over a corpse.

A mummy. His knees had pulverized its pelvis, one fist broken into its rib cage. Glittering like mica, tiny flakes of fossilized skin and flesh clung to his own lean, desiccated arm. Impelled by dream logic, instead of leaping up with a shout of horror, running away, he bent closer to search out traces of his tears on the cadaverous face. Black as pitch, lacquered by time and dehydration to the glistening imperviousness of chitin or obsidian, the craggy surfaces and angles appeared unmarked, as if the tears evaporated before they struck. The air was that dry.

Slow-rising fear made him wish to flee, but flight seemed impossible. With a tremor of dry nausea, he saw marks on the mummy's glistening black cheeks, stains where varnished skin appeared to be decaying, crumbling from black glass to brownish powder. It was only a moment—if there was time in this place—before the bruises were disturbed further, from within.

Threads or tendrils like writhing fingers poked through dissolving skin, white flushed a sickly pink at the blunt tips, wriggling, reaching.

He wanted to pull back but could not.

They had heads, the tendrils, like minute serpents, coiling, seeking. But then, one after another, the heads split open and unfurled tiny leaves, ghostly pale, yearning for a light more nourishing than they would find in this dim desolation.

Reassured somewhat that the tiny shoots were merely terrible, inexplicable, not malevolent, distracted by thirst and his consuming need to move on, he hardly noticed the continued flaking away of fossilized skin around the mummy's eyes. But as pallid seedlings grew and leafed out with unnatural vitality, a kind of radiance bubbled up within stony sockets, stirring dust and mica into minute whirlpools, and the broken, vine-cumbered mummy regarded him with brown eyes he seemed to know.

❖

There's some stickiness because Sam saw part of what happened when Luke and Levent jumped into the Aegean. Sam's pretty amazingly laid-backly okay with his kid being a fag (polar opposite of Luke's mom), but he's not going to stand for Luke going all colonial predatory on somebody who's essentially their employee. Who can't say no. Eventually Luke manages to work his dad around to crediting the True Story of how Levent came to be embracing Luke in deep water off the stern of the *Esin*, but it's still sticky.

Of course Luke doesn't let on to any of the subtext. Like how much he absolutely does want to jump Levent's bones. After the fact, it occurs to him maybe Levent wanting a friend in Berkeley (*going* to Berkeley) might undermine the colonialism argument, but he isn't going to bring it up again. Wary of being seen to admire Levent, all nautical and active and sexy as the *Esin* sails south, he buries his head in his iPod and a book Perla loaned him about the local ancient civilizations. He can't concentrate, though, because he keeps catching corner-of-the-eye glimpses of Levent's long legs and handsome big feet and wondering why, if it was such a pleasure to hold him, Levent had let go.

Can't concentrate until his eyes catch on a line describing exactly the horrible place in his dream: the endless ochre desert in half light, low sepia sky, distant peaks that might be palaces or ziggurats half seen through clouds of dust. No water anywhere, the unceasing whisper of unheard voices. He's never opened this book before—how did it get into his head?

He flips back a page, two, searching for context. There's a cross-hatched drawing of an ancient artefact, a broken stone slab engraved with the image of two women in elaborate costume standing either side of a bare-chested man (a crack runs through his face, ruining it) whose long lance or spear pierces the body of some huge animal. Luke can't make out what it is and the caption doesn't tell him: the women are named Ninnin and Llad, the man Dimuz.

The pages-long passage that follows is translated from a series of fragmentary records collated into *The Story of the Rivalry of Ninnin and Llad*. It's an academic translation, painful to read, impeded by square brackets around multiple possibilities for uncertain words, curly brackets around hypothetical reconstructions of missing phrases, footnotes full of scholarly quarrels. Luke figures out right away the sepia place is the land of the dead where Llad rules, but it's heavy going between the indirect ancient manner of telling a story and modern interrogations. After maybe a quarter hour's struggle, he gives up—he's on vacation!—and slaps the book shut.

But still, how did Llad's terrible kingdom get into his dream? Was it a dream? He truly doesn't remember falling asleep or waking, no transitions or interruptions in the *Esin*'s skipping progress.

Luke looks up. No sign of Levent, possibly just as well. His dad lies flat out, oiled and basted, baking brown. Perla's propped on her elbows beside him, reading her own book.

Decisive for a change, Luke sits up. Putting the iPod to sleep and pulling out the earbuds, he says, "Perla?"

Her big sunglasses turn. "Yes, Luke?"

"You've read this, right?"

Perla nods, but Luke already knew it. It's a standard text. Her real life doesn't have anything to do with ancient Anatolian history—she's a financial adviser—but she minored in archaeology at her mom's university.

"I'm feeling really vay-cay-stupid. There's this myth, I guess, translated from original sources, that I can't make sense out of."

Interested, Perla sets her book aside and sits up. One of the things about his stepmom, in the four years Luke's known her, is that she has a higher opinion of his intelligence than he does. "Which one?"

"The Rivalry of Ninnin and Llad."

She nods again. "Not Lycian—older. Probably Sumerian origin, though the Mesopotamian myths are interestingly different. Ninnin's a version of Innana, Llad Ereshkigal." Then she seems to see Luke's expression and laughs. "Sorry. Not helpful, huh?"

"I just want to know the story."

"Okay. You're right. That translation isn't meant for readers. So Ninnin and Llad, they're goddesses and sisters. Llad, the older one, watches over the dead in the underworld. It's not like our Hell, all burny and fiery and eternal torments—really, it's kind of worse."

Luke shudders, remembering. "Yeah, I got that."

"It's like endless boredom until you wear away from the tedium, and it's everybody who ever died, not just the bad seeds. No Heaven to balance it out."

"I don't believe in Heaven," Luke protests.

"You've been arguing with Roger, have you?"

"I don't *talk* to Roger." Uncomfortable, Luke stares at his hands. "I'm really glad to be here with you guys now instead of back home."

"Luke," Perla says. "A: Don't listen to Roger. He's an ignorant bigot terrified of a world bigger than he's willing to understand. B: You're here because your dad and I wanted you with us. No fear, I'll let you know if you get in the way. And C: Did you figure out *Ninnin and Llad*'s a gay-pride story?"

"Huh—*what*?" Whiplashed, Luke swallows. "And, uh, thanks."

"Luke," Perla says again, but doesn't go further.

After an uneasy moment, Luke prompts, "Llad's the goddess of the dead…"

"And her little sister Ninnin"—Perla sounds relieved—"well, Ninnin's responsibilities aren't so well defined. She's a fertility goddess. One of her traditional epithets is *mother and daughter and sister of passion*. Somehow she comes into possession of a baby boy named Dimuz, it's not clear how, nor why she decides it would be better for her sister to raise him in the underworld instead of her doing it in the high houses of the gods."

"A baby in that place?"

"It doesn't seem to warp him much, but you can't expect psychological coherence in ancient myths. Dimuz grows up to be the most beautiful young man ever, a noble paragon in every way those people valued, and when he's around your age Llad sends him back to Ninnin in the upper world. Inappropriately, at least according to our way of looking at it, she tries to seduce him. He spurns her."

"He's gay?"

"They don't come out and say it. Didn't have the words. He prefers to spend time with his men friends, warring and hunting and drinking and so forth, and there's never any talk about him enjoying temple prostitutes or other women like all the other heroes. So, yeah, most open-minded scholars read Dimuz—the Dimuz in this story, there are others where it's not so obvious— as the least ambiguous strictly homosexual figure in the ancient record."

"Score!" says Luke.

"Luke, sometimes you're just too adorable to tolerate."

From his prone position a few feet away, Luke's dad says, "I know, right?"

"Shut up, both of you." Luke's squirming inside his skin.

Perla and Sam both laugh. Sam gets up to sit by his wife. "Enough embarrassing the kid," he decides. "Get on with the story."

Grinning, Perla leans against him. For just a second Luke's envious of them for having each other. Acceptance and positive reinforcement are all very well—no, spectacularly excellent (Roger and his mom glower in the back of his mind), but *he* wants somebody to lean against. Levent. He imagines this ancient gay culture hero, Dimuz, might be as handsome as Levent.

"Ninnin decides it's her sister's bad influence that turns Dimuz away from her," Perla is saying, "so, rashly, she goes down to the gates of the underworld. Even though she's an immensely powerful goddess, she has to abide by the rules: she can't enter death in all her living, divine glory. The demon guardians strip her of her splendid clothing and jewels and send her off into the endless desert as naked as any of the uncounted dead souls wandering there. It takes almost forever for her to walk to Llad's palace. By the time she arrives she's just like the other dead, remembering nothing of her life or who she was, only that she desperately wants *something*. Llad doesn't recognize her.

"Meanwhile, back in the real world Ninnin's absence is having terrible effects. Without her divine vitality, an unending chilly drought overcomes the land. Crops and animals die. Famine spreads. The remaining gods become alarmed. They decide only Dimuz can fetch Ninnin back from death and rescue the upper world, so they carry him off from whatever good time he was having to the gates of the underworld.

"The guardians recognize Dimuz as their old playmate and their mistress's ward, somebody who belongs, so they're pleased to let him through with all his honor and glory and humanity intact. When he tells them why he's come, they search out Ninnin's fine clothing and jewels in their treasure house and adorn him like a queen. Then they send him out into death.

"Because of who he is, it takes Dimuz much less time to reach his foster mother's palace. He finds the shade of Ninnin right away. When he dresses her up in her own robes, she begins to remember who she is. He takes her to Llad, who agrees to escort her back to the world of the living. And then Dimuz reacquaints himself with the companions of his youth and proceeds to have himself a fine time."

"In Hell?" asks Sam.

"It's not Hell," says Luke, annoyed by his dad's interruption.

"He's a hero, having a fine time is the point of his existence." Perla shoves Sam a little with her shoulder. "And like I said before, you can't expect coherence or verisimilitude or plausibility in the fragments of ancient myth."

"Sorry." Sam is contrite. "Go on."

"While Dimuz enjoyed himself, the two sisters made the long, weary journey to the high houses of the gods. All around them, the world came back to life—gentle rains fell, seeds germinated, baby animals romped. Both goddesses were dissatisfied. Ninnin recalled the burdens of her responsibilities in the world and felt a strange nostalgia for the restful unknowingness of death. Llad was confused, repulsed, by the vast vitality and multiplicity of the upper world as life returned to it. Ninnin was angry that Dimuz still didn't desire her, preferred death to her, and Llad slowly understood that she, too, longed for Dimuz's arms.

"But they made the best of it because, being gods, they had no choice. Fascinating sidelight. We've got Dimuz, one of the first gay men in recorded literature, and also one of the earliest clear references to lesbianism: the text says quite clearly that Llad and Ninnin *comforted one another* during the nights of their journey and continued so even after they reached the gods' precincts, because *only she recognized her sister's terrible longing for the man neither could have.*"

What Perla finds fascinating Luke thinks is squicky and demeaning, but she doesn't take it further so he doesn't say anything.

"The thing is, with Llad not in the underworld, the balance of the universe is off again. Now the upper world is *too* alive. Without death, it grows fat, rotten with excess, diseased. The other gods become alarmed again. They petition the sisters of life and death to make things right. So they return to the terrible gates and call Dimuz. He laughs at their attempts to bargain with him—they're gods, they only know how to demand—but ultimately agrees that if Llad returns to her place he'll spend part of each year in life, part in death.

"So Dimuz returns to his loves among living men—distant from but visible to the longing Ninnin—and then, after the season

passes, goes back through the terrible gates into the welcoming
arms of the dead, but not of death, Llad, permitted only to gaze
on him from a distance, yearning."

"Whoa," says Luke. "That's really sad, in the end."

His dad nods—then brightens, with a sly glance at Luke.
"For everyone but Dimuz."

"He is Adonis," gravely says the last voice Luke expects,
"Dimuz. The beautiful youth all women mourn when he goes
into death. You tell the story well, Perla Hanım."

Looking over Luke's shoulder, surprise unhidden by her
sunglasses, Perla says, "Thank you, Levent Efendi. Yes, Dimuz
is a version of Sumerian Tammuz, who's the ancestor of Adonis.
The Greeks tried to rationalize the stories, though, according to
their view of the universe."

Finally, still jumpy, Luke turns his head. Beautiful almost-
nude Levent, handsome as Dimuz, meets his gaze and smiles
sweetly. "Roisin Hanım asked me to tell you she's prepared a
mid-morning snack."

❖

The *Esin*'s sharp prow cuts through the Aegean. Spray
billows over Luke and his dad and stepmom when they return to
the foredeck. Sails boom and ropes clatter. Altan Efendi bellows
basso-profundo Turkish commands from the bridge and Levent
leaps to obey, or Roisin Hanım if she happens to be in position
and not encumbered by a tray of fruit juices for the Americans.
It's all very like the previous days' sails except no longer so novel,
so Luke can imagine himself becoming bored.

Except he's wondering just how much of Perla's story Levent
overheard. The gay stuff? And what was that about Adonis? All
Luke remembers about that myth is that Adonis was beautiful,

went hunting, got killed by a wild boar, and the wild anemones blooming at the time took on the color of his blood in mourning.

Anemones. He hasn't had a good look at Levent's tattoos. They're flowers—anemones? He's pretty sure none of the blossoms are blood red. He'll have to try to get closer (which he wants to do anyway, of course) because he'll recognize anemones. Perla used to grow them in her garden before she sold that house to move in with his dad.

It seems only a moment later—Luke deep in dopey fantasies of cavorting with Levent in a meadow bright with flowers, so he has to lie flat on his belly—when, under power, sails furled, the *Esin* putters between two small rocky islands into a round cove surrounded by high cliffs. Luke jumps up and runs to the rail. From the flying bridge atop the deckhouse, Altan Efendi lets out a bellow of satisfaction: no other Blue Voyage gulet is there before them. He has Levent drop anchor where the water is deep and blue, but only ten yards toward shore the bottom of the cove bellies up nearly to the surface, turning the water lemon yellow for another fifty yards before it ripples against the tawny beach.

Luke's antsy all of a sudden. He wants to plunge into the tempting water, rinse the scum of dream sweat and sunscreen from his skin. Wants to stagger onto solid land that doesn't rock and roll underfoot, just for a change, to find running fresh water and smell green growing things, not endless salt and himself.

As if divining Luke's impatience, from above Altan Efendi booms, "We will go ashore in a few minutes, genç efendim. Let my wife and Levent just finish loading our luncheon into the dinghy."

Startled by the voice breaking into his tunes, Luke looks up from the green-blue water and pulls one earbud out. The captain waves genially and Luke removes the other bud. "Can I help?"

"I believe they have everything in hand."

Nevertheless, Luke grabs his book and sunscreen, the tray of juice glasses because it's there, and wanders aft. Perla and Sam have already vanished—down to their cabin to pull themselves together or whatever. As Luke rounds the deckhouse, Levent is just lowering a big red cooler over the taffrail. He happens to glance up.

Levent's grin hits Luke right in the eyes and he stumbles, blinded. The tray goes flying. Luke hears an unlucky glass encounter the rare metal fitment and musically shatter. The other two merely thud on wooden deck. Somehow he's on his knees and one stinging palm.

The pang in his hand isn't just impact. Before he can determine what it is or whether it should bother him more than embarrassment, someone has an arm under him, lifting him up, somebody's concerned voice is saying something Luke doesn't understand.

"I'm sorry, I…tripped?"

"It was my stupid fault, Luke," Roisin Hanım is muttering, her brogue thick and melodious. "Some sailor I call myself, leaving things strewn about for the unwary to trip over. Sit up now, let me see." She has him sitting back against the deckhouse bulkhead, she's holding his hand in both of hers.

"I'm bleeding," Luke observes. It doesn't seem to concern him much although there's rather a lot of it pooling in the palm Roisin holds up, dribbling between numbed fingers.

"Yes. An unfortunate encounter with broken glass." Leaning over his hand, she's being very calm. "Levent."

"Here." Looking frightened but resolute, Levent sets the enamelled-metal first-aid kit on the deck, unlatches it. "What do you need, Hanım?"

"Your eyes, my dear. I don't trust my own. We wish to be sure there are no fragments of glass or splinters in Luke's wounds. Tweezers, if you find anything."

She's not simply holding his hand, Luke realizes: she's clamped fingers and thumb tight around his wrist in a kind of flesh-and-bone tourniquet. He wonders, should he be worried?

Breathing thinly through his teeth, Levent squints over Luke's palm, swabbing up blood with a wad of cotton, probing gently with fingertips, then the pointed tips of a pair of bright steel tweezers. There's a momentary wince when he pulls something out of Luke's flesh but whatever it is so small Luke can't see it. Levent goes back to work.

Now nausea begins to rumble in Luke's belly and a fog of some kind of great weariness creeps up his unnaturally extended arm. If his tears nurtured vines within the fossil flesh of the mummy in his dream, he wonders, what would blood provoke?

"Ow," says Levent.

Luke blinks back to alertness.

"What is it, dear?"

Levent doesn't reply. Wielding the tweezers with the wrong fingers, thumb and middle, he picks out another invisible fragment and drops it into Roisin's free, open hand. "I believe that's all," he mutters, peering hard, then sets the tweezers aside. His fingers are gummy, rusty with thick stains. "Luke Bey's hand needs to be washed. Then we can look again."

"Yours too," Luke blurts just as Levent sucks the bloody index finger into his mouth. Roisin lets out a little gasp and Luke, angry with himself, says, "You cut yourself!"

When Levent withdraws his finger it's not really clean, filmed with saliva and diluted blood, but cleaner than the others. Knuckles left red smudges on his chin. He regards the index finger's tip for a moment, his expression blank, and mutters, "A minuscule scratch."

"Let me see."

Levent smiles—not the grin that turns Luke into a quivering pile of yearning, just a twitch of the lips that's somehow more affecting. "Of course, Luke Bey." A tiny bead of blood forms on the pad of the finger Levent's showing Luke before it dissolves into red feathers penetrating the slick of spit. "See? It's nothing."

Roisin hmmphs and releases Luke's wrist. "Go wash your hands, boys," she says, pushing Luke away—into Levent's arms.

As Levent helps him upright, Luke sees the thing he must have tripped over. Kicked nearly into the scuppers, the flat basket had scattered crumbs of earth across the deck, but not much. Less than two days after he watched the seeds sown, the basket's already crowded with seedlings, their roots knitting the soil in place. Then Roisin moves into his sightline, hiding the thing. "Tread carefully, boys. Watch for more glass. I'll clean it up in a moment."

It can't have taken any time at all. Perhaps glasses are always being broken aboard the *Esin*. Altan Efendi didn't come running from the bridge to see what was up, Perla and Sam didn't pop out the door Levent's leading Luke through, his steady arm strong around Luke's back, holding him upright as though he was unsteady.

He is unsteady. It's just a scratch, a couple of scratches. He's unsteady because Levent is holding him. He's unsteady because Levent licked his blood, both their blood, off his finger. Sucked the finger into his mouth like it was something else.

Unexpectedly, Levent half pushes Luke right past the galley. At the top of the companionway, Luke almost balks but then clatters down, half dragging Levent after, and pushes open the door of the little head next to his cabin. There isn't really room for two full-sized people inside, so Luke has to practically climb onto the toilet lid before Levent can close the door behind them. Clambering down, he wonders, hopeful, why the door needs to be closed, and pulls a mad notion from the back of his mind. "Let me see your finger again."

Just reaching for the faucet, Levent hesitates. His lips tilt into the unearthly, close-mouthed smile and he lifts his right hand. Before Luke quite sees the tiny jewel-like blob of blood, before he's quite sure what he's going to do, the finger's sliding between his lips.

It doesn't really taste like blood. He doesn't think it does. Salty.

Levent's eyes narrow a bit and his smile widens just enough to reveal the wet pearls of lower teeth. In Luke's mouth, the finger twists, scratching at his tongue. Lower, outside his mouth, Levent's thumb pushes into the fleshy spot under Luke's chin. Slowly, Luke's face is drawn forward. This time they're really going to kiss.

"Let's wash up, Luke Bey," Levent says, voice low and amused, and Luke realizes he's about to plaster a bloody palm print on Levent's chest.

The finger pulls free with a liquid slurp.

Shoulder to shoulder, they wash their hands under trickles of tepid water. The soap stings Luke's wounds. Levent makes sure he does a thorough job. When Luke's hand is clean, the tiny cuts welling sluggish blood, Levent inspects it meticulously. He finds no more glass. Before he smears it with antibiotic ointment (Luke hadn't noticed him bringing the first-aid kit with him) and mummifies it in cotton gauze, he raises the palm to his lips and kisses it. "I feel your accident was my fault," he murmurs.

Luke can't process the suggestion, as ludicrous as it is accurate, and merely gapes while Levent tends to his hand. Levent's fault? Because he's distractingly beautiful and Luke's an infatuated klutz? A glimpse of pastel colors prompts him. "Tell me about your tattoos," he blurts, desperate.

"My flowers?" Levent turns up his left forearm as if to inspect the tattoos himself, faintly surprised by their blossoming under his skin. "They're pretty, aren't they?"

They grow up from the tangle of blue veins at his wrist, five sinuous stems intertwined with shorter stems of foliage like Italian parsley, each surmounted by a single open blossom: lavender, white, blue, pale blushy pink, blue again. "We call them *mountain tulip*, dağ lalesi, though they aren't tulips. I don't know the English name."

"Anemone," Luke says, certain now.

"Really? We have a flower called anemon. It's similar, I suppose, not as showy, and it blooms in the spring, not summer like these."

"One variety of anemone—the prettiest." Luke grazes one of the blue blossoms with the tip of a finger. Its purple-black center gleams, surrounded by a corona of blue-black stamens. Levent's skin is warm. "Or windflower. That's the antique English name, because the petals bruise so easily. You don't have a red one."

"Not yet."

Something's happening. Levent's other hand's coming up, open and defenseless as a windflower, to brush fingertips against Luke's stubbly cheek. "There's a story about the red flowers," he says, eyes still lowered, "an old, sad, Greek story."

Luke wonders if the tiny cut on Levent's index finger is still open, painting his own cheek with filaments of red. "The blood of Adonis."

Unsurprised, Levent raises his eyes, his chin. They kiss.

They jump apart when heavy footsteps sound on the companionway outside the closed door and Luke's dad says, "Luke? We're all waiting."

"Sor—" Luke can't get in a breath. "Sorry, Dad. Just a minute."

Sam's feet thunder back up the stairs. Levent's grinning at Luke, as if they were merely friends, before he turns to latch and heft the first-aid kit.

"Kiss me again," Luke demands.

"Your parents and my employers are waiting."

"Kiss me again."

"Very well. With great pleasure."

❖

Sam and Perla and Levent swim ashore but Luke's ordered into the dinghy with Altan Efendi and Roisin Hanım. He feels clumsy, the hand bandaged into a useless paw so he couldn't row if they needed him to—they don't, Altan powers up the noisy outboard—and gazes yearningly after Levent's supple golden back and flutter-kicking feet. That luscious ass, his trunks the same scarlet as an anemone's petals. Two brief kisses. No tongue, even. Barely an embrace.

It's hardly a moment before Altan grounds the dinghy prow-first on the beach. Luke's no help fetching out the cooler and baskets, not even spreading the beach blanket. "How did this happen?" his dad wants to know, inspecting the white gauze wrapped around his son's hand.

Luke's relieved not to see any blood spots seeping through. He imagines Roisin has already told the story and Sam only wants confirmation. "I tripped and broke a glass and fell on it. It's not much, really. Lev—" It's hard to say the name without making it a revelation, as if his friend were just anybody. "Levent overdid the bandages. It'll be fine tomorrow, just scabs."

Salt water drips from Sam's hair onto the gauze, darkening it. "You're sure?"

"Positive."

"Okay." Sam squeezes, then releases the bandaged hand. "Let's have lunch."

After they eat, a bewildering array of savory finger foods (some, Roisin confesses, from cans), and drink (Turkish beer for the grown-ups, sour-cherry juice for the boys), Altan and

Levent ferry baskets and cooler and dirty dishes back to the gulet. Talking—what about? Luke wonders, then stops wondering— Perla and Roisin wander along the beach, Perla in her swimsuit splashing through the shallows while Roisin Hanım on dry sand is still wearing a shirt and white pants. Is her modesty, if it is modesty, Turkish or Irish, Luke wonders, Muslim or Catholic?

Looking away, he stops wondering. The *Esin* floats serenely at anchor on the blue bay. Tethered to its flank, the dinghy wallows when substantial Altan Efendi clambers down into it, casts off, steers back toward the beach. No Levent. Washing dishes in the galley, presumably. Disappointed, Luke sighs.

"Are you having a good time, Lukey?" Sam asks.

"Huh?" For a second, more than a second, Luke doesn't hear the question, doesn't recognize it's a question. "Yeah! Absolutely." He remembers something about his dad. "I don't even remember...wotzisname." He does remember Douglas. Fondly, even. He's not an utter amateur because of Douglas. Risking a glance, he sees Sam doesn't appear convinced. "Thanks for not leaving me with Mom and Roger for two weeks, Dad, really."

A crease folds the skin between Sam's eyebrows. "They're rather...unevolved, aren't they?"

"They don't believe in evolution. Let's not talk about them. What about you? You and Perla. I'm not getting in the way too much, am I? I mean, it's your honeymoon."

Sam shakes his head, a don't-worry-about-it shake. "You and Levent seem to have made friends pretty quick."

Luke persuades himself not to gulp or blush, not to look away from his father's regard. "Like Perla says, they're friendly people, the Turks. And he's a great guy, Dad. Really bright. Smarter than me, I bet, I can barely speak English"—Luke's best grades and SAT scores, his only admirable grades, are in English—"let alone a second language. He's going to college this fall, you know."

"That's good." In Sam's world every young person should go to college.

"In the States, Dad. Berkeley. Half a mile from our house."

Sam's eyes widen.

"So, like, it's not just these few days on the boat. He'll need friends in California. I like Levent a lot, Dad, and I think he likes me."

Sam shakes his head, an I-was-afraid-of-that shake. "Lukey, look—" Another shake, and Sam squeezes his eyes shut for an instant. "*That way*, Luke? Do you think you like him that way?"

Luke blinks. He hates when Sam talks to him like he was a little kid. It makes him angry and rash. "Levent is extremely handsome, Dad, he has a really great body, of course I'm attracted to him." *He's attracted to me, too. He kissed me. Twice.*

Looking intent and fierce, protective, like a papa bear, Sam reaches for Luke's arm, the wrist of his good hand. "His tattoos, Luke. Five flowers, here—" He traces their position on the flesh of Luke's forearm. "Altan Efendi told me, he was proud of the boy. One flower for each of the foreign tourist girls he fooled around with over the last five summers aboard the *Esin*. I don't want your heart broken again, Lukey."

"Oh." He can't think. *It wasn't broken the first time you thought it was*, he thinks.

"I'm sorry, baby. Better to know, though, right?"

He kissed me. Perla didn't say anything about Turkish BFFs kissing each other, just holding hands and hugging. "Yeah, I guess." He musters up some bravado. "Well, you know, I do have a couple of straight guy friends. Who're good-looking enough I'd be willing to fool around with them if they were interested. So it's like that. Levent's still going to need a friend in Berkeley. It's fine."

"Is it?"

Of course it's not, you stupid man. The thought makes him feel bad as soon as it forms. He loves his dad. Sam loves him, cares for him, as he is, imperfect and dumb and gay, not as he *should* be. "It's fine, Dad. I'm fine. You want to go for a swim?"

"Your hand?"

Luke's already tearing off the gauze Levent wound with too much, with false, care. "Salt water's good for little cuts."

❖

Dozing on the warm beach afterward, all sunscreened up (the stuff stung in his cuts worse than the sea's salt), Luke seems to recall another ominous dream. Dripping blood-warm salt water, he had clambered out of the cove onto the rocky, scrubby flank of one of the small islands. Any moment he expected to reach its crest and gaze out over the wine-dark Aegean. (*Wine dark.* What did that mean exactly?) But he kept scrambling and the moment never came. After a while he ceased smelling the sea, only the salt crust on his skin dissolving as he sweated. Salt made the scents of the dry brush he blundered through, the green herbs he trod on, more vivid and strange.

Suddenly he seemed to hear voices and rushed ahead. Suddenly he was running up a narrow, rutted alley instead of a hillside, with tall, plastered, windowless walls on either side, packed earth and pebbles underfoot. The voices came from overhead, yelling, keening, women's voices: *We mourn. We mourn him, cut down in youth and beauty.* He tried to halt, to look up for the grieving women, but found he couldn't. As he ran up the steepening street, panting, baskets and terra-cotta dishes began to fall from the sky—from the tops of the walls. Dirt scattered from the vessels as they struck the street, dirt and the wilted plants that had been rooted in them.

Something hit him in the back of the neck and he fell to his knees, crying aloud. But now the street had vanished, or he had vanished from it: his knees crushed fragrant green grasses and all around him ghostly white anemones bloomed, bobbing on their long, springy stems. He plucked from the grass a shard of red terra-cotta, its surface crusted with dried soil engraved with the hair-thin worm tracks of countless roots. Littered across the grass were clumps of dying or dead young plants, earth still clinging to their roots, limp and yellowed as if they were rotting or dried out, grey.

He heard laughter, masculine laughter. It was familiar, he thought. It was Levent, he was certain.

When he rose and saw the youth standing at a little distance in the meadow of white anemones, leaning on a tall wooden staff, he nearly ran, calling, but remembered what his father had told him. Levent, if it was Levent—his back was turned, his naked ass as spectacular as Luke had imagined—was not alone.

One woman wore black, not black clothing but darkness, the other brilliance. They were arguing in voices like harsh, incomprehensible thunder, not with the young man before them but each other, and the subject of their argument—Luke couldn't doubt it—kept laughing, scornful. At last, he seemed to shrug, said something low and bitter, and began to turn away.

Both women roared. Luke didn't see how it happened. Instead of two unearthly women, a single enormous beast coughed, suddenly impaled on the tip of the youth's staff—his spear. It scrabbled at the ground with its hooves, tearing up soil and grass and pebbles, grunting horribly as it forced the lance deeper into its chest. Small eyes gleamed red and red blood drooled around its tusks. Although its foot was anchored in the ground, the youth could barely hold his spear as the huge boar—or was it a sow?—made it bow and tremble.

The spear splintered. Unprepared, the sow nearly stumbled before her stumble became a rush. The youth laughed again before her sharp teeth opened his flank.

"No!" Luke yelled, waking himself up.

We mourn. We mourn him, cut down in youth and beauty.

All the white anemones flushed blood red.

❖

It's hard to be cold toward Levent, especially because he keeps seeing his friend ripped open by the wild pig's tusks, but Luke has a certain amount of self-respect and manages somehow. Despite Levent's obvious confusion and hurt. After the long sail into dusk and then night to the next anchorage, after the very late supper, before Perla and Sam finish their coffee and Turkish white wine, Luke excuses himself and goes belowdecks. Angry with himself for being taken in, with Levent for encouraging his stupid delusion, he undresses, brushes his teeth, climbs into the narrow bunk.

Can't sleep. The stifling cabin still smells pukey. He'll never sleep again.

A very long while later, he hears his dad and stepmother come down the companionway. He knows it's them—they pass the door of his cabin to enter the *honeymoon suite*, not much bigger than his cabin and oddly shaped, the bed triangled into the *Esin*'s pointed prow. Then, louder, Altan Efendi's tramping feet, turning at the bottom of the stairs toward crew quarters in the stern. Luke thinks, can't be sure, he hears Roisin Hanım's lighter tread echoing her husband's. He waits, counting seconds in his head until he loses track, then waits longer. Everybody aboard *must* be asleep.

Barefoot and naked, Luke slips off the bunk and eases his door open. Trailing the fingers of both hands along the bulkheads to either side, he tiptoes through the dark, manages not to stub a toe on the lowest step, climbs the companionway to the deckhouse. Still no lights. First he goes to the forward windows and peers through. Moonlight and starlight just suffice to reveal the slumbering lump of Levent on the starboard sunbed.

Coming out the deckhouse door, Luke's distracted by the smell of something stronger than the Aegean's salt—something green. The keklikotu? He doesn't think he's ever smelled fresh oregano, only dried from the shakers on the tables in pizza joints. It's not that, not as sharp and unpleasant until cooking tames it, more like lawns and January meadows after rain.

Oddly curious, he finds the rungs bolted to the bulkhead and climbs. Levent isn't going anywhere. He doesn't know what to say to Levent anyway. When his head rises above roof level, he smells the oregano, recognizes it—the pot is right there—but it's muted, overwhelmed by the other scent. Not the geraniums by the flying bridge, definitely not geranium. New grass and something blander, and something like the tongue-shrinking tang of licorice.

It's the basket, Roisin's basket. On hands and knees, cautious, Luke approaches. What did Levent say? *Woman's business. Hanım's business. I am not to know. Not to inquire. Not to touch.*

Moonlight and starlight bleach the overcrowded new foliage to silver. Luke didn't know any seeds sprouted and grew so fast— two, not quite three days. Slender blades like grass, tiny whorls of lobed leaves like fancy French lettuces, sprays of feathery stuff on swaying stems. He leans closer.

"Don't touch!"

Startled out of his wits, heart hammering, Luke collapses, rolling onto one shoulder. Darker and denser than night, eclipsing stars and half the crescent moon, Levent looms over him.

"I told you, it's woman's magic, dangerous for men."

"Magic?" Luke blurts. Then, outraged, "You like girls!"

A loud intake of breath. "I don't dislike them."

"You *don't* like boys. Me! You sleep with girls! Altan Efendi told my dad and Dad told me."

"In some ways, Efendi is a very stupid man." Levent hunkers down to his haunches. "Luke Bey. Is that what it is? I have slept with women—well, not much sleeping—any man can, you could."

"No, I couldn't. I wouldn't."

"It wasn't my choice, Luke. What I desire women don't have."

"What?"

Reaching before Luke can shy away, Levent strokes his cheek. "Stubble. Beard stubble on your handsome face. Sexiest thing ever. Drives me wild." His fingers feather down over Luke's chin, neck. "A flat, strong chest with a little hair on it. Or a lot, if you should happen to grow a lot as you get older. Muscles. Something else."

Luke chokes the word out: "Dick."

"In a word. In my hand, in my mouth, in— You're not wearing any clothes, Luke Bey."

Almost embarrassed but more thrilled, and hornier than that, Luke sits up. "Are you? Levent Bey."

"More than I could wish."

"Take them off."

"Willingly. When we get down from the roof, away from... *that*."

Luke's already scrambling to his feet—keeping a safe distance from the innocuous basket of seedlings and earth—when he remembers he's angry. With Levent. Who just called him sexy. Beautiful Levent. Who sexed up a different tourist girl every summer. "What about your anemones?" he demands. "Like trophies, one for each girl."

"Please, Luke." Levent's already on the ladder, his head level with Luke's knees. "Not now and not here."

Unmollified but still horny and acutely ready to be convinced, Luke follows. Inexplicably, it's when he's hanging halfway down the ladder that it properly penetrates that he's nude—naked as a jaybird in mating-season display. What if his dad—or, horribly worse, Perla—was struck by insomnia and felt a need to stroll up on deck?

Levent has already vanished around the deckhouse. Luke scurries after, finds him waiting with apparent calm seated on the port sunbed. The one Luke slept on last night. The folded blanket sits beside him. Levent hasn't removed his swim trunks.

Wanting more than anything ever to sit right beside him but stubbornly determined to remain angry, Luke snatches the blanket. Flipping it half open, he wraps it around his waist and sits on the other sunbed. Without sun, with a yard between them, he can't make out Levent's expression as the other boy launches into speech.

"When Adonis—Dimuz goes down into death, all women mourn. They use their private magics to call him back, ensure he returns life to the world—"

"No," says Luke, impatient with mythology. "Just tell me this. It's boys you really like? Me?"

Rising to his feet, Levent pulls apart the drawstring of his scarlet swim trunks, pushes them down.

❖

"I had a fascinating talk with Roisin Hanım yesterday," Luke's stepmother says.

"Oh?" says Luke, not really interested. He's still glowing, thinks he is, though he's tried to keep the brilliance damped. Exhausted, too. They didn't really do anything, him and Levent on the sunbed on the *Esin*'s foredeck, nothing Luke hadn't already done with Douglas—didn't do, actually, quite a few of the things Douglas had taught him—but they were awake all night anyway. Barely remembered, when dawn began to grey the sky, that Levent needed to pull his trunks back on and pretend to have slept, Luke scuttle frustrated belowdecks to put on something himself.

"The *Esin* and the summer Blue Voyages aren't what support them at all," Perla goes on. "Roisin calls the boat Altan's charming, expensive hobby. Roisin's shop in Didim brings in the significant part of their income."

"Oh?" Just a polite noise, a prompt. Luke hadn't wanted to debark from Altan Efendi's hobby, ride in an open Jeep up to visit the Lycian rock-cut tombs in the cliffs above the little fishing village—lose sight even for a moment of Levent. Levent sat right beside him through breakfast, nudging him now and again, throwing an arm around his shoulders, all the jokily affectionate bro-touching Turkish boys were permitted, frustrating as all hell. But also, under the table, now and then caressing or tickling him, rubbing his calf against Luke's, knocking their ankles together, trailing his toes across the insanely sensitive tops of Luke's feet. Even more frustrating. "What does she sell in her shop?"

"Levent hasn't told you? Roisin's a tattoo artist—she did his anemones."

"Really?" Startled, Luke looks up. They're sitting, stepson and stepmom, at the base of a grey cliff overlooking the village on its bay far below. Luke had pled tiredness and a false soreness in his scabby palm when Perla's mother with unnatural vigor for her age wanted him to climb with her to the high, sheer tombs. Sam had been eager but Perla said she'd seen it all before and stayed with Luke. "Roisin Hanım doesn't have any tattoos. Altan Efendi either."

"Altan's old-fashioned. Traditional Islam disapproves of body modification about as much as traditional Judaism." Perla regards the inscription engraved in ancient Lycian letters around her own right wrist. She confessed once that it wasn't entirely grammatical, something her mother still gives her grief over, but refused to translate it. "Roisin's ink isn't where you can see it. She didn't do it herself, of course. Her teacher in Cork city, before she came to Turkey on holiday and fell in love."

Luke wonders if *he's* in love, on holiday in Turkey. He knows he was never in love with Douglas. In the harbor below, he can pick out the *Esin* moored among other Blue Voyage gulets—the fishing boats left with the tide—but not any of the people aboard. If they're aboard. Is Levent thinking of him, doing make-work boat maintenance with Efendi or carrying packages in the market for Hanım? "Why anemones?" he asks, feeling a stab of terror as he recalls the unexplained girls the blossoms represent. "Why did she ink anemones on Levent's arm?"

"For Adonis, of course," Perla says, as if it were an explanation.

"What?"

"Look at the rooftops in the village, Luke."

"What?" He can't see that far.

"They don't call him Adonis, probably, or Dimuz either, the women of the Aegean and Mediterranean coasts, when they plant his midsummer gardens. It's just custom, tradition, what's always been done."

"Gardens?" Luke's trying to see anything on the roofs far below. "Roisin's basket of seedlings on the deckhouse roof?"

"It's a fertility ritual, of course. They're all fertility rituals. Older than Turks and Islam in Turkey, older than Judaism probably. Roisin learned it from her mother-in-law, I imagine. The seasons of fertility, for sowing and harvest, are very different here than in Ireland. As the killing heat of midsummer approaches, the women remember Adonis under all his names and none, the god who dies every year, taking the world's virtue with him, and then is reborn.

In his memory, they plant small gardens of seeds that germinate and sprout quickly, grain and herb, wheat, barley, lettuce, fennel. They die quickly, too, young like ever young Adonis. Too hot, not the season, perhaps the gardeners *forget* to water them for a day or two. Then, midsummer night, in a cataclysm of grief, they hurl the withered little gardens into the street or the sea and mourn the momentary death of beauty. It's very cathartic."

She's done it herself! Luke thinks, surprised. Usually he thinks of Perla as a pragmatic businesswoman, less romantic and given to fantastical gestures than Luke's own dad. Also: *She's not telling me everything.* It's women's business, women's magic, not for men to know. They're grieving, those women, the beautiful men who don't desire them, working magic to change their natures.

❖

"Are you absolutely sure about this?" Sam asks.

It's two months later and an old argument. Since Luke returned home he's had sporadic messages from Levent, when the *Esin* on its Blue Voyages moored overnight in a town with an Internet café or cellular network robust enough to support his smartphone. They weren't all the same, the messages, but they said the same thing Luke replied: *I miss you, I can't wait to see you again.* Last week, from his own computer in İzmir where he was making final preparations for departure, Levent wrote: *It was the blood, yours and mine, strengthening my natural inclinations. Plus Hanım's bad luck in not reserving Efendi's boat for a family with a daughter those two weeks. Plus my good luck it was YOU instead. Or maybe she took pity on me and arranged it all.*

"I'm sure," Luke says. He's hyper, antsy. Levent's already in the States—he landed in New York last night, called from the airport hotel. His voice sounded more foreign, somehow, as if being in an English-speaking country exaggerated his Turkish accent. "Absolutely positively."

They've driven down from the Berkeley hills, Luke and his dad (Perla's at work), across the Bay Bridge, through the city, south to SFO. Sam expected Luke to want to drive, but Luke didn't trust his dad to keep safe all the way the flowers he bought this morning: six perfect out-of-season blood-red anemones with dense black hearts. He's holding them now, Luke is, jiggling on his toes with impatience as they wait in the arrivals area.

"He's sleeping in the guest room, you know."

"Of course he is." *It won't be* sleeping *in my room.* For two weeks, until Levent moves into his residence hall on campus. Two weeks to learn everything else about each other, to explore and experiment, to fall ever more in love. "Thank you, Dad. So much."

"Well." Sam pats his son's shoulder gingerly. "He does seem like a good kid, and I can only applaud the good influence that has you actively thinking about college yourself. But promise me, Lukey, promise me you'll warn him in no uncertain terms that I love my boy very very much and will not tolerate him ever hurting you."

"There he is!"

There he is! Luke can't run to him because Sam's holding his shoulder. He holds up the flowers in their crackly cellophane cone, grinning like anything, squirming like a little kid. From the crowd of other passengers, Levent beams. He hefts the overnight bag on his own shoulder, then lifts his left hand to wave. On the pale skin of his inner forearm, upside down, five pastel anemones are eclipsed by the sixth, scarlet as blood.

For Sandra McDonald, who wanted a happy ending

Contributors

'NATHAN BURGOINE (redroom.com/author/nathan-burgoine) lives in Ottawa, Canada, with his husband Daniel. His previous short fiction appears in *Fool for Love*, the 2010 *Saints and Sinners: New Fiction from the Festival*, and *Men of the Mean Streets*. In the summertime, 'Nathan enjoys watching the squirrel antics while writing outside.

A Navy veteran, SAM CAMERON spent several years around the world gathering stories. She writes short fiction and novels for young adults, including *Mystery of the Tempest* and *The Secret of Othello*. Currently she lives in Florida, where it is always summertime and the beaches stretch along the ocean forever.

MARGUERITE CROFT is a San Francisco Bay Area writer. She has a short story forthcoming in the *Flushed* anthology and can be stalked on Twitter as @albionidaho. She loves eating orange and vanilla frozen yogurt cones during summer lightning storms.

ALEX JEFFERS (sentenceandparagraph.com) lives in New England—why, he no longer knows. He has published many works of short fiction and four books: *Safe as Houses*, a novel; *Do You Remember Tulum?* and *The New People*, novellas; and *The Abode of Bliss*, a sequence of linked stories. An as yet untitled collection of unlinked stories is forthcoming in summer 2012. He was born in the middle of July and is only properly happy when the weather is hot hot hot.

L Lark (l-lark.com) is a writer and visual artist currently living in South Florida, a place with its own fair share of monster sightings. Links to her projects, publications, and blog can be found on her website. Her favorite summer activity is watching thunderstorms form over the Everglades.

Allergic to peas and Tom Cruise movies, **Dia Pannes** enjoys writing short fiction. Her first sale was to *Speaking Out*. Living in upstate New York, she does enjoy going to local fairs during the warm nights of summer.

Aimee Payne grew up in a podunk town in Ohio that she couldn't wait to escape. She is working on an MFA in Writing for Children and Young Adults from Vermont College of Fine Arts. This is her first published story. She lives in Jacksonville, Florida, with fellow writer Will Ludwigsen and a too-large assortment of rescued dogs and cats. Because she lives in Florida, the thing she enjoys most about the summer is good air-conditioning. She misses spending the summer in her grandma's pool with her brothers and sister, though.

Christopher Reynaga is a recipient of the Bazzanella Literary Award for Short Fiction and a graduate of Clarion West. He has had fiction appear in the *American River Literary Review* and has a story forthcoming from *Cemetery Dance*. His favorite part of summer is skinny-dipping in the great, green waters of the creek bend.

Shawn Syms has completed a short-fiction collection and is at work on a novel. His fiction has been shortlisted for the Journey Prize and has appeared on LittleFiction.com and JoylandMagazine.com. His journalism, essays, reviews, and other writing have appeared in over thirty other publications. Shawn's favorite thing about summer is big burly bears in skimpy little tank tops.

ANN ZEDDIES spent the first three summers of her life on a mountain-top in Idaho, and still remembers them fondly. Unbeknownst to her, she was being irradiated by fallout from nuclear test sites. So now she has super-powers. Ghosts of summers past appear in all her works, if you examine them closely. She wrote *Deathgift*, *Skyroad*, *Steel Helix*, and *Blood and Roses* under her own name, and *Typhon's Children* and *Riders of Leviathan* as Toni Anzetti. Her most recent story was "Waiting to Show Her" in *Speaking Out*. Now she lives in western Michigan, where the Lake Michigan shore is the very essence of summer. Jumping into big waves on a sunny day is one of her favorite things ever, and she will stretch summer into October just to do it one more time.

Editor **STEVE BERMAN** thinks summertime is wonderful because it recharges the solar batteries in his cat, Daulton. This is his third anthology for young adults. He plans to do more, but not necessarily in June, July, or August, when he likes to read a great deal. He lives in southern New Jersey but never goes to the beach.

Soliloquy Titles From Bold Strokes Books

Boys of Summer, edited by Steve Berman. Stories of young love and adventure, when the sky's ceiling is a bright blue marvel, when another boy's laughter at the beach can distract from dull summer jobs. (978-1-60282-663-2)

Street Dreams by Tama Wise. Tyson Rua has more than his fair share of problems growing up in New Zealand—he's gay, he's falling in love, and he's run afoul of the local hip-hop crew leader just as he's trying to make it as a graffiti artist. (978-1-60282-650-2)

me@you.com by K.E. Payne. Is it possible to fall in love with someone you've never met? Imogen Summers thinks so because it's happened to her. (978-1-60282-592-5)

Swimming to Chicago by David-Matthew Barnes. As the lives of the adults around them unravel, high school students Alex and Robby form an unbreakable bond, vowing to do anything to stay together—even if it means leaving everything behind. (978-1-60282-572-7)

Speaking Out edited by Steve Berman. Inspiring stories written for and about LGBT and Q teens of overcoming adversity (against intolerance and homophobia) and experiencing life after "coming out." (978-1-60282-566-6)

365 Days by K.E. Payne. Life sucks when you're seventeen years old and confused about your sexuality, and the girl of your dreams doesn't even know you exist. Then in walks sexy new emo girl, Hannah Harrison. Clemmie Atkins has exactly 365 days to discover herself, and she's going to have a blast doing it! (978-1-60282-540-6)

Cursebusters! by Julie Smith. Budding psychic Reeno is the most accomplished teenage burglar in California, but one tiny screw-up and poof!—she's sentenced to Bad Girl School. And that isn't even her worst problem. Her sister Haley's dying of an illness no one can diagnose, and now she can't even help. (978-1-60282-559-8)

Who I Am by M.L. Rice. Devin Kelly's senior year is a disaster. She's in a new school in a new town, and the school bully is making her life miserable—but then she meets his sister Melanie and realizes her feelings for her are more than platonic. (978-1-60282-231-3)

Sleeping Angel by Greg Herren. Eric Matthews survives a terrible car accident only to find out everyone in town thinks he's a murderer—and he has to clear his name even though he has no memories of what happened. (978-1-60282-214-6)

Mesmerized by David-Matthew Barnes. Through her close friendship with Brodie and Lance, Serena Albright learns about the many forms of love and finds comfort for the grief and guilt she feels over the brutal death of her older brother, the victim of a hate crime. (978-1-60282-191-0)

The Perfect Family by Kathryn Shay. A mother and her gay son stand hand in hand as the storms of change engulf their perfect family and the life they knew. (978-1-60282-181-1)

Father Knows Best by Lynda Sandoval. High school juniors and best friends Lila Moreno, Meryl Morganstern, and Caressa Thibodoux plan to make the most of the summer before senior year. What they discover that amazing summer about girl power, growing up, and trusting friends and family more than prepares them to tackle that all-important senior year! (978-1-60282-147-7)